HAVEN'S DECEIT

The Haven Chronicles: Book Three

by

Fi Phillips

Burning Chair Limited, Trading As Burning Chair Publishing
61 Bridge Street, Kington HR5 3DJ

www.burningchairpublishing.com

By Fi Phillips
Edited by Simon Finnie and Peter Oxley
Cover by Burning Chair Publishing

First published by Burning Chair Publishing, 2024

ISBN: 978-1-912946-41-9

Also by Fi Phillips

Haven Wakes – The Haven Chronicles: Book 1
Magic Bound — The Haven Chronicles: Book 2

Dedication

This book is dedicated to my readers. For keeping me on my toes with their comments, supporting my writing with their purses and book reviews, and making me feel like a real author. Thank you.

Chapter One

The photograph of Blessing was exactly as Steve remembered her. She was seated at the table in Hartley's kitchen with a tome of a book open before her. She rested her head on one hand, peering up at the photographer from behind a curtain of pale blonde hair. She was smiling. It was the unsure but honest smile that Steve had become so familiar with. He missed that smile.

"When was this taken?" he said.

"Do you know, I really have no idea." Hartley stood at the sink with his hands plunged into soapy water. It was the first time that Steve had ever seen the shopkeeper do the washing up. "It's the essence of her though, don't you think? It'll do well for the Tree of Remembrance. I just need to find a fitting frame and ribbon. Gold, do you think? Or maybe blue."

"Isn't it too soon for that?" said Steve. "Blessing might still—"

"Don't start that again." Hartley stopped his clattering and splashing and gave a deep sigh. "She's gone. We agreed."

I didn't agree, Steve thought. *I just gave in because it seemed easier.* "I mean, there's still hope."

"I can't do this now!" Hartley dragged the apron from around his rotund body and threw it on the floor. "It's too much."

"I'll do the washing up," said Steve, pushing back his chair. "I don't mind."

"That isn't what I meant," said Hartley, turning to face him. "You say that there's still room for hope, but sometimes hope is just too painful to bear." He wiped a hand across his eyes, gave a nose-crinkling sniff, and pointed to the door to the shop. "I have work to do," he said. "In there."

"Of course," said Steve. "Sorry."

"I just…" Hartley shrugged. "I have no words, dear boy."

"I won't say it again." Steve picked up the pinny from the floor. "Want me to dry?"

"No, leave it," said Hartley. "It'll dry in its own good time."

"Coffee?" said Steve. "Or I could make some toast. Or we could go for a walk."

"Later," said Hartley. "I'm not up to any of that right now."

"Sure," said Steve. "Whatever you need." He straightened out the apron and hung it on the coat-stand. "Do you mind if *I* go for a walk? I won't be long."

"Take as long as you need, Steve," said Hartley. "Not that I want rid of you, but walking the streets of Darkacre often clears out the psychological cobwebs."

"That's what I thought." Steve unhooked his jacket from the coat-stand and slipped it on. He wanted to say more but he didn't know what that 'more' should be. The weight of their loss was too heavy to shift with just words.

*

The Darkacre air was as it always was. The only change Steve had ever noticed was that some days in the magical community were cold, while others were pleasantly warm. Today was a cold day. He dug his hands into his pockets and set off without thinking about where he was heading.

Maybe his judgement was coloured by his mood, but the cobbled streets of Darkacre seemed quieter than usual. No. 'Quieter' wasn't exactly right. They were more reserved, as if the cobbles and the terraces of red-brick houses felt Hartley and Steve's loss but didn't know how to help; they just looked away instead.

It had been three days since he and his friends, plus the Council, had faced Parity in Sanctuary. Three days since the portal to another world, one that terrified the magicals, had been opened. And of course, it had been three days since Blessing had sacrificed herself to save them all. Except that last one—Blessing's sacrifice—still didn't feel real to Steve. It didn't matter how many times he was told that she was gone, he just couldn't believe it.

"Oi, oi, mate." Steve was so deep in his thoughts that, when a hand grasped his shoulder, he batted it away and readied himself for a fight.

"Don't creep up on me like that!" said Steve as he recognised the teenager.

"Sorry." James held his hands up as if he was at gunpoint. "Didn't mean to scare you." He slowly lowered his hands and backed a couple of steps away. "I just wanted to say hi and how are you and…" He shrugged. "You know."

"Sorry," said Steve too. "I was thinking about…" He shook his head. "Stuff."

"Yeah, well. There's a lot of stuff been going on, hasn't there?" James' usual grin was nowhere to be seen. He looked as lost and miserable as Steve felt. "Hartley not with you?"

"He needed space," said Steve. "We've been stuck in his shop since we got back. He's even doing the washing up."

"Blimey, things must be bad." The edges of James' mouth twitched into an almost-smile. "Fancy a wander?"

"I'm not sure I'm good company at the moment."

"We don't have to talk," said James. "Just tootle."

"Tootling sounds good," said Steve.

Walking in companionable silence, the two teenagers wandered their way to the gate to the city. Frobisher sat in his deckchair, wrapped up in a couple of jackets and a thick, woollen scarf. He nodded to them as they passed but he didn't say a word.

When they reached the small square that housed the community school, the space was empty, the building silent, and the door locked.

"It's the weekend, mate," said James when Steve asked where everyone was. "Did you lose track of the days?"

"I suppose I did," said Steve.

"Not surprising after what's happened. I don't suppose…" For once, James looked unsure what to say. He chewed at his bottom lip for a moment then blurted out his next words. "Have you heard from the darkling?"

"No." Steve shook his head. "I thought you might have."

"Not a word," said James. "When you came home and she wasn't with you, I thought…" He shrugged. "Frobisher has hardly left the gate. Says he wants to be there when she comes back. He's grown attached to her. We all have."

Steve remembered the last time he had seen the darkling as she faced off against their pursuers. *I will hold off the Hidden for as long as I can, and then I must take up the reins of my old mission.* That was the final thing she had said to him.

"She wasn't with us at Sanctuary," said Steve. "She went off on her own quest. I wanted to talk to Hartley about her but he's…" He stopped. "It didn't seem like the right time."

"Aren't you worried about her? I know she can look after herself but…" Again, that shrug. "I want to know she's okay."

"Me too," said Steve. "I'll try to talk to Hartley. He'll know what to do."

It wasn't until they reached the community garden with its patchwork of fenced-off plots that Steve realised what had felt so off during their walk. Nobody worked the soil in the garden or chatted with their neighbours. The place was as quiet as the school had been.

"There's no one about," he said. "Not anywhere, except for you and Frobisher."

"Noticed that, did you?" said James. "Not surprising, if you think about it. Since Hartley and Blessing were taken by the Council, people have been on edge. Staying indoors. Keeping to themselves. I suppose this must have been how it felt in Myrkhof before they sealed it off from the workaday world."

"Myrkhof is another place like Darkacre, isn't it?" said Steve.

"Just the same," said James, nodding. "You can get to it from the, er…" He frowned. "What do you call it? Up north and a bit over. The Scandinavian States. Where it looks like Christmas all year round. You know, snow and reindeers. Well, not so much of the reindeers these days, but lots of snow."

"Why did the Council seal it off?"

"They didn't want a repeat of the Xav Mallorick scandal," said James. "He's well and proper jailed now. No one knows where. His community was sealed off first, and then Myrkhof. Over two hundred families turfed out of their homes."

"That's seem a bit harsh," said Steve. "It wasn't their fault."

"That's the Council for you."

"I heard Naomi Onai say his name at the Gathering," said Steve. "Who was he?"

"Don't know much," said James. "Happened before I was born. Far as I know, he wanted to tell the world about magic. Make a better place for workadays and magicals together. Something like that."

"That doesn't sound so bad."

"The Council got wind of what he was up to," said James. "Locked him away. I heard that he wasn't taken to the normal Council prison. He was sealed up by himself somewhere."

"Like in a wall?" said Steve. "To die?"

"No, no, no," said James. "Nothing like that. Just a special prison, somewhere."

"You don't think the Council will do that to Darkacre, do you?" The thought hit Steve's stomach like a sudden blow. "Seal it off?"

"That's what people here are worrying about." James shrugged and then shook his head. "But no. Frobisher would stop them."

"It's my fault." Steve suddenly felt as if the weight of Darkacre was on his shoulders. "If I'd handed over the Reactor to Abel, or Hartley. If I'd stayed at school and not gone off on an adventure. If—"

"*If* is a nasty word, mate." James grasped Steve by the shoulder and gave him a gentle shake. "You did what you did, and you did good. Can't change any of it. Nobody here blames you. You're one of us now, one of the family."

Family, Steve thought. He liked the sound of that.

"I need to find my mum and dad," he said.

"Goes without saying." James released him and nodded. "So what are you waiting around here for?"

"I think it's too soon. After…" He looked down at his feet. "Hartley is upset."

"We're all upset, mate. But life goes on. Blessing wouldn't want anything less. I say you tell Hartley how you feel."

"Really?"

"Really. He'll understand."

"Thanks, James." Steve nodded as he backed away from his friend. "I will. And I'll ask about the darkling."

"Make sure you do," James called after him. "Good luck."

The weight on Steve's shoulders felt a little lighter as he set off at speed along the cobbled street.

Chapter Two

"You'll be safe at school." Hartley's unbuttoned shirt cuffs, still damp from washing the dishes, flapped around his wrists as he expressed himself.

"I wasn't safe there when Braeden Kendra's thugs came after me." Steve sat with his elbows on the table and his head in his hands. "I don't want to go back to school. I want to find Mum and Dad."

"Steve, I wouldn't know where to start looking for your parents. The darkling? Now, that's another story. I can start asking around about her, on my own. The school must be incredibly worried by your absence."

"They weren't worried last time," said Steve. "Annoyed, but not worried. They didn't even call the police."

"What about your friend, Jonathan? Won't he wonder where you are?"

"I suppose so." He sat back with a humph. *He's right*, Steve's mind piped up. *Jon will be on his own. Without you there, Curtis is sure to bully him.*

"Look at it this way." Hartley pulled out the chair next to Steve and sat down. "I know your parents didn't leave you in my care—"

"No, they didn't."

"But I also know that they wouldn't want this kind of life for you." Hartley sighed. "School is where they can find you when they return."

"They could find me here in Darkacre."

"Oh Steve!" Hartley slammed a fist on the table and stood up again. "You're impossible to reason with."

"So are you!"

"What we need is a cool head with a sensible mind to make this decision." Hartley returned to his pacing. "A referee whom we will both listen to."

"I know someone like that." Steve stood up and nodded towards the door at the back of the kitchen that Hartley used as his personal and magical exit from Darkacre. "Do you think you could travel us to Eleanor's apartment?"

"Eleanor?" Hartley stopped in his pacing. "Of course. We've been there before."

"Then do it," said Steve. "Let Eleanor decide. If she says I have to go back to school, I will. But if she agrees with me…" He left the sentence unfinished.

"Fine," said Hartley, flexing his hands as he strode to the door. "But if she agrees with me, that will be an end to this."

"Of course," said Steve. *No way*, he thought. *This is just the beginning.*

*

Eleanor's apartment was just as Steve remembered: smart, stylishly co-ordinated, and efficiently arranged.

"Master Haven. Mister Keg. Welcome. I do hope you are both well." Eleanor's personal robot, a cleaning model called Hetty, zoomed out from the kitchen area as soon as Steve and Hartley arrived. The small robot was just above knee-height and travelled on four of its eight limbs.

"Hi Hetty," said Steve.

"Is it supposed to do that?" said Hartley, moving to stand behind the sofa. "How does it know our names?"

"Eleanor told Hetty to remember us in case we needed a place to stay. You were there when she said it."

"Was I?" Hartley slowly came out from behind the sofa. "Hello," he said with a weak wave. "Hetty, was it? How do you do?" He looked at Steve and shrugged.

"How do I do what?" said Hetty. "I am programmed to carry out many domestic tasks."

"Is Eleanor here?" said Steve.

"Eleanor is not here," said Hetty. "You are welcome to wait."

"Don't mind if we do." Hartley dropped onto the sofa with a little bounce. "Do you make tea, Hetty? To drink?"

"Yes, Mister Keg. I can make tea. Would you like a pot or a cup?"

"A pot would be delightful," said Hartley. "And are there biscuits?"

"I'm sorry. We do not have biscuits," said Hetty.

"That's a shame," said Hartley. "Cake?"

"I am programmed to bake cake."

"Well, if it isn't too much bother," said Hartley. "I wouldn't want to put you to any trouble."

"Hartley, what are you doing?" said Steve as Hetty returned to the kitchen area and gathered ingredients. "We're not here to make cake."

"Of course not," said Hartley. "Hetty is making it for us. Marvellous things, these robots. Don't you think?"

*

By the time the front door opened, Hartley and Steve were sat at the crumb-covered kitchen counter with two-thirds of a Victoria sponge cake and an empty pot of tea. Hetty the robot remained in her docking station, her charge exhausted by all the baking and serving.

"You're here," said Eleanor, staring at Steve.

"Hi," he said.

"I am also here," said Hartley, removing a blob of jam from his beard with his finger. "Hetty is a marvel."

"Hartley persuaded her to bake cake," said Steve.

"She offered," said Hartley, licking the jam off his finger.

"How did you get here so quickly? No, scrub that." Eleanor glared at Hartley. "*Why* are you both here?"

"It was Steve's idea," said the shopkeeper. "I insisted he'd be safe back at school, but he disagrees."

"I want to find Mum and Dad," said Steve.

"I don't understand," said Eleanor, glaring at the crumbs and mess. "Hetty—"

"She's sleeping," said Hartley. "She was very industrious."

"He means that she's charging," said Steve.

"Why does she need charging? I thought you said she just baked a cake."

"And made us a pot of tea," said Hartley.

"It started out as just baking a cake," said Steve. "But then Hartley asked her what else she could make. I hope you like biscuits. There's a lot of them in your cupboards."

"I see." Eleanor looked at the messy kitchen counter for a second longer, sighed, and gave a little shrug. "Steve, why didn't you talk to me about your parents when I saw you just now? I don't want you to get into trouble with the headmaster again."

"Just now?" said Steve. "What do you mean 'just now'?"

"When I visited you at school today."

"I haven't been at school today."

"Yes, you have."

"No, I haven't."

"Steve, I saw you there. In your room. With your teacher."

"Which teacher?" said Steve.

"The one who visited the Haven Corporation with you. Mr Tobias."

"Why's he still around?"

Steve remembered the last time he had seen the teacher. He'd grown to like Mr Tobias, trusted him even, until he'd revealed himself as one of the Council's enforcers, a Hidden. If it hadn't been for the darkling's help, Mr Tobias would have stopped Steve's escape from school.

"Where else would he be?" said Eleanor.

"I don't know what's going on," said Hartley. 'But I can confirm that Steve hasn't as yet returned to his school. And that teacher you spoke of? He's a Council spy."

"But he seems so nice. Are you sure?"

"One hundred per cent," said Steve. "He tried to keep me at school when Hartley and Blessing were arrested. The darkling fought him off though. Then Frobisher—"

"Stop, stop!" Eleanor marched to the sofa and flung herself down on it. "So you're telling me that the person I just left at school, with your pretend teacher, isn't you?"

"No," said Steve. "I mean, yes. I mean, who did you leave at school?"

"Well, it looked like you. Exactly like you. Maybe more obedient and polite than you. I suppose that should have been a clue."

"Thanks," said Steve.

"A lot has happened since we last met," said Hartley. "Maybe I should tidy away while Steve explains."

"Me?" said Steve. "You were there too."

"You can both tell me what's happened," said Eleanor. "Hetty? Damn, I forgot."

"Tea?" said Hartley.

"Coffee," said Eleanor. "And strong. I think I'm going to need it."

*

Eleanor sat at the cleaned kitchen counter with an empty cup and saucer. Steve had dealt with the crumbs and crockery while Hartley had started on the coffee. The shopkeeper's clanking around in her kitchen had disturbed Eleanor so much that she had finally taken over.

"I wanted to tell you about Parity. Hence the school visit," she said.

"What have they done?" Steve's stomach tensed at the

11

mention of the covert organisation. They were supposed to maintain balance between the magicals and the workaday world, but Elrick Olen and his agents had had their own self-serving agenda.

"Parity." Hartley tutted as he refilled his cup from the slim porcelain coffee-pot. "I suppose it was too much to expect that those people would be out of our hair."

"That's just it," said Eleanor. "They're gone. They cleared out of the Haven building and took their robots with them. What do they call them? Their hounds."

"When did this happen?" asked Hartley. "Which day?"

"Tuesday," she said.

"And today is?"

"You are out of touch, aren't you?" she said. "I suppose it's all this gallivanting around and adventuring."

"Something like that," said Steve with a smile.

"Today is Friday. Parity left three days ago."

"That makes sense," said Hartley. "The same day that they accosted us at the Sanctuary."

"Where's the Sanctuary?" said Eleanor. "And what do you mean 'accosted'? What have you two been up to?"

"So much," said Steve.

"Do I need more coffee for this?"

"Lots of the stuff," said Hartley. "And probably biscuits."

*

By the time they had finished telling Eleanor about the Council's arrest of Hartley and Blessing, their travels to the Augur and Keeltown, and Parity's involvement, the sky that was visible through the apartment's large window had darkened to a velvety blue and the automatic blinds had lowered to conceal the cityscape.

"I know this may be difficult to get your head around, Eleanor," said Hartley. "It's a complicated situation."

"Not at all," she said. "We have two cultures that necessarily interact but with the need for one to remain concealed from the other. It stands to reason that a third party like Parity is needed to maintain a level of balance and diplomacy between those worlds."

"Oh, you do understand," said Hartley. "That's good," he grumbled.

"I even understand the Council's investigation into what happened at the Haven Corporation. But their response was rather heavy handed."

"Heavy handed?" said Steve. "They put Hartley and Blessing in cells. They were going to—"

"As I say, heavy handed." She stood up and began to pace in front of the sofa. "What I still don't understand is how you appear to be in two places at the same time, Steve."

"That is a tad peculiar," said Hartley. "Even by my standards."

"Someone who looks and acts just like you is at your school right now, and yet here you are supping coffee in my apartment. How do you explain that?"

"Well, I'm not to blame," said Hartley. "This time."

"I can't explain it," said Steve. "But maybe the other me can. We need to go back to school and confront him."

"But your school is closed at this time of night," said Eleanor.

"Not to Hartley," said Steve. "He can travel us in there."

"Where did I travel you to last time we visited your school?" Hartley drained his cup of coffee. "That's the only place I can take you, I'm afraid."

"The headmaster's office."

"What if the man catches us?" said Hartley. "It could become very awkward."

"There's no need to worry about being discovered," said Eleanor. "The headmaster is away on holiday. I had to speak to that horrible secretary to arrange a visit to the school. She was in a terrible mood when I arrived because the headmaster hasn't left her with the code to get into his office."

"Did she tell you that?" said Steve.

"No, but your teacher…" She paused. "The person pretending to be your teacher, a teacher, whatever he is, he told me."

"That's decided then," said Steve.

"Is it?" said Hartley.

"Wouldn't you want to know if someone was pretending to be you? Wouldn't you want to know why?"

"I would," said Eleanor. "I find it quite disconcerting that I've been speaking to a complete stranger."

"Fine," said Hartley. "But if this gets me in trouble with the Council again, or the Hidden, I'm blaming you."

Chapter Three

When Steve and Hartley stepped out of the headmaster's stationery cupboard, they found themselves in a completely dark room. It smelled of cleaning fluid, beeswax, and expensive aftershave.

"And you're sure you can get us out of this room?" said Hartley, closing the cupboard behind them.

"There's a keypad at the door."

"We need light," said Hartley. There was a breath, a cough, and a bright green point of light pinged into the air.

"What did you do?" said Steve as the point of light whizzed around in front of his eyes.

"It's an orb," said Hartley. "I've been practicing."

"It's a dot," said Steve.

"Give me a chance." Hartley slapped his hands around the light and blew between his cupped palms. When he opened them, a green orb the size of a sprout hovered an inch above his hand.

"It's very small," said Steve.

"I suppose it is." Hartley sighed. "Never mind, I have a torch." He squashed the orb between his finger and thumb. It disappeared with a squeaky fart.

Steve waited for Hartley to retrieve the torch, smiling a little as he listened to his friend complain under his breath about the need to use 'technology'.

"Here we are," said Hartley. "And light!"

Instead of the sound of a button being pressed or a switch flicked, Steve heard something that always brought trouble into his life. It was the noise of a Hidden's arrival.

"You just couldn't resist, could you?" said a familiar voice as a cold, white light flooded the room.

Mr Tobias stood between the friends and the door to the school corridor. He was dressed as Steve remembered him, in a smart suit that was a little worn, a shirt that had been dulled by much washing, and a tie that bore the school emblem. A large light orb hovered above his outheld hand.

"We're not here to cause trouble." Hartley pulled Steve to his side.

"Relax," said the teacher with a slight smile. "Good to see you again, Steve."

"Is it?" said Steve. "I bet I got you into trouble for letting me escape like that."

"A little."

"Why are you still here?" said Hartley. "You can't spy on my young friend anymore."

"True," said Mr Tobias. "But I have a new purpose. It's all about keeping up appearances."

"What do you mean?" said Steve.

"It's probably easier to show you." In a blink, Mr Tobias had released the orb and moved across the space so quickly that Steve yelped as he felt the man's grasp on his shoulder. He heard Hartley protest and then they were no longer in the headmaster's office.

*

"This is weird," said Steve.

"Decidedly," said Hartley.

"It was necessary," said Mr Tobias. "My superior didn't want the school to raise the alarm when you went missing."

Steve and Hartley stood on one side of the room. Mr Tobias and the other person stood opposite.

"Pleased to meet you," said the other person. "I'm Steve

Haven."

"No, you're not," said Steve. "*I'm* Steve Haven."

"But are you sure?" said the other person.

The other person looked exactly like the image Steve saw in the mirror every morning. There wasn't anything—no gesture, no turn of phrase, not one detail—that didn't look or sound like Steve.

"Stop playing with our guest." Mr Tobias rolled his eyes. "Sorry, Steve. He's always like this."

"Like Steve Haven?" said Copy Steve.

"Like a performer," said Mr Tobias. "You know you love it."

"What's not to love?" said Copy Steve as he sat at Steve's desk and crossed his legs with a flourish. "I have clean clothes to wear and a comfortable bed to sleep in. They feed me. They educate me. I have friends." He shrugged. "That's paradise to someone like me."

"And what exactly is that?" said Hartley. "Leshy? Bakeneko? Or just a plain old shapeshifter?"

"There's nothing old or plain about me," said Copy Steve. "I am fabulous. But yes, I'm a shapeshifter."

"I have to admit that he's good at what he does," said Mr Tobias. "No one has guessed the truth. Not that these workadays would notice the truth. Not even your friend, Jon, has realised that you've been replaced."

"Right," said Steve. On the one hand, he was pleased that Jon wasn't on his own but on the other, he had to admit that he was a little bit offended his friend hadn't noticed.

"So are you coming back to school, Steve?" said Mr Tobias. "Had enough adventures?"

"But I've hardly settled in," said Copy Steve.

"I think it would be best," said Hartley, laying a hand on Steve's shoulder. "We both do."

"No, we don't." Steve shuffled out of Hartley's grasp and crossed his arms. "You just want rid of me."

"Do I sense a disagreement?" said Copy Steve. "Well, if

anyone wants my opinion—"

"We don't," said Hartley and Steve at the same time.

"Sorry for speaking," said Copy Steve with a tut.

"I want to find my parents," said Steve. "I know that—"

"Let me stop you there," said Mr Tobias, raising his hands. "As a member of the Hidden, I should tell you that the location of your parents is of utmost importance to the Council. I'm therefore expected to report any plans or information I glean from you. But as your teacher, I fully understand your feelings. I'd also like to point out that there is a perfect solution right under your nose."

"Oh, you mean me," said Copy Steve after a moment. "I suppose 'perfect' should have been the clue."

"Would that be all right?" said Steve. "Wouldn't the Council mind?"

"Of course," said Mr Tobias. "If they ever found out."

"I've never known a Hidden to act against their employer," said Hartley. "What makes you different?"

"You assume that my loyalty is to the Council."

"Obviously," said Hartley.

"And it is," said Mr Tobias, "but only part of the Council. I work for Kiri Ema. While the other Council members would prefer that you are both contained, Kiri doesn't agree. So let's say that this encounter never happened. I have no idea where you are or what you intend to do."

"That is unexpected and rather generous," said Hartley.

"You mean I can stay?" said Copy Steve. "I'd hate to return to that cold, smelly hostel."

"You can stay," said Steve. "You can be me, for now."

"This is going to be such fun." Copy Steve clapped his hands.

"Come on, Hartley." Steve marched across to the cupboard door that still bore faded chalk marks from when he'd tried to travel out of it just a few days before. "We can get out this way."

"I see." Hartley ran a hand across his beard as he looked from Steve to Copy Steve and finally addressed Mr Tobias. "Just how fervently do the Council wish to find Mary and Elijah Haven?"

"Let's say that Elijah Haven's investigations rang certain alarm bells for the Council. So when he, and then his wife, went missing, it made most members of the Council very nervous."

"I presume that by 'most', you mean Blaike Harn, Jonah Ledwitch, and Naomi Onai?" said Hartley.

"And Volund Wolff," said the teacher. "Kiri Ema has refrained from admitting any opinion on the matter."

"Come on," said Steve. "We've got things to do." He jerked his head at the cupboard door.

"It seems there is to be no discussion," said Hartley with a sigh. "Fine. Have it your way, Steve." Hartley stomped across the room and ran his hands around the frame of the cupboard door.

"Before you go," said Mr Tobias. "I hope there's no hard feelings between us, Steve. I know we parted on difficult terms."

"That's one way of putting it," said Steve.

"Kiri Ema asked me to take the part of a teacher here. She feared for your safety. When I tried to stop you, I was simply following orders."

"Here we are." Hartley opened the cupboard door wide. Over the threshold, what should have been a standard wardrobe with hanging clothes and a pair of shoes instead displayed the interior of Eleanor's apartment. "Shall we?"

"I hope you're going to close that when you're finished," said Mr Tobias. "I don't want to handle any more unexpected visitors."

"It'll be back to a wardrobe once we've departed," said Hartley. "I always tidy up after myself. Usually," he admitted.

"In that case, all there is to say is goodbye, Steve," said Mr Tobias. "And good luck."

"You too," said Steve. "And Steve?"

"Yes?" said Copy Steve.

"Look after Jon. Don't let the other boys bully him. He's a good person and a good friend too. Promise?"

"Of course," said Copy Steve, suddenly looking a little

serious. "He's my friend too."

"I can't keep this door open forever, you know," said Hartley. "It'll be noticed."

"Take care of yourself," said Mr Tobias as Steve reached for the open cupboard door. "Or as much care as you can take when you're travelling with Hartley Keg."

"I'll try," said Steve.

He took one last look around his room. He'd been happy here, for a while. With a nod, he turned his back on the safety of the school, stepped through the cupboard door, and started out on a new adventure.

Chapter Four

After a surprisingly comfortable night on Eleanor's sofa, Steve sat at the glass dining table in her apartment. Just like the rest of her home, the room was modern, sophisticated, colour co-ordinated, and neat. Or at least it had been neat until Hartley had descended on it.

"I thought we could spread out in here," she said as she poured herself a coffee from a cafetiere into a matching cup. "And discuss the way forward over breakfast."

"Sounds marvellous." Hartley crunched noisily on a slice of toast, his third, sprinkling his beard with crumbs and splatters of butter. "What are we talking about?"

"Steve, you haven't eaten. I know I'm not your mother but…" She looked at the empty plate in front of him. "Hetty can make whatever you like."

"You haven't eaten either." He sat with his hands around a glass of milk that he'd hardly touched. Now that he was free to go look for his parents, his stomach felt like a knot made up of more knots.

"I don't do breakfast," said Eleanor. She watched him for a moment more, her fingers playing on the handle of the cup. "Okay," she said. "I have good news and I have bad news. And I have other news. Which do you want to hear first?"

"Good?" said Hartley around a mouthful of toast.

"The good news is that I've tracked down where your mother travelled to. To be completely honest, I've known for a few days now."

"That's great," said Steve, releasing the glass of milk as the knots in his stomach loosened. "Where is she?"

"I'm not sure where she is right now, but her flight took her to Nuova Venezia."

"Venice?" said Hartley.

"New Venice, to be exact."

"You've lost me," said Hartley.

"New Venice is a modern reconstruction of the old city," she said. "When the original Venice finally sank—is sank the right word?—or when it became obvious that it would be destroyed by the elements, a New Venice was created."

"A raised city like Caercester?" said Hartley.

"Better than that," said Steve. "It flies."

"Without magic? How odd."

"Don't you want to hear the bad news?" said Eleanor.

"Not really, but okay," said Steve. Suddenly, Hartley's chewing noises were making his stomach rumble.

"There's a waiting list to visit Nuova Venezia. It's such a popular resort for holidays, especially for the rich and famous, that you need permission to enter."

"How long is this waiting list?"

"Months," said Eleanor.

"I'm sure there's a work-around," said Hartley. "I know I can't travel us there but there are bound to be other means." He tapped a finger to his nose. "If you know people."

"Do you know people?" said Steve.

"I might," said Hartley.

"I'll take that as a no," said Eleanor. "Maybe your darkling friend can help."

"Ah," said Hartley. "That may prove difficult."

"We don't know where she is," said Steve.

"We parted company during our last adventure. I believe she was on her way back to the Haven Corporation."

"Whatever for?" said Eleanor. "After Parity's departure, I thought the Haven Corporation was all done with that kind of thing. Even the Council haven't been in touch lately."

"The darkling was worried about Parity's interest in the basement," said Steve. "That's where Winters' lab was before…" He shrugged. "You know."

"That would explain a number of things." She tapped her nails on the side of her cup. "Okay then," she said.

"Are you going somewhere?" said Hartley as she snatched his cup from his grasp and tidied the breakfast things into the centre of the table.

"We all are," she said. "There's something you need to see."

*

Steve was worried. After Eleanor had ushered them into her car, she had hardly said a word other than to give instructions to the driver of the midnight blue vehicle. It wasn't as if Steve hadn't tried to talk to her.

"So why don't you use the Haven vehicles?" he'd asked as the car lined up at traffic lights between two rows of automated vehicles.

"We both know the answer to that," had been her curt reply. Then, after a moment of staring at the glass that separated passengers from the driver, she said, "I'm not sure I altogether trust automated vehicles anymore. Your Uncle Rex felt the same. This was his car. As head of the Haven Robotics Corporation, Rex liked to keep up a certain appearance. Martin was his driver for years. Before that, Martin's father drove Rex around."

"Lovely car," Hartley called out to Martin. "Excellently manoeuvred too."

That was the last time Eleanor spoke on the journey. It wasn't until the vehicle pulled up outside the Haven Corporation building that she said anything more.

"Thank you, Martin. Well, come on then," she barked at Steve and Hartley as the driver opened her door and she slid out of the car in a smooth, sophisticated move.

"Thanks." Steve hurried out as Eleanor marched away and

disappeared through the doors of the building. "Come on, Hartley."

"I'm getting there," said his friend with a wide grin for the driver. "Thank you, Martin."

The driver nodded in response and closed the car door behind them. He didn't say a word. He just watched the two of them rush through the parting glass doors.

"Can I help you?" the receptionist robot called from its glass desk which sat in the centre of the entrance lobby.

"They're with me," Eleanor called from the lifts at the back of the reception area. "Hurry up, Steve. Hartley."

"I do hope you enjoy your visit to the Haven Robotics Corporation," said the robot as they rushed past.

"What's the hurry?" said Hartley as Eleanor pressed her finger to the lift call button. "Where's the emergency?"

"No emergency," said Eleanor as the lift doors slid open. "But I hate wasting time, especially if you two are heading off on another jaunt."

"I wouldn't call it a jaunt," said Steve as they stepped into the lift.

"More of a quest really," said Hartley.

"Whatever it is, you need to see this first." Eleanor pressed her finger to the button marked 'B' for basement. "You may be able to help us understand."

"'Help' is my middle name," said Hartley. "I'm always happy to assist."

"I'll remember that," said Eleanor as the doors slid shut and the lift began to drop.

*

Even Eleanor noticed the change in Hartley as the lift doors opened into the basement. His face paled. His eyes glazed over. He looked unsteady on his feet as he braced himself against the lift wall with one hand.

"Are you all right?" she said.

"This is wrong." Hartley clamped a hand on Steve's shoulder to steady himself even more. "This feels like when we visited Nereid 8."

"Is it a magical thing?" Eleanor backed out of the lift. "Should we distance ourselves?"

"I think so," said Steve. "I mean, yes, it's probably a magical thing, but no, he isn't going to explode."

"It's in there." Hartley jerked his head towards the open lift doors.

"What is?" said Eleanor, looking around.

"The device that's draining my magic." Hartley dropped to the floor and sat in the middle of the lift with his hands pressed to the sides of his head.

"Well, that's inconvenient," said Eleanor. "I wanted his opinion."

"How bad is it, Hartley?" Steve crouched beside his friend. "Can you make it any further or shall we send you back up in the lift?"

"Back up, back up." Hartley was rocking now, with his eyes clamped shut.

"Come on, Steve," said Eleanor.

"I can't leave him like this."

"Yes, you can," she said, returning to the lift. "I'll take Hartley back upstairs. You head off into the basement. Keep going until you can't go any further. Mr Cady will fill you in."

As Steve stepped out of the lift and the doors slid shut behind him, he tried to calm the nerves that gripped his stomach. *I'm not alone*, he thought as he began to walk. *Mr Cady is down here.* He halted at the doorway that led through into a well-lit corridor beyond. *Winters is gone. Parity is gone. There's nothing down here to worry about.* He nodded his head to convince himself.

Then why are you down here? said the niggling voice in his head. *What does Eleanor want you to see?*

Shut up, he thought back. *You're not helping.* But he couldn't deny that the voice was right. Eleanor had brought them down here in a hurry and as Hartley had said in the lift, this felt wrong.

*

'Wrong' had been an understatement. Steve had followed the increasingly familiar route through the corridors of the basement. What had been a neglected space the last time he was here—running for his life in an attempt to rescue his friends—was now refurbished with brand new lighting and freshly plastered walls. That in itself wasn't wrong. If anything, it was expected after the explosion. Of course the basement would have been repaired. That made complete sense. It was what Steve discovered in the final room that was wrong.

"Steve, good to see you again." The robotics engineer that Steve had met only a few days before pumped Steve's hand enthusiastically. "Is it just you?"

"Yup, just me, Mr Cady," said Steve, staring past the man. "Hartley and Eleanor had to go."

At the other end of the room was a white wall that reached all the way to the low ceiling. It was completely smooth, broken only by the gaping mouth of an open door. It was the door to Winters' laboratory, the one that Steve had seen destroyed only months before, along with everything that lay beyond.

A robot crouched in front of the door, its limbs drawn underneath it like a resting dog. A smear of red dirtied the joint of one of its limbs.

"Fascinating, isn't it?" said Mr Cady. "There's no record of the basement being used for anything other than storage. Eleanor suggested we break in with brute force, but I knew cracking the access code would be much more satisfying. It only took Sam a couple of minutes."

"Sam?" said Steve.

"Surgical assistant model. S. A. M. I like to call them Sam. Very dextrous. Perfect for hacking door keypads." Mr Cady's smile weakened as he spoke. "Not so perfect for dealing with what we found in there."

"Winters' laboratory," said Steve. "Or at least it was that before…" He mimed an explosion with his hands and said "Poof".

"That would explain why Parity was interested." Mr Cady tapped a finger on his chin as he nodded. "But," he said, pointing his finger in the air, "why would the Council be involved?"

"The Council?" said Steve, wondering just how much Mr Cady knew about, well, everything.

"The people in charge of the magical world that your friend Hartley belongs to," said Mr Cady with a smile.

"Eleanor told you," said Steve.

"She did," said Mr Cady. "At least, enough to understand that magic exists—which I find fascinating—and that there's a whole culture based around it."

"So you know that Winters was a magical?"

"No, I didn't." Mr Cady clicked his fingers. "That explains it of course. This gets better and better."

Glad someone thinks so, thought Steve.

"The lab is empty," said Mr Cady. "Except for one thing. Or rather one person."

"What?" said Steve.

"She's rather excitable," said Mr Cady. "Exhausted but…" He shrugged. "Sam tried to help but she didn't like that. Lashed out. Injured herself." He sighed. "She's your age. Maybe a little older. Could you talk to her? Sam can restrain her, if needed. Careful now," said Mr Cady as Steve rushed to the open door. "She's unpredictable. Best stay calm. Very calm."

Chapter Five

When the door opened, the darkling had tried to react. She wanted to jump to her feet and attack whichever Parity operative had returned to taunt her, or hurt her, or simply put an end to her life. She wanted to do that, but she couldn't.

She had no idea how long she had remained in the white, starkly-lit room. It felt like a week, or weeks even, but she hoped it was merely days. Her initial outrage and fear at being imprisoned had exhausted her body and her spirits. Her human hunger built and then turned into a gnawing nausea. Her limbs trembled. Her lips were dry and cracked. She had next to nothing to fight back with, not even a clarity of thought.

But when the robot entered the room, a weak wave of adrenaline strengthened her enough to swipe a fist at it, bloodying her knuckles as they scraped across the joints of one of the machine's limbs. Cradling her hand, she had retreated with as much speed as she could manage, shuffling across the floor until she backed into the wall of the laboratory.

"All is safe, Mr Cady," said the robot in its synthetic voice. "The room is empty except for the sole inhabitant. She is in need of care."

"Inhabitant?" The man she had seen talking to Eleanor Palmer ran into the room before skidding to a halt. "Hello," he had said in a kind but wary voice. "Are you all right?"

"No." Her mouth felt dry and the words difficult to form. "No, I am not."

"That's what I thought," said the man. "Here. Let me help you."

The darkling hissed and snarled at his outheld hand like a cornered beast.

"Right, you are." The man retreated a little, called for the robot, and then they had left her alone.

She didn't know how long the door had remained open with the man pacing in the room beyond. Her gut instinct was to run, but the robot barred her way, its limbs coiled beneath it as it waited just outside the door. It wasn't until she heard someone new join the man that she left the safety of the wall.

"Miss Darkling." Steve stopped for a moment at the doorway. "Where have you been?" He ran across the room, engulfing her in a tight hug.

"Here," was all she could manage.

"So you know her?" said the man, peering into the laboratory.

"Yes, she's a friend," said Steve, releasing her. "This is Mr Cady. You can trust him. We're going to get you out of here. Get that thing off you."

"This." She touched a hand to the collar that the Parity operatives had fitted around her neck. "Hurts."

"I thought you said this was a laboratory, Steve," said Mr Cady.

"Parity prison," she said as Steve helped her to stand.

"Oh dear," said Mr Cady. "Eleanor won't like that, but it does tell us why Parity were down here."

"Can you walk?" Steve wrapped one of the darkling's arms around his shoulders.

She nodded, leaning into him. "Thank you."

"No need," said Steve. "You've rescued me so many times. I'm just returning the favour."

*

The girl Steve helped through the basement corridors seemed nothing like the darkling he had come to know. Yes, she looked like the darkling's solid form; but she was frail, and scared, and depending on him to look after her.

Something had changed about her appearance, too. Her eyes had always picked her out as something other than human. They had been indigo in colour and larger than a person's eyes had any business to be. Now, they were a violet blue and of a normal size. Unless you knew she was a darkling, you would have assumed that she was just another teenage girl. She walked with one arm around Steve's shoulders and the other hand clasped to the metal collar that encased her neck. She stared at the walls as if they were a threat, but Steve saw nothing out of the ordinary in them.

"Hartley will know what to do," he said, just as much to reassure himself as the darkling.

"I could have a look at the device round her neck," said Mr Cady who walked ahead of them. Since they'd found the darkling, he had fluttered around the two young people in an attempt to help.

"Thanks, but we know someone who can get it off quickly," said Steve.

"That's good," said Mr Cady, sounding more disappointed than pleased. "I'll get the lift doors." He nodded to himself and headed off at speed.

"Where is Hartley?" the darkling whispered.

"With Eleanor," said Steve. "The basement affected him. I thought he was going to faint."

"Parity did something to the basement walls." She struggled to speak, pulling at the collar. "Drains magic, just like the white room."

"That would explain it," said Steve as they reached the final space that held the lifts. "James will have that collar off in no time. Then, you can get well in shadow form."

"Here we are." Mr Cady stood at the lift doors, holding them open with one hand. "We can go straight up to Eleanor's office from here.

"We'll have you back in Darkacre in no time," said Steve. "You're safe now."

"Safe," she said with a nod. "That sounds good."

*

The darkling sat on a velvet chaise longue in Eleanor's office. It was the only comfortable-looking piece of furniture in the immense room. Steve hovered at her side. He felt too happy to sit down and didn't want to stray too far from his friend. At the back of his mind, another emotion niggled at him. Guilt. He shouldn't be this happy when Blessing was still… He put an end to that thought. The darkling was back. Best concentrate on that.

Hartley sat in front of the darkling in a stiff leather chair that he had dragged across the room. His eyes were watery but there was no denying his happiness. He held the darkling's hand, alternately patting it and laughing.

"So we can add torture and imprisonment to Parity's record." Eleanor paced up and down in front of her desk, with her hands on her hips and the occasional shake of her head. "Unbelievable."

"But they're gone now," said Steve. "And Miss Darkling is back."

"I'm sorry." Eleanor stopped pacing and turned to the darkling. "We haven't met before. I'm Eleanor Palmer. I'm…" She shook her head. "It doesn't really matter who I am, other than that I'm glad you're here and safe."

"Thank you," said the darkling. She looked as if she might fall asleep at any moment. "I am happy also."

"Hartley, can't you do something about the Parity collar?" said Eleanor. "It's quite barbaric."

"James can help with that," said Steve. "He's from Darkacre," he continued when Eleanor frowned. "He's good at this kind of thing."

"He is my friend," said the darkling. "I trust him."

"Darkacre, it is then," said Eleanor. "I can call my car."

"No need," said Hartley, releasing the darkling's hand. "I just

31

need a suitable doorway." He pushed himself to his feet, clasped one hand to his mouth as he retched and the other to his head. "No," he gulped as he sat down heavily. "Whatever Parity did to the basement still has its hold on me. Maybe in a few minutes' time."

"I think the girl has waited long enough, don't you?" Eleanor returned to her desk. "I'll call the car around. Steve, you can tell Martin where to go."

"Well, if you're sure," said Hartley. "We wouldn't want to be a nuisance."

"Too late," said Eleanor with the tiniest of smiles.

*

The darkling sat on a dining chair in Frobisher's parlour. James examined the collar around her neck, tutting and sighing to himself.

"Can't you get the collar off?" said Steve. "It looked easy when you got rid of Hartley's."

"It was," said James. "This Parity collar is a different matter though. See this?" He tapped his finger on the point where the collar fastened. "The locking mechanism is plastic."

"So?" said Steve.

"Magic doesn't work on plastic. Not my magic anyway. If I teleport the collar, the plastic bits might stay on her neck."

"Please try." The darkling's head dipped as she slurred the words. Her eyelids felt as heavy as the collar around her neck and the emptiness in her stomach.

"*Try*, I can do." James stood up straight, lips pursed in thought, and then he gave one decisive nod. The collar, or at least most of it, disappeared. The plastic portion fell to the floor. As the metal part of the collar materialised in James' hands, the darkling slumped to one side. Steve caught her before she fell off the chair.

"Frobisher, it worked," said Steve.

"That's good," said the gatekeeper. He stood at the window, holding back the patched-up curtains with a finger as he peered out at the street beyond. "I do wish he'd come in. People will think there's something up."

"Be fair," said James as he and Steve helped the darkling to the fireside armchair. "You did tell on him to the Council. He's got reason to be ticked off."

"You don't have to rub it in." Frobisher closed the curtains with a tut. "How'd you feel?" he asked as he crossed the room.

"Heavy," said the darkling. It wasn't a perfect description, but it was the nearest she could come to the physical sensation she felt.

"After-effects are only to be expected," said Frobisher. "Now that monstrosity is off, you can rest up in shadow."

"True," she said, looking at her hands as she willed them to return to her native form.

"Go on then," said Frobisher.

"I am trying."

"What's wrong?" said Steve.

She closed her eyes, drawing her arms around her. She took a deep breath all the way down into the base of her stomach, then released it in one drawn-out, desperate attempt to return to shadow. She remembered what it was to be formless, to be of no substance at all. She pictured herself moving across the floor of Frobisher's parlour, collecting in the puddle of darkness under his sideboard, and repairing all the damage that the collar and Winters' laboratory had inflicted on her.

She opened her eyes. She still sat on the chair. Steve, James, and Frobisher stared at her with a range of worried and puzzled expressions.

"I cannot," she said so quietly that it was almost a breath. "I need Blessing's help."

"Blessing is—" Frobisher began.

"Not here," said Steve, cutting the gatekeeper off. "I'll get Hartley."

"Not enough," she said as Steve headed for the door. "I need a g…"

Her head lolled forward onto her chest as the world melted away from her sight, and she slept.

Chapter Six

"You never should have brought her here."

Hartley stomped up and down the gatekeeper's parlour. Frobisher had disappeared into his kitchen. Steve could hear the old man rattling around with pots and pans and crockery. The darkling lay on the sofa in a deep sleep, barely breathing.

"She needed James' help." Steve sat on the fireside armchair, his arms crossed. "Where else would we take her?"

"Fair point," said James.

"And look what happened," said Hartley. "No offence, James, but—"

"Well, tough, because I am offended." James leant on the back of the fireside armchair. "You and Frobisher need to sort this disagreement out. It's doing no one anything good."

"That man." Hartley wagged a finger at James. "That man will never—"

"Tea." Frobisher stood in the open doorway, eyes fixed on the tray that he carried. "For those as wants it." He gave a sniff and carried his load to the small, low table that sat in between the armchairs and sofa.

"Not for me." Hartley turned his back on them all, facing the curtained window.

"Fine." Frobisher unpiled the stack of cups and saucers, sat on an armchair, and began to pour the tea. "Steve?"

"That would be great."

"Me too, Fro'," said James.

"Hartley, are you sure?" said Steve.

"I prefer coffee," said Hartley with his back still turned. "Tea is for old men."

"Oi," said James. "I'm not old."

"Thank you, Frobisher." Steve picked up a cup of tea. "You're very kind."

"Kind?" spluttered Hartley, turning on them. "After what he did. How can you say—"

The darkling sat up with a cry, her back rod-straight and her eyes as wide as they could physically be. Steve struggled not to spill his tea as he jumped a little, his cup rattling on the saucer.

"It's all right now." James rushed to the sofa and took her hand. "You're here. At Frobisher's. You're okay."

"I was in the white room," she said. "They shut the door on me. I was alone."

"But now you're not," he said. "You're with family."

"Why don't you have a cup of tea?" said Frobisher. "Tea always helps."

"Thank you," she said. "That is kind."

"Enough with calling that man 'kind'," said Hartley. "After what he—"

"Hartley Keg." Frobisher stood up and faced the other man. "You are a braggart and a very disruptive man."

"How dare you," stormed Hartley. "I should—"

"But." Frobisher stopped Hartley's rant with a raised hand. "I owe you an apology."

"Oh." Hartley took a short, wide-eyed breath. "Go on."

"I made a bad judgement call when I told the Council about your involvement with the Haven Corporation incident." He gave a sad nod. "And I will forever regret the loss of that poor, dear girl as a result of my actions."

"Fro' mate…" said James.

"No, it's true. All of it," said the gatekeeper. "But now we have our other dear girl back after all she's gone through. And I think that's a reason for celebration. Even if we're still broken-hearted over Blessing." His voice broke a little as he said her name. "Friends?" He offered Hartley his hand.

Hartley stared at the gatekeeper's hand as a tear rolled down his face. He sniffed, rubbed a hand across his nose, and nodded. "Thank you, Frobisher," he said as he shook the man's hand.

"Now you," said Steve.

"Pardon?" said Hartley.

"Say you're sorry too."

"You've been a right pain," said James. "Apologise."

"Hartley Keg does not apologise." He pulled himself up to his full height, which meant that the top of his head brushed the low ceiling of the parlour. "Very often." He gave a small cough to clear his throat. "I'm sorry. To all of you. I've not been myself since…" His words ran out.

"We know," said James. "We all miss her."

The friends shared a moment of silent grief, and then Frobisher broke the spell and returned to his pouring.

"Milk and sugar, Miss Darkling?"

"Do I like milk and sugar?" she asked. "Or tea?"

Frobisher sploshed a drop of milk into the filled teacup and added a sugar lump. "Shall we find out?"

*

By the time that Frobisher tidied away the tea tray, James' younger brother Michael had arrived home and was grilling the darkling for details.

"Your eyes look so different." He stared at her face as if it was the first time he had seen her.

"I'm sure Miss Darkling doesn't want to be treated like a zoo animal, Michael." Hartley shared the settee with the two of them.

"She doesn't mind, do you?"

"I suppose not."

The darkling had never considered the way she looked, other than whether her solid form was sufficiently crafted to act as a disguise. Now, knowing that this was her only form, she felt unsettled.

"And you can't change any more?" said Michael.

"It would appear not," she said. "I am just this."

"Only for now," said Hartley. "And there is no 'just' about it."

"He's right. In a fight, you'd still kick James' ar—"

"Oi!" James cut off his brother as Hartley chuckled. "Language."

"You would though," Michael told the darkling with a wink.

"Leave the girl alone," said Frobisher, peering in from the kitchen. "She needs to rest." Frobisher said that last word as if he wasn't entirely sure what 'rest' meant for the darkling, now. "Come help me wash the tea things."

"Do I have to?" Michael complained as he followed the gatekeeper out of the parlour.

"So Blessing is really…?" The darkling wasn't sure how to finish the sentence. "She is gone?"

"I'm afraid so," said Hartley.

"I see." Even without her ability to read their auras, the darkling could sense the tension between her friends. "If I had been there…" She shook her head. "I am sorry. I let you down."

"No, you didn't." James sat down beside her on the settee and grabbed her hand. "Don't you think that. Don't you dare."

"He's right," said Steve. "Even if you'd come to Sanctuary with us, Parity would have put one of those collars on you. You're not to blame."

"Thank you." The darkling was surprised by the tremble in her voice and the tightness in her throat when she thought of Blessing. Her eyes were leaking again, just as they had when she was first imprisoned in the laboratory. It was strange and discomforting. "What will you do now?" she managed.

"Back to school for you, Steve?" said James.

"No way," said Steve. "That's sorted, isn't it, Hartley?"

"It would appear so," said the shopkeeper.

"Sorted, how?" said James. "Come on, spill."

"I've got a replacement," said Steve. "While I'm away."

"This sounds juicier by the moment. Fill me in, why don't you?"

As Steve told them about the shapeshifter and the Hidden who posed as a teacher at his school, with the odd interruption from Hartley, the darkling tried to make sense of what she felt, both physically and emotionally. She felt the warmth of James' hand on her own and found it comforting. She heard the camaraderie between Steve and Hartley as they shared the telling of their discovery. She felt more vulnerable than she had ever felt before, but that vulnerability was accompanied by an idea that she was safe here with these humans.

"And Eleanor knows where Mum went so it makes sense to go after her," said Steve. "I'm not sure how, but—"

"Hold on now. Who said anything about going after your parents?" said Hartley.

"I did," said Steve. "I've been saying it all along. And now I don't have to worry about school, there's nothing stopping me."

"Well, I can't travel you there." Hartley slumped back into the settee. "I've never been to this New Venice before. Nowhere near."

"You'll find a way," said James. "You're Hartley Kez."

"Flattery will get you nowhere," said Hartley. "Certainly not to New Venice."

"Sounds like you don't want to go," said James. "Maybe you're scared."

"I am not scared," said Hartley. "And I won't be goaded into a decision either."

"There is nothing to stop the two of you from going," said the darkling.

"You too," said Steve. "You can come with us."

"I am not sure that I could help. I am only this."

"Yeah, but like Michael said, you're still kick-ass."

"I do not know what that means," said the darkling.

"It means that you're the best fighter of us all," said Steve. "It means that you're strong and won't take any nonsense."

"Even the Hartley Keg kind of nonsense," said James.

"I resent that insinuation," said Hartley but his lips curled into a faint smile. "If we did decide to go to Venice, I'd have to figure out the nearest location on the Continent to open a doorway to."

"Sounds right up your street," said James. "You being a traveller an' all."

"Right," said Steve. "We can do this then. And you'll come too," he said to the darkling. "Won't you?"

"If you think I can help."

"Of course, you can, dear girl," said Hartley. "But I think there's someone you need to meet before we go. Someone who can help with your current conundrum."

*

Effie and Norman Gard were as different as they were alike. Effie was a tall woman with big arms, a rosy smile, and a voice that could beat Hartley's own enthusiastic boom. Norman was a head-and-a-half shorter, wiry, and prone to nodding at everything his wife said. The quality they shared was the warmth with which they welcomed Hartley, Steve, and the darkling into their home.

"Effie, my dear." Hartley placed a swift kiss on her cheek. "Norman." He shook the man's hand. "How are you both?"

"Good," said Norman with a nod.

"You know us," said Effie. She led them past a steep narrow staircase and into a parlour that was a riot of potted plants, glass vases, and embroidered surfaces. "Life is always for the taking."

"It is." Norman followed the four of them into the parlour, nodding his flat-capped head.

"How can we help?" Effie took a seat at a two-person square table that sat snug under the front window, crossing her slippered feet at the ankles. Norman took a perch at the dresser on the other side of the room.

"My young friend here is in need of some advice." Hartley placed his hands on the darkling's shoulders, drawing her in front of him. "From Mimi."

"Oh, that kind of advice, is it?" said Effie. "What kind of fae are you, if you don't mind me asking?"

"I am a darkling," said the darkling. "I think."

"It's a complicated situation," said Hartley. "I thought Mimi might be able to shed some light."

"I'll get her." Norman left the room with a nod. The darkling heard his footsteps trundle up the narrow staircase.

"Let me look at you," said Effie, holding out her hands to the darkling.

"Go on." Hartley nudged the darkling forwards.

"I won't bite." Effie laughed. "Not if you're in my good books."

The darkling moved closer, stopping a pace away from the table. She wasn't used to being the centre of attention.

"Darkling, but not a darkling," said Effie.

"That's right," said Steve. "For now."

"Your eyes look quite human," said the woman. "Not sure if that's a good sign or bad. How do you feel?"

"Feel?" The darkling wasn't sure how to answer. "The room is sufficiently warm. My clothes are comfortable. I have a little pain here." She brushed a finger across her forehead.

"No, how do you *feel*?" said Effie. "Happy? Sad? Scared?"

"Confused," said the darkling after a moment's thought. "Revealed."

"Sounds about right," said Effie. "Yes, Mimi will be a help."

"How?"

"She was a darkling herself," said Effie. "I'll let her explain. Gods know it still confuses me."

*

When Mimi first entered the cluttered parlour, the darkling

thought there had been a mistake. The girl was younger than Steve, maybe eleven or twelve years old. With her short cropped blonde hair and light brown eyes, she appeared to be altogether human. There was nothing about her that suggested she was or ever had been a darkling.

"Hello." Mimi remained in the doorway to the hall. She looked at everyone in the parlour in turn, a smile lifting her lips each time she caught someone's eye.

"Mimi, we've got a visitor." Effie nodded towards the darkling. "She's a lot like you."

Mimi frowned as she stepped into the room. "Do you mean...?" She looked more intently at the darkling's face. "Do I know you?"

"Maybe," said the darkling. "From before."

"Hartley, how are you for onions?" Effie stood up, crossing the room at speed to take Hartley's arm. "And pickle." She drew him with her to the door at the back of the room.

"You know me," he said, beckoning to Steve to follow them. "I'm always delighted to stock up my pantry."

"I think they want us to talk," said Mimi as the door closed behind the others. "Shall we?" She took the seat that Effie had just left and gestured to the empty chair on the other side of the table.

"Thank you." The darkling pulled out the chair, running her hands across its back.

"It is safe to sit."

"Of course." The darkling looked at the closed door that her friends had disappeared through. She could hear Hartley's laughter and a clattering of pots.

"Sit," said Mimi. "Please."

"Very well." The darkling sat on the chair, folding her hands on her lap.

"How long has it been since you…?" Mimi tilted her head.

"Hours. Days," said the darkling. "I do not know how much time has passed."

"For me, it has been over a year since I lost my…" Mimi paused, glancing around with a frown. "Powers? Essence?" She shrugged. "Since I became human."

"How?" asked the darkling.

"That is unimportant," said Mimi. "What matters is that I survived, just not as a darkling. I am human. A workaday even." She smiled. "Effie does not like that word, but it is a fair representation of what I am. I have no magic. I age. My hair grows. I eat food to nourish my body. These are all lessons that I had to learn. You will too."

"I do not want to," said the darkling. "When my shadow self returns—"

"*If* it returns," said Mimi.

"It must." The darkling felt her face growing red. She clamped her hands into fists, surprised at the pain as her nails dug into her palms.

"For me, the change was final," said Mimi. "For you, it may be different. What were you wearing after you lost your darkling self?"

"These." The darkling touched the hoodie she wore.

"And were those clothes part of the solid form you always took?"

"In recent years, yes."

"Then that is the first change you must make," said Mimi. "Put on fresh clothes."

"But these are part of me," said the darkling. "Formed from my shadow self."

"And that is why you will keep them safe and close by," said Mimi. "But you can't wear the same clothes all the time, now that you are human. You and they will begin to smell." She leaned closer and said in a quiet voice, "Until I became human, I had no idea how bad people can smell."

"New clothes." The darkling felt the tension in her hands release as she nodded. "I can do that."

"You will feel lost without the ability to read people's auras, but in time you will learn to read the tone of their voice and the way they hold their body instead." Mimi began to count things off on her fingers. "Sleep. I found it strange but when your body is too tired, it will make you sleep. And perhaps dream."

"What is a dream?"

"It is a story that your mind tells while you sleep."

"That is strange," said the darkling.

"Humans are strange," said Mimi. "Generally. You will get hungry and thirsty," she continued. "And without shadow, you must find other ways to heal. You will need a hairbrush to keep tangles away. Your hair is different to mine, curlier, so maybe you should ask for a comb."

Mimi continued to list all the ways that the darkling would have to adapt to her new life as a human. The more the girl talked, the more she sounded like just that: a young girl excited to spend time with a new friend.

"And you will need a name," Mimi finished. "That was easy for me. I was already known as Mimi. What do your friends call you?"

"Hartley calls me 'Miss Darkling'."

"That is not a name," said Mimi. "That is like calling my brother 'Master Nuisance'." She giggled. "Have you ever had an actual name?"

"Once," said the darkling. "A long time ago."

"Did you like it?" said Mimi. "Being called that?"

"They told me it meant 'dear one'." The darkling nodded. "Yes, I liked that."

"As darklings, we had no need for names. We simply knew each other because of the whole that we are part of. Humans are different. They like to be seen as someone unique and separate from others. Even the most humble human stands firm in their identity. So for now," said Mimi, "while you are this, having a name will serve you well."

"Should I tell my friends what my name is?" said the darkling.

"Well, if it will stop them from calling you Miss Darkling," said Mimi. "That has got to be a good thing."

Chapter Seven

"That is decidedly odd."

Steve, Hartley, and the darkling stood at the entrance to Keg's Emporium. The door to the shop was ajar. Steve could smell the dusty interior with its scent of old books, polish, and coffee.

"Do you often leave the door open?" said the darkling.

"Unlocked, yes, all the time," said Hartley. "But never open like this."

"Were you expecting anyone?" asked Steve.

"No more than usual," said Hartley. He peered around the door. "There's no one in sight. I'm sure it's fine. Only way one to find out."

He pushed the door wide open, jangling the bells that hung above the door frame. Nobody jumped out at them or pulled back the curtain that closed off the kitchen at the back of the shop.

"Just a slight mishap," said Hartley with a grin. "Nothing to worry about."

The minute that the words left his mouth, four Hidden appeared in the shop, accompanied by the usual vacuum release sound of their arrival. Hartley speedily retreated from the door, bumping into Steve and the darkling.

"Not so fast."

Jonah Ledwitch blocked their way. The Council member was as smart as he always appeared, dressed in a suit with his auburn hair slicked back into a pigtail. Steve was used to Hartley towering over everyone, but Jonah Ledwitch was just as tall. His thin frame only accentuated his height.

"Jonah," said Hartley. "To what do I owe this…? What's up?"

"I'll explain inside if you and your friends will join me." Jonah looked Steve and the darkling up and down. His lips spread into a broad smile that was more disconcerting than cheering.

"Of course," said Hartley. "After you, Jonah."

"Oh no, after you. I insist."

"As you wish." The four Hidden watched in silence as Hartley stepped into the shop, followed closely by Steve and the darkling. "No need for any trouble, is there?" he said with a forced smile. "No need at all."

"What's happening?" Steve whispered as the three friends walked through the shop.

"Not sure," Hartley whispered back. "Best stay close."

"What was that?" Jonah called after them as he entered the shop, closing the door behind him and turning the key in the lock.

"I was just saying that you've caught us at a disadvantage." Hartley pulled back the curtain to the kitchen. "We weren't prepared for guests."

"I'm not here for niceties, Hartley." Jonah followed them, his hands folded behind his back. "We won't take up too much of your time."

Hartley stepped through into the kitchen, heading straight for the door at the back of the room. Before he reached the table in the centre of the space, the four Hidden appeared. Two of them blocked his route to the door.

"Coffee?" Hartley turned around, his wide grin hiding any disappointment he might have felt.

"No," said Jonah. "There won't be time for that." He nodded and the four Hidden moved as one. Two of them grabbed Hartley by the arms. The others pushed Steve and the darkling away from their friend.

"What are you doing?" said Steve.

He tried to go to Hartley, but one of the Hidden barred his

route, shoving him further away. The darkling almost dodged the Hidden who faced her but before she could reach Hartley, she was grabbed around the waist and dragged away.

"This is preposterous." Hartley struggled in the clutch of the other two Hidden. "Unhand me."

"You brought this on yourself, you know." Jonah took a seat at the table in Hartley's kitchen. He stretched out his long legs as if he was relaxing at home. His eyes shone with a glee that matched his unpleasant grin. "You pushed us too far."

"I thought the Council weren't interested in us now Bless…" Steve stopped short of saying his absent friend's name. "That's what Blaike Harn said."

"The boy's right," said Hartley. "We're not under any caution from the Council. You have no right to detain us."

"Your actions gave me every right," Jonah snarled.

"You can't tell him what to do," said Steve.

"Of course we can." The legs of the kitchen chair squealed on the tiled floor as Jonah stood up. "We are the Council. Bring the old fool to me."

"What are you going to do?" Hartley dug his heels in, but the Hidden easily dragged him across the kitchen.

"I'm going to make your life difficult," said Jonah. "With the hope that you'll stay out of trouble and the Council's way in future." Jonah flexed his fingers as the Hidden dragged Hartley even closer.

Steve dropped to his knees on the kitchen floor and scuttled between the legs of the Hidden as they scrambled to grab him. He heard the darkling grunt as she kicked out at the Hidden who stood in her way.

"That's enough of that!"

Steve flinched as a fiery orb sparked into existence only inches from his face. He could feel its heat on his face. Before he could retreat, one of the Hidden grabbed him by the collar and dragged him away. When he looked at the darkling, she was just as trapped.

"Careful with the fire, Jonah," said Hartley, eyes wide. "We don't want to burn down the place."

"Don't we?" Jonah circled a finger, and the orb moved towards the curtain drawn across the doorway to the shop.

"Jonah!" Hartley struggled in the grasp of the Hidden. "This is my home. When Blaike Harn hears of this—"

"She wouldn't care." Jonah clicked his fingers, and the orb disappeared. "But I'm not here for that. Bring him to me."

"Release me!" Hartley complained as the Hidden dragged him around the table. "I have rights. You can't do this!"

Jonah grabbed Hartley's wrists, pulling them upwards. Hartley let out a yelp at the man's touch. Two thin funnels of white smoke unwound from the Council member's grasp. Hartley's face paled until it matched the colour of the smoke. His mouth fell open and his eyes watered.

"What are you doing to him?" Steve struggled in the Hidden's grasp. "This isn't right. Stop!"

With a ferocity that silenced everyone in the room, the light from the kitchen ceiling lamp blazed and the kitchen chairs all dashed away from the table, clattering to the floor. Jonah released Hartley with a gasp. He looked at his hands as if they weren't his own and then, with a snarling grimace, he grabbed Hartley's wrists even more tightly than before.

He's burning him, thought Steve as the funnels of smoke, now filled with glowing embers, returned.

"There." Jonah released Hartley, shook his hands as if ridding himself of grime, and then folded them behind his back. "That wasn't so bad."

"Bad?" Hartley held his trembling arms before him. "I challenge... I..." The Hidden released him and his legs gave way. He dropped to his knees on the stone floor.

"What have you done to him?" The Hidden still held Steve in place. "Hartley, are you okay?"

"No, no." Hartley turned his hands back and forth with increasing speed. A thin, glowing bangle encased each of his wrists. "What have you done to me, Jonah?"

"Hampered your magic," said Jonah. "More than that. These cuffs will gradually drain your magic over time. Best get used to the life of a workaday."

"This is…" Hartley's voice quaked as he spoke. "Barbaric."

"Barbaric," said Jonah with a sneer. "I'd rather think of it as a fitting punishment for the crime."

"What crime?" said Steve. "We haven't broken any laws."

"That is debatable," said Jonah. "Hartley has been a thorn in my…" He paused with a sudden intake of breath. "In the Council's side for far too long. It was necessary to discipline him for tampering in our process."

"But this," said Hartley, his hands outheld. "For a traveller. This is beyond cruel."

"There will be no more adventures, no more causing trouble, and no more interference in Council matters," said Jonah. "It's time for you to retire, Hartley. Put your feet up. Do what people your age do. Old people," he added.

"You can't do this," said Hartley, but there was no sense of defiance in his voice; only sadness.

"It's done," said Jonah. "There was always going to be a consequence for your deviant behaviour. I'm just sorry that it took this long to catch up with you." He nodded to two of the Hidden who instantly went to him and grasped him by the shoulders. "Now if you'll excuse me, I have more important matters to attend to." With a second nod, Jonah Ledwitch and the Hidden disappeared.

Chapter Eight

"I'm sorry." Steve didn't know what else to say. He felt like a spare part; worse than that, a spare part without a plan.

"As am I." Hartley sat at the kitchen table with his shirt sleeves rolled up. He examined the bangles that encased his wrists, turning them back and forth. The bangles no longer glowed, but they fitted so snugly to his wrists that they appeared to be joined to his skin.

The darkling prowled around the kitchen. She hadn't sat down since Jonah Ledwitch and the Hidden had left. She was making Steve nervous; more nervous. He sat on the chair beside Hartley, jiggling his legs and tapping his feet.

"We could talk to Kiri Ema," he said. "She seems to be on our side. And I'm sure Volund Wolff wouldn't agree with this. I know they're only two out of five Council members, but it might be worth a try."

"Steve is right," said the darkling.

"I daresay." Hartley rolled down his sleeves and fastened one. The other was missing its button. "In the meantime, there's only one thing to do."

"Eat something?" said Steve.

"Travel," said Hartley as he marched across the room. He ran his hands over the frame of the iron door at the back of his kitchen.

"But Jonah Ledwitch said you couldn't."

"Never mind what that bully said." Hartley grasped the door handle. "Who's to say he wasn't lying? I need proof. Ready?"

"Are you?" said Steve.

"I'm Hartley Keg. I was born ready." And with that, he pulled the door open.

For the briefest of moments as the door swung back on its hinges, Steve thought everything was going to be okay. Hartley looked so sure of himself, so certain that he'd be able to magically open that doorway to another place, that Steve tried to believe it too. Even the darkling stopped in her pacing.

The iron door slammed back against the wall. The space within the door frame was completely filled with bricks cemented in staggered rows. There was no unexpected exit, no breeze of a far-off land, and no sign of Hartley's travelling magic.

"He wasn't lying. Damn!"

With a roar, Hartley slammed the door shut. Steve felt the force of the slam through the floor. The shopkeeper folded his hands into fists, shaking them as he gave the door a swift kick. His face went the colour of a very ripe strawberry, and then a blueberry.

"Calm down," said Steve. "Please. We'll sort this out. We'll—"

"Calm down?" shouted Hartley. "Calm down? How can I…?"

Hartley blinked his wide eyes like an owl, slapped a hand to the side of his head, and staggered back against the wall.

"What is wrong?" The darkling was across the room and at Hartley's side before Steve had a chance to stand up. "Hartley, talk to me."

"This is bad," said Hartley as he slid down the wall to sit on the floor. "I feel so weak. It just came over me in a rush. This is worse than the collar that the Council put on me. It's like…" He shook his head.

"Like what?" said Steve, crossing the room to crouch down in front of his friend.

"It's like I don't have a scrap of magic in me."

"You're Hartley Keg," said Steve. "Of course you have."

"I'm serious," said Hartley. "It's not there. I feel…" He sighed. "I feel empty."

Hartley gave a loud sniff that made his shoulders rise and wiped a hand across his eyes. The darkling slipped from a crouching position to sit on the floor beside the shopkeeper. She rested a hand on his shoulder and Steve could see that she was close to tears herself.

"We'll sort this out," said Steve. "I promise we will."

"Of course." Hartley shrugged. "You're a good boy, Steve."

"Let's get you up." Steve reached for Hartley's hands and then stopped. He wasn't sure how painful the bangles were. "Come on." He grabbed Hartley's free arm and nodded to the darkling to do the same.

"I think I need my bed," said Hartley as he was dragged to his feet. He swayed a little on the spot.

"Nope," said Steve. "You're going to sit down with the darkling and me so we can work out what to do next."

"Next?" said Hartley as if Steve had suggested something beyond his understanding. "I'm not sure there is a next."

"There is always a next," said the darkling. "We just need to find the right one."

"See?" said Steve. "The darkling agrees. We're going to sort this out. Together."

But as he and the darkling part-pulled, part-supported Hartley across the kitchen, Steve realised he had no idea what that 'next' might be. Even the annoying voice in his head was silent.

*

After several cups of strong, gritty coffee and as much positivity as Steve and the darkling could raise, Hartley seemed a little more like himself. The three friends sat around the kitchen table, working on their next step.

"Can we appeal?" said Steve. "Take this in front of the Council?"

"The Council did this to me." Hartley held out his wrists.

"They're not going to listen to reason. They don't do U-turns."

"Perhaps Jonah Ledwitch lied," said the darkling. "He may have worked alone. Not on behalf of the entire Council."

"It's possible," said Hartley. "I can't imagine Kiri Ema would have agreed to this." He shook his head. "But one Council member isn't enough. I'd be setting myself up for failure. Why bother when I can't win?"

"Why bother?" said Steve. "Because this isn't right. It isn't fair. Why aren't you angry about this?"

"I *am* angry." Hartley sat back with a harumph. "I'm also slightly nauseous, humiliated, and at a total loss. I need to think about this, put the old noggins to work," he said with a nod of his head.

Steve sat back, trying to stifle a sigh. The coffee had worked wonders on Hartley, but it had made Steve even more jittery. The energy that had made him jiggle his legs had moved into his stomach. He needed to do something, anything, to rid himself of the discomfort.

"I'll clear these away." He grabbed the cups, stacking them noisily.

"Leave them," said Hartley. "Our conversation isn't finished."

"But you said—"

"That I'm at total loss about how to fix this." He flapped his wrists around. "But we came to an agreement, didn't we?"

"To go find my parents?"

"To try to find your parents by visiting New Venice," said Hartley. "I may not be able to travel us there personally, but we can reach our destination by more vehicular methods. The tramline will take us to the southern coast, but we'll need another way to cross the sea to the Continent." He nodded with a grin. "I may know a man with a boat."

"*Do* you know a man with a boat?" asked the darkling.

"I do," said Hartley. "Have you heard of Port London?"

"Of course," said Steve. "Is that where your man with a boat lives?"

"Lives, no," said Hartley. "But with any luck, we'll catch him there. I'll send a squirrel mail ahead. In the meantime, we best prepare ourselves for a long journey. Steve, is your pocket still working?"

"Yes." Since the tailor Tiberius had altered one pocket of Steve's jacket, it had the magical ability to hold as much as Steve needed it to, and only he could retrieve items from it. "Still working."

"Excellent," said Hartley. "Who needs luggage when you have pockets?"

Most people, thought Steve. *But then we're not most people.*

Chapter Nine

Steve sat on the edge of the single bed, holding his trainers. Even if he couldn't have heard Hartley in the kitchen rattling pans on the hob, the smell of bacon would have told him that it was breakfast time.

He looked around at the small bedroom as he pulled his trainers on. This was the room where he had woken after being attacked by Braeden Kendra's thugs. It seemed like years ago, but in truth less than a couple of months had passed. The same miscellany of pictures hung aslant on the walls. Steve had tried straightening them but every morning when he woke, each picture would lean at its own individual angle. The old armchair, where he left his clothes on a night, sagged comfortably in a corner. Its leather had split in places and been patched up with mismatched swatches of suede or velvet. The metal-framed bed was creaky but comfortable, swathed with blankets and quilts. There was no way to tell that this bedroom belonged to a teenage boy, but it felt altogether more like home than any room at boarding school had ever seemed to Steve.

And you want to leave all this? The voice in his mind poked at his moment of happiness. *To go off on a chase that might lead nowhere?*

"Or it might lead to Mum and Dad," Steve muttered. "I can't not do anything when there's a chance—"

There was a tap at the door. "All right in there?" Hartley opened the door an inch and peered through.

"Just getting dressed." Steve stood up. "And talking to myself."

"I'm obviously rubbing off on you," said Hartley. "In a good way, of course."

The kitchen smelt more of burnt fat than bacon when Steve walked in. Hartley rushed back to the stove, using the tea towel that was flung over his shoulder to swipe at the smoke that rose from the hob.

"I hope you like your breakfast on the crispy side." Hartley jabbed at the contents of the smoking pan with a fork. "Bacon? Fried Onions? We're out of eggs but there's cheese and bread in the pantry."

"Just bacon," said Steve.

At the large table that dominated the kitchen, the darkling mopped the grease from her plate with a slice of bread. The darkness of her short, curly hair stood out against the white blouse she wore. On the table beside her plate was a flat parcel packaged up in brown paper and string.

"New clothes?" Steve pulled out the chair beside her and sat down.

"Hartley found them for me." She stuffed the final bite of bread into her mouth and looked at her greasy hands. She pushed back her chair and lowered her hands to the pale blue trousers she wore.

"Don't." Steve caught her wrist. "It'll stain. Hartley, cloth."

"I have seen Hartley wipe his hands on his clothes," she said.

"Yeah, but he's not always a good example to follow." Steve caught the tea towel that the shopkeeper tossed to him. "Here. Use this."

"Thank you." She carefully wiped her hands. "I am still getting used to this."

"Me too," said Steve. "Something to post?" He pointed to the parcel.

"These are my old clothes," she said, placing a protective hand on the parcel. "They are part of me. I must keep them close. If I change back to my darkling self, these may do the same."

"I've agreed to carry them in my pocket." Hartley placed a plate of bacon in front of Steve with a fork, then grabbed the darkling's plate. "Good?" he asked her.

"He means the food," said Steve as the darkling looked confused.

"It is adequate," she said.

"I'll take that as a compliment," said Hartley, returning to the hob.

"'Adequate' is one way of putting it," said Steve as he tackled a rasher of bacon with his fork. When it refused to be stabbed or broken in two, he put his fork aside and picked the rasher up with his fingers.

"Now then." Hartley sat down at the table with a plate of blackened bacon, crispy fried onions, a dollop of pickled something, and a lump of cheese. "Do we have a plan?"

"We find Mum and Dad," said Steve.

"That's not a plan. That's a goal," said Hartley, stuffing a piled-up fork of food into his mouth. "What should our first step be?"

"Eleanor said Mum is in New Venice. So go there, I suppose?"

"Where is New Venice?" asked the darkling. "Is it in the city?"

"No. It's on the Continent," said Hartley. "We can take the tram to Port London." He sighed, casting a forlorn look at the door at the back of the kitchen. "It won't be a quick journey, but needs must."

The three friends sat in a companionable silence for a few minutes. Or as silent as it ever got when Hartley was eating. Steve finished his bacon, licking his fingers clean. The darkling watched the shopkeeper with a slight frown on her face.

"Hartley?" she eventually said. "There is grey in your beard."

"I beg to differ," he said as he wolfed down the last morsel on his plate. "Maybe it's food."

"No, it's definitely grey hair," said Steve. "I can see it too."

"No, no, no." Hartley went to the small mirror that hung by the curtained door to the shop. "That's disconcertingly new," he said as he scowled at his reflection. The shopkeeper's beard had been a vibrant chestnut brown since Steve had known him, but now the bottom inch or so was completely grey.

"Are you all right?" said Steve. "Is it the bangles?"

"I'm fine," said Hartley with a shrug. "Don't fuss."

"Sorry," said Steve as his friend turned away from the mirror and clapped his hands together.

"Preparations," said Hartley. "Specifically, you."

"Me?" said the darkling as Hartley pointed a finger at her.

"You," he said. "Come with me."

*

"I am not sure that this is suitable." The darkling stood in the middle of the kitchen wearing a knee-length waterproof coat. It had obviously been made for someone who carried more weight than the darkling with her slim build.

"The zip still works," said Hartley, walking around her. "It's got pockets, albeit not as magical or useful as my pockets. And the hood doesn't leak." He slapped his hands together "Perfect."

"What he means," said Steve, "is that it was the only coat he had in stock."

"That too. Now then. If we can't use my door, we'll have to leave Darkacre the standard way." Hartley rolled his eyes. "Frobisher will be highly amused, so best not tell him unless we have to."

"You do have my parcel?" said the darkling as Hartley pulled on his tweed jacket.

"Here," he slapped one of his pockets. "Safe and ready for when you need it."

"Don't worry," said Steve. "No one can get to your things. Only Hartley. He's like padlocked luggage on legs."

"I'm not sure if I appreciate being called luggage," said the shopkeeper.

"Hartley!" There was a shout, a clashing of the bells that hung over the shop door, and then the clatter of footsteps moving at speed.

"There you are." Michael barged into the kitchen and bent

over for a moment to catch his breath. "We need you."

"What is wrong?" said the darkling.

"It's Frobisher. He's in trouble."

"Where?"

"At the gate. He's arguing with them."

"Arguing with who?" said Steve.

"The Hidden."

"You really should have started with that," said Hartley. "Come on, my boy. Lead the way."

*

At the gate that linked Darkacre to the city of Caercester, Frobisher struggled with one of the Hidden. From his stance, Steve could tell that the old gatekeeper was pleading rather than objecting. James stood a couple of paces away, hands clenched into fists.

The Hidden raised a gloved hand and swiped Frobisher across the face, driving the old man to the ground.

"Oi!" James thundered into the Hidden, pushing him back into his companions who barred the gateway. "Leave him alone."

"James." Frobisher clambered to his feet. "Leave it."

"He's just an old man." James squared up to the Hidden, fists and chin raised in defiance. "Why'd you have do that? That's bullying, that is. That's intimidation. I'll report you."

"James." The darkling grabbed his arm. "Stop."

The Hidden who had struck Frobisher lunged towards the two of them. Steve thought they were going to haze his friends or hit them. Instead, the Hidden turned away after a second to join their companions at the gate.

What are they doing? Steve moved closer to the gateway. *They're not... They wouldn't...*

The city image that was visible through the gateway slowly dimmed to a shimmering mist. With a slam of stone on stone, rows of grey bricks began to build in the gateway, racing upwards

60

to fill the space.

"No." Frobisher had his head in his hands. "Not here," he wailed.

"Gatekeeper, by declaration of the Council, Darkacre is sealed until the current investigation is complete," said one of the Hidden. "Supplies will be—"

"You can't do that!" James struggled in the darkling's grip.

"Stop it." The darkling fought to hold him back. "You will get yourself into trouble."

"Agreed." Frobisher nodded.

"Agreed?" said James. "You can't give into them."

"There's nothing I can do," said the old man. "Come inside. We need to talk."

"But—"

"Now." Frobisher's voice had returned to its usual snappiness, but his eyes told a different story. "There's nothing we can do here. Come away."

*

Frobisher held a damp flannel to the side of his face where the Hidden had struck him. He sat in a fireside armchair in his parlour, turned away from the others.

"It's not right." James hadn't calmed down since their return to Frobisher's home, despite the best efforts of his companions. "They should've warned us first. Given people the chance to leave. They can't just do this."

"Unfortunately, they can. They can do whatever they like. I'm testament to that." Hartley pulled up his sleeves and displayed his bangled wrists. "Jonah Ledwitch took great pleasure in hampering my powers. And he said he had the Council's backing."

"Not all of them," said Frobisher, dropping the flannel from his face. "Kiri Ema would never have agreed to that."

"How do you know?" said James, throwing his hands in the

air. "I bet she agreed with the rest of them. I bet—"

"You're wrong!" Frobisher lurched to his feet. "She's not like all the others with their pomp and rules. For one thing, she didn't sign that notice pinned to the gateway. The others did. Even Volund Wolff. But not Kiri Ema. She has honour and a good heart. She cares about communities like Darkacre."

"Fine." James clamped his arms crossed. "But what good does that do us when we can't leave Darkacre?"

"He's right," said Hartley. "I can't travel us out. I've tried." He avoided Frobisher's glare. "I was only trying to travel into the city. But not even that works."

"Let me see those." Frobisher beckoned Hartley to him. "Do they hurt?"

"Thankfully, no." Hartley bent down and showed his wrists to Frobisher. "But when I tried to use magic, just the tiniest doorway magic, they weakened me."

"They don't just hamper your magic, do they?" said Frobisher. "Your beard is going grey. You're aging."

"I'm fine." Hartley straightened up. "You don't need to worry about me."

"You are the most worrying person I've ever met, Hartley Keg." Frobisher shook his head. "Looks like we all need help now."

"Would Kiri Ema help us?" said the darkling. "If she is our ally?"

"Maybe," said Frobisher, nodding. "If she could."

"So where does that leave us?" said Hartley. "If Darkacre is sealed, we have no means of sending a message to her. Nothing can get out or in that isn't conveyed by the Hidden."

"What about the door to the Council controlled area?" said Steve. "The Confluence. Is that sealed as well?"

"Theoretically, it should be." Hartley raised his eyebrows at Frobisher.

"Only one way to find out," said the gatekeeper.

"And if it is open," said the darkling. "What do we do then?"

"Go talk to Kiri Ema," said Steve.

"I agree," said the darkling.

"As do I," said Hartley.

"As heart-warming as this camaraderie is," said Frobisher with a tut, "we'd best see if that door's open first. If it's sealed, none of us are going anywhere."

Chapter Ten

A smattering of Darkacre residents remained in the street that led to the sealed gateway. Some spoke in hushed voices. Others simply stared at the poster the Hidden had left behind.

"They look lost," said Steve. He and his companions stood outside Frobisher's front door. "Scared."

"What did you expect?" snapped James. "Sorry," he said, patting a hand on Steve's shoulder. "It's not your fault."

"They are scared," said Hartley. "And most likely in shock at the Council's actions."

"But if the door to the you-know-where is working," said James. "Well, we can get everyone out of here."

"Not so fast," said Frobisher. "Can you imagine what would happen if there was a sudden influx of Darkacre people into the Confluence? It would be bedlam."

"So?" said James. "How would that be worse than this?"

"Besides," said Frobisher. "As soon as we do that, the Council will seal that gateway off too."

"Quite," said Hartley. "As things stand, we have a tactical advantage. Best not to show our hand until we have to."

"And that's if the door is even open. And then unguarded," said Frobisher.

"So how are we going to do this without anyone seeing?" said Steve.

"Leave that to us," said James. "Michael, you're with me."

"What are they going to do?" said Steve as the brothers walked towards the people gathered in the street.

"What they're good at," said Frobisher. "Be annoying."

"Oi!" James cuffed Michael across the back of his head. "I'm still your big brother. You can't talk to me like that."

"Yes, I can. I'm just as good as you are." Michael pulled himself up to his full height, even rising up onto his tiptoes. "I'm better." He shoved James in the chest.

"I can't believe you said that. After all I've done..."

As the four or five residents turned to stare at the boys, Frobisher touched a hand to one side of the gateway. With a shudder, a modest wooden door with no embellishment appeared under his hands.

"So far so good. Let's see if it goes anywhere." He pulled the door open a fraction. Light spilled through from the other side.

"It worked," said Hartley. He sounded a little disappointed. "My door didn't work."

"Only you could be offended by success, Hartley Keg." Frobisher opened the door wider. "Go on then."

"Aren't you coming with us?" said Steve.

"Not this time," said the gatekeeper. "I'm the only one in Darkacre who can open this door. I need to stick around in case people need a way out."

"I've never used this door before. Where does it lead to?" said Hartley.

"Customs and security in the Confluence." Frobisher stepped back to let them pass but kept a firm grip on the door handle.

"Won't it look suspicious?" said Steve. "Us coming from Darkacre, when it's been sealed by the Council?"

"Probably," said Frobisher. "But you're not entering the Confluence proper. Get in this way and then get out through the exit. After that you can send a squirrel mail to Kiri Ema."

"Well, when you put it like that, it sounds just the ticket." Hartley slapped his hands and rubbed them together. "Onwards," he said with a wide grin before he disappeared through the doorway at speed.

"Thank you, Frobisher," said the darkling. "For everything."

"On you get," said Frobisher but without his usual brusque

tone. "You take care of these two."

"I will."

"Don't dither," said Frobisher as Steve hesitated to follow the darkling. "Best make it quick. Someone might come along and see us."

"Right," said Steve but he still didn't move.

"Hurry up." Frobisher tapped his foot. "I've things to do."

"Are we doing the right thing, Frobisher?" said Steve. "Going to find my parents when Darkacre is in trouble?"

"The way I see it," said Frobisher with a frown, "you have to find your parents. Family matters. And this way, you can get a message to Kiri Ema. You're not abandoning us. You're just going to fetch the cavalry."

"Thanks, Frobisher."

"Now, hurry up. My arm's getting stiff holding this door open."

With a final nod to Frobisher, Steve stepped through the door and entered the Confluence.

*

"Well, you see, officer—"

"I'm not an officer. I'm a guard."

When Steve stepped through the doorway, he bumped into a wall. He thought it was a wall anyway.

"Sorry," said the wall. The wall, or rather the golem, turned around to face Steve. The creature looked amiable enough, but its lofty height, probably around seven feet tall, was enough to intimidate most people.

"That's okay," said Steve.

The golem tilted its head as it continued to stare down at him. "Are you with them?" He pointed to Hartley and the darkling.

"I am," said Steve as Hartley vigorously shook his head and mouthed 'no'. "We were just on our way out of the Confluence."

"That does not make sense," said the golem. "This area is only used by those who wish to enter the Confluence. Your presence is suspicious."

"We were just being nosey," said Hartley. "I wanted to show off the efficiency of the Confluence customs area to my young friends here."

"I think you are lying." The golem called to an identical golem guard who stood to one side of the lift door that Steve and his friends had walked through. "Take them for questioning."

"What's going on?"

Steve recognised the voice straightaway. So did the golem who barred their way. The creature spun on the spot and made a sudden but deep bow.

"These are my friends," said Kiri Ema. "Why have you accosted them?"

There was no sign of the over-sized Council robes that Kiri had worn when Steve had last seen her. Instead, she was dressed in jeans, a grass green kaftan top, and a long string of beads. Her feet were bare. The only element of her appearance that hadn't changed was her white hair which sat in a messy bun on the top of her head, secured by her wand.

"Apologies," said the golem, refusing to look Kiri Ema in the eye. "We had no idea who they were. This one," he said, pointing to Hartley. "He said that—"

"Relax," said Kiri Ema with a widening smile. "You were just doing your job. Well done."

"Thank you, Councillor Ema," said the golem, retreating to its post at the side of the lift door and gesturing for its companion to do the same.

"Well, my dears," she said, smiling at Steve and the others. "I really think we should be on our way, don't you?"

"Absolutely," said Hartley. "Steve, the door?"

"Allow me." The golem turned to the lift door and tapped the circle of gold set into the centre of the polished wood. The door slid aside with as little sound as an exhaled breath of air.

"Thank you, thank you," said Hartley as Kiri Ema pulled him into the lift. "So kind."

"Yeah. Thanks," said Steve as he backed into the lift with the darkling at his side.

"So, Hartley Keg," said the Council member as the lift door slid shut. "What shenanigans have you been getting yourselves into this time?"

"Shenanigans?" said Hartley with a laugh. "What makes you think—?"

"Darkacre has been sealed," said the darkling. "We needed a way out so that Steve can find his parents."

"Honesty and brevity," said Kiri. "I like that. But as for you, Hartley Keg..."

"Yes?" he said.

"Thank you for brightening my day." She laughed. "I needed a reason to smile. It's been a difficult one, heartbreaking even."

"Is that because of Darkacre and what Jonah Ledwitch did to Hartley?" said Steve.

"Darkacre. The Council's attitude to the people they're supposed to serve. Even Volund Wolff has fallen into line, although I fear Blaike Harn may have used her powers to influence him, poor bear. No, I couldn't stay here one moment longer." She shook her head. "But as for Jonah Ledwitch, what has he been up to now? Hm?"

"I assumed you knew," said Hartley, pushing back his sleeves. "These monstrosities."

"Hartley, I had no idea." She took his hands. "This is Blaike's latest attempt at hampering. But it's untested."

"That makes me the lab rat," said Hartley with a sigh.

"And it works?"

"Annoyingly well."

"And it is aging him," said the darkling.

"So I see." Kiri touched the bottom of his beard. "Hartley, I am so sorry."

"It wasn't your doing." He released her hands and drew down his sleeves. "You have nothing to apologise for. Anyway, enough of my problems. We need your help for something else. We plan to leave Caercester, but without my doors, it's a little more convoluted. I don't suppose you could convey us to the tram station?"

"Just a ride? Is that all?" said Kiri as the lift came to a barely perceptible halt and the door slid aside.

"Crossing the city without the worry of falling under the eye of the Hidden and the Council—the rest of the Council— would be more than enough, Kiri. And very much appreciated," said Hartley.

"Fair enough," she said as she stepped out of the lift with the others close behind her. "A ride I can do."

Steve hadn't considered where the lift would take them. He assumed it would be straight out into the city of Caercester or some well-kept, guarded, lobby. Instead, he found himself in what appeared to be an old-fashioned eatery.

"Ah, the Five Points," said Hartley with a sigh. "I've missed this place."

"What is it?" said Steve.

"More a case of what was it?" said Hartley. "Originally, it was a tavern. Purchased from workadays in the know, and run by our own people as a way to hide the city entrance to the Confluence."

"We had some good times here, Hartley," said Kiri, staring around.

The interior of the tavern was empty except for a dust-furred bar that ran the length of the room and a couple of broken stools that lay on their sides. The walls were covered in wood panels and the whole area was illuminated by a cobweb-ridden chandelier.

"That we did." Hartley gave a long sigh. "Shame it had to stop."

"There was no *had to* about it," said Kiri, heading off to a pair of double doors with boarded up glass panels. "It was all bureaucracy and narrow-mindedness. I thought when I joined the Council I could make a difference, get rid of all those unfeeling rules." She shook her head as she pulled the doors open. Sunlight flooded into the tavern, illuminating the dust that hung in the air. "I was a fool."

"You were hopeful," said Hartley as he grasped one of the doors. "There's a difference."

"You're very kind to say that, old friend." She smiled up at him with a slow shake of her head. "But you're wrong. The Blaike Harns of our world were never going to let me in. I should have known that at my age. Should've stayed home instead."

"But where's the fun in that?" said Hartley.

"I do like you, Hartley Keg. Always the optimist," she said as she started through the doors. "Just like all of us fools."

*

The outside of the Five Points Tavern reflected its neglected interior. It looked like a derelict old pub. With its broken-down brick and plaster façade, it was something to be ignored by most people, an eyesore, and a smudge on the gleam of the modern city. Two tramps huddled by the doors to the pub, bundled up in ragged clothes. They watched Kiri and the others with suspicious eyes.

The road outside buzzed with e-buses and driverless cars. None of the passengers seemed at all interested in Steve, his friends, or the Five Points Tavern. Neither did the human and robot pedestrians on the other side of the road.

"You're in luck. I just returned from my final ride around the city," said Kiri proudly.

"So I can see." Hartley stayed behind Steve and the darkling. "Are they safe?"

Kiri's ride was a roofed carriage, the kind of vehicle that Steve had seen in history books. He was sure that it was normal for them to be pulled by horses or cattle. This one wasn't normal though.

"Aren't they beautiful?" Kiri stood between the two creatures that were fastened up to the carriage. "I keep them here to remind me of home."

The large—very large—birds extended their long necks towards her, lowering their heads so that she could scratch them both under the chin.

"Ostriches?" said Hartley.

"Moa," said Kiri. "Giant moa, to be exact."

"I thought they were extinct," said Steve as the birds lifted their heads to stare at him and his friends. The nearest moa made a low, guttural noise as it tilted its head and blinked at him.

"In the workaday world, they are," said Kiri. "But we have a mob of these beauties in my home community back in New Zealand."

"That's so…" Steve couldn't find the right way to express how he felt. "So…"

"Cool?" said Kiri. "Awesome?"

"All of that," he said with a grin.

"But if these birds are extinct," said the darkling, "will they not stand out in the city?"

"The carriage and the birds are hidden by an enchantment. All that workaday eyes can see is a standard e-bus," said Kiri.

"That is clever," said the darkling.

"I thought so," said Kiri. "Open her up, please," she said to the golem who waited beside the carriage.

"Of course, Councillor Ema."

"Just Kiri," she said. "I'm not on the Council anymore."

"As you wish." As the golem opened the carriage door, a set of wooden steps built themselves down to the level of the road, one piece at a time.

"Are you sure that you won't remain?" said Hartley as Kiri climbed the steps. "You've been the people's voice on the Council for so long."

"And what good did that do anyone?" She glanced back at the doors of the Five Points Tavern and gave a long sigh. "There's nothing more I can do here. Aata?"

"Yes, Kiri?" said the golem.

"Take us to the nearest entrance to the tram station. After

that, bring me back here. I need to pack."

"Of course, Kiri."

As Steve followed the others into the carriage, he saw the golem whisper to each of the birds before gently petting each creature on its neck. When the steps clattered back up into the carriage and the door closed behind him, Steve had just enough time to drop into a seat before the birds set off at speed.

Chapter Eleven

The tram station was just as Steve remembered it: immense, cavernous, and filled with a miscellany of magical passengers who chattered on the long, wooden benches or crowded on the platforms on either side of the tram track. Compared to the clean, metallic lines of the city stations he was used to in his workaday life, the tram station was chaotic, colourful, and altogether joyful.

The Inspector, dressed in her head-to-toe hooded midnight-blue cloak, towered over a trio of bearded men who gesticulated madly and widely with their arms to make themselves understood. It wasn't until the three cheered—one of them also gave a little jump into the air—and moved away that Hartley steered Steve and the darkling towards her.

"My dear Miss Inspector," said Hartley, taking her gloved hand. "It's so good to see you again."

"Is it?" As Steve had learned on their last visit to the tram station, the Inspector was invisible. There was no face to see inside the hood. Her voice, however, told the whole story. "Do you have a ticket this time?"

"Ticket? No," said Hartley, holding out his hand as the Inspector began to protest. "But I do have this." On the palm of his hand, a bright purple seed around the size of a kidney bean pulsated with a light of its own. "Kiri Ema thought you might accept this instead."

There was a little inhalation of air from somewhere inside the Inspector's hood. "A dragonic tulip." She picked up the seed between finger and thumb as if it was the most precious, and possibly explosive, item she'd ever seen. "I thought these were extinct."

"Will it suffice as our tram fare? Miss Inspector?"

"Yes," the Inspector said in an awestruck voice. She gave a little cough. "It'll do," she said as she closed her gloved fingers around the seed. "Just make sure you have the fare for your return journey."

"It almost sounds as if you care, my dear." Hartley gave her a wink.

"The next tram is here." She moved away as the ground began to vibrate and a warm breeze spread through the space. "Best be on your way."

As a series of interconnected tram carriages sped into the station, Steve and his friends joined the crowds of passengers waiting for a ride.

"This one will do." Hartley grabbed Steve's sleeve with one hand and linked the other through the darkling's arm. "Best stay close. The trams don't stop for long."

He pulled them along with him, jostling shoulder-to-shoulder with the crowd, until suddenly they were at one of the open tram doors.

"It looks full," said Steve as Hartley pushed him into the carriage. "Sorry," he said as he bumped into a cow that filled a large proportion of the carriage. At least, he assumed it was a cow. It was the size of a cow—it even smelt like grass—but the creature's body was so engulfed in thick fur that it was difficult to tell which end was which.

"Space for three little ones?" called Hartley. "Coming through."

The party of three that accompanied the beast all nodded in response but didn't speak. One held a rope which disappeared into the beast's fur.

With a jolt, the tram carriage leapt into motion, and they were off.

Two stops further along, the beast and its owners left the carriage, albeit with a great deal of heaving, pushing, and coaxing. When the doors closed and the tram pulled out of the tiny station, the darkling spoke her first words since entering the carriage.

"What is that?"

"The smell? It's not me," said Hartley. "I assume it's the aroma left behind by the muckle."

"No, that buzzing noise." She turned around, tilting her head to hear better. "It is coming from you, Hartley."

"I can hear it too," said Steve.

"I wonder." Hartley pushed Steve away and spread his arms wide. "Give me space. Incoming."

"Incoming what?" said Steve.

With a ping and a bark-bark-bark, a squirrel popped into existence above Hartley's head and dropped onto the shopkeeper's shoulder. It continued to bark as it flapped its sparking tail around.

"What happened?" said Steve as Hartley dove his hand into his jacket pocket.

"The poor creature travelled onto a moving tram. Never a good idea." Hartley pulled out a squirty bottle and doused the squirrel's smouldering tail. "Is that better, little one?"

The squirrel chattered as it examined its wet tail and then it pulled a rolled-up piece of paper from the sash that it wore.

"Thank you kindly," said Hartley. "Perhaps you'd best wait until we reach the next station before you leave."

The squirrel gave a 'tsk' and a chatter as it ran down Hartley's sleeve and launched itself at one of the hanging, leather handles. It furled its body into the strap, clinging on with its front paws.

"Let's see." Hartley unrolled the piece of paper, nodding to himself as he read.

"What's the message?" said Steve.

"It's a reply." Hartley furled up the note again and popped it into his pocket. "My man with a boat has agreed to meet us in Port London."

"Will they give us passage?" said the darkling.

"Probably," said Hartley, "It depends how expensive the fare is. We may have to rely on my charm and talents."

"Charm and talents?" said Steve.

"Absolutely," said Hartley. "Charm and talents, my boy. Charm and talents."

*

Steve expected the tram station at Port London to reflect the size of the city. He at least expected it to be bigger than its equivalent in Caercester.

"So is this a workaday station or a magical one?" he asked, barely resisting the temptation to shout 'halloo' down the long corridor they had stepped into.

"Oh most definitely a magical one," said Hartley. "The workaday world travels above us and below. This space exists only to connect the tram line to Port London."

On the facing wall and in both directions as far as Steve could see were a multitude of doors. All of them were made from lacquered wood polished to a shine. Each bore a metal destination plate. The nearest doors were marked Kings Cross, Parliament Towers, and The Palace.

"How do we find the right door?" The darkling stared down the corridor to their right. "You do not have your travelling magic to help us."

"Admittedly I am without my magic," said Hartley. "But that isn't a problem with these doors. They work for anyone who knows how to use them. Even a workaday. Watch." Hartley elbowed Steve with a wink, cleared his throat, and then he called out in his best booming voice, "Tower Bridge."

There was the sound of gears releasing and then the doors slid to the right, one after another, gathering speed until they were a blur. There was a judder and a thud-thud-thud, and the doors slammed to a halt. The door that stopped directly in front of them was marked '*Tower Bridge—Under*'.

"See?" Hartley grinned at the darkling. "Simple." He knocked on the door then stepped back, gesturing for the others to do the same. "Just in case," he said.

The door unexpectedly, to Steve at least, slid aside instead of opening on its hinges. Steve raised a hand to shield his eyes from a cold waft of grimy air that made him shiver. He squinted into the light and realised that he could see the outline of a figure standing beside Hartley. It was only the outline because Steve could see straight through the figure into the space beyond.

"Port London," said Hartley with a widening grin "It's been far too long."

As the shopkeeper stepped through the doorway, the outlined figure followed. It stayed so close to Hartley that it was almost touching him. The figure raised its hands as if it was about to grab the elderly magical.

"Hartley, stop!" said Steve as the darkling pulled him through the doorway and he heard the voices of people passing overhead. "We're being followed," he blurted out as the station door shut behind them.

"I saw it too." The darkling pulled Steve away to a grimy-windowed wall that ran the length of the space they stood in. "I think it is a grayling."

"Really?" Hartley looked around the space. "I didn't see anything."

"Is there any other way out of here?" asked the darkling.

"Just the way we came in," said Hartley, looking around. "Once the entrance closes on this side, it returns to being a normal door. The grayling is trapped in here. It can't leave without us seeing that door open."

"We can't leave either," said Steve. "Don't forget that."

"Spread out." The darkling tilted her head as she prowled towards the doorway. "If it cannot leave, it will either try to wait us out or attack."

"Probably the former," said Hartley. "Graylings are cowards, the lot of them. It wouldn't dare—"

"Shut your mouth, old man!"

The voice was so close to Steve's ear that he jabbed the speaker with his elbow as he span around. He heard rapid footsteps—he wasn't sure whether they belonged to the darkling or their unseen attacker—and then a grunt as the darkling wrapped her arm around the throat of a thin woman dressed all in brown.

"Let me go." The grayling's voice was grating and unpleasant to listen to. "If I get my hands on you—"

"Really?" said the darkling. "You think you could better me in a fight? Do you wish to find out?"

"Easy now." Hartley stepped closer to the struggling grayling but kept himself out of her reach. "There's no need for unpleasantries, Miss Darkling."

"It is a grayling. It cannot be trusted."

"I'd expect that sentiment from your kind," said the grayling.

"Ladies, ladies, this squabbling is getting us nowhere. All we want to know is why our friend here was following us."

"I wasn't following you. I just took advantage of your tram ticket." The grayling stopped struggling. "Then she attacked me!"

"To be fair, you attacked us," said Hartley.

"You called me a coward."

"I taunted you into revealing yourself." Hartley rubbed a hand across his beard. "Tell me this. If we were to let you go, what would you do?"

"Leave," she said. "Quickly."

"You cannot trust her," said the darkling.

"Please." The grayling held out her hands to Hartley. "Don't let her hurt me. I'm scared."

"There's no need to be scared," said Hartley. "As long as you're telling the truth."

"I am. I promise."

"Of course, there's an easy way to solve this dilemma. Now, which pocket did I put it in?"

As Hartley looked down at his jacket and patted the pockets, the grayling hissed. She braced herself on the darkling's arm around her throat and kicked out. Planting her feet on Hartley's chest, she pushed herself up and over the darkling.

Hartley fell into Steve, almost knocking the two of them to the ground, as the darkling lost her grip on her prisoner.

"Works every time." The grayling sneered at them as she reached into her sleeve. "Stupid humans. Your sympathy is always your undoing." She pulled out an item that looked like a glow-stick.

"No!" The darkling kicked out at the grayling's hand, knocking the glow-stick out of her grasp.

"Grab it," Hartley barked as the glow-stick hit the ground and bounced in Steve's direction.

"Give that to me." Once again, the grayling struggled in the darkling's grasp, spitting and snarling like a cornered rat.

"Got it." Steve caught the glow-stick, holding it out to Hartley.

"Careful, careful." Hartley held the device between thumb and forefinger as he took it from Steve. "We don't want to set it off."

"But it's just a glow-stick, isn't it?" said Steve as Hartley raised it to the light of the window.

"No, no, no. This is a flare charm," said Hartley. "You break it, as you would a normal glow-stick. However, it's a thousand times brighter and sends out a message that identifies your location. Do you see the writing on it?"

Steve stared at the glow-stick, or flare charm as Hartley had called it. At first, all he could see was the plastic casing and the colour of the green fluid within but as he continued to look, he began to make out a line of writing. This wasn't the alphabet he knew but a series of shapes and bent lines that flickered in and out of view as if they really didn't want to be seen.

"This last one…" Hartley pointed to a symbol of an upward pointing arrow at the bottom and a downward pointing arrow above connected by a line on the left. "This is the symbol for the Hidden. She would have brought them to us." Hartley pocketed the flare charm "First, they hamper me so I can't use my beloved doors and now this. It seems that the Council have more interest in our movements than they're willing to admit."

"What are we going to do with it?" The darkling grunted her words through gritted teeth as she fought to keep her grasp on the grayling. "We cannot let it return to the Council."

"Of course you're right, my dear." Hartley reached into his pocket. "We can't have her tell the Council where we're going."

"Or why." The darkling tightened her grasp on the grayling's throat. "Shall I despatch her?"

"Whoa, we can't do that," said Steve. "We're the good guys, remember?"

"He's right." The grayling sounded genuinely scared this time. "You wouldn't do that. You can't."

"Why not?" Hartley stood within an arm's reach of the grayling now, his face devoid of his usual charm. "It would solve our problem."

"No." The grayling shrank away from him as much as she could in the darkling's grasp. "I won't tell them. I promise."

"Unfortunately, we can't afford to take your word for that."

"Best take the boy away," said the darkling. "He does not need to see this."

"On the contrary, Miss Darkling," said Hartley. "I think he needs to understand the reality of the situation, the gravity of our dilemma."

"Hang on." Steve could feel his chest tightening and his mouth was suddenly dry. "You can't hurt her."

"Hold her still," said Hartley. "This will only take a moment."

"Hartley, stop—"

Steve dashed towards them as Hartley pulled his hand from his pocket. The darkling released her captive and turned away with an arm across her face as Hartley blew a handful of blue dust in the grayling's face.

"What did you do?" said Steve as the grayling crumpled to the floor.

"Sleep elixir," said Hartley, brushing the last of the dust from his hands. "What did you think I was going to do to her?"

"I…" Steve stopped. The tightness in his chest had been replaced by the beating of his racing heart. "You scared me."

"Not as much as he scared that," said the darkling as she glared at the sleeping grayling. "We had best bind it before it comes round."

"No need for that. She won't wake for a few hours," said Hartley. "But just for my peace of mind." He retrieved what looked like a dog collar from his pocket and fastened it around the grayling's neck.

"What's that?" said Steve, imagining Hartley leading the grayling around on a leash.

"It's a truth-see charm," said Hartley. "It'll keep her visible so we can leave with the assurance that she hasn't followed us. I fashioned that one myself," he said proudly.

"Out of a dog collar?" said Steve.

"Well, needs must," said Hartley. "It does the job and that's what matters."

"But you don't have your magic," said Steve. "How can it still work?"

"Once a charm, or a potion, or a device is created with magic, it can generally be used by anyone. Even a workaday or someone who's having a bad magic day."

"Or a non magic day," said the darkling.

"You don't have to rub it in, you know." Hartley rolled his eyes and gestured to the heavy iron door they had arrived through. "Shall we?"

"Perhaps you should go first." The darkling backed away from the door.

"Are you worried that the iron door will harm you?" said

Hartley.

"As a darkling, a fae, iron can be a challenge," she said. "But now I am this…" She shrugged.

"There's only one way to find out," said Hartley.

Steve watched the darkling touch her fingertips to the door. She didn't react in any way that suggested pain or discomfort. After a moment, she grabbed the handle and pulled the door open.

"Where are we exactly?" said Steve as the darkling disappeared into the dim space beyond.

"Exactly?" said Hartley. "I believe those who use this place called it the Underhang. Port London is above us, polished and pristine, and mostly unaware of the old world that exists below."

"Like the river lane in Caercester."

"On a grander scale, but yes, just like that."

"How long will the truth-see charm keep the grayling visible?" Steve looked back at the slumbering woman.

"Until she finds a way to remove it," said Hartley, "but don't worry, the sleep dust will keep her down for a while. We'll be long gone by the time she wakes."

"There's a door at the bottom of this flight," the darkling called up to them. "Should I open it?"

"That's the one," Hartley called back as he stepped through the iron doorway. "Coming?" He raised both eyebrows at Steve. "The captain is waiting."

"The man with the boat?" said Steve.

"Indeed. That's if you still want to visit Venice."

"Of course, I do," said Steve. "It just feels different this time."

"You mean without…" Hartley sighed and shook his head. "Can you manage that door on your own?" He called down the staircase.

"I can manage." Steve heard the darkling's grunting reply. It didn't sound as if she could manage at all.

"Let's go," said Steve, stepping through the doorway onto a dusty, gridded iron landing. "We don't want to miss our lift."

"That's the spirit," said Hartley. "Onwards," he called as he charged down the staircase.

Steve watched the darkling and Hartley pull at the handle of the door below. Hartley couldn't travel them around anymore. The darkling had lost her shadow powers.

And Blessing is gone, his mind added to the equation.

But they're not, thought Steve. *And even though they're hampered, they still want to help.*

He nodded to himself and trotted down the stairs as the door flew open at his friend's efforts and a grey, misty light crept into the bottom of the stairwell.

Chapter Twelve

"So this is Tower Bridge."

Steve kept turning around to take in the old, humungous relic as they passed over the bridge. The river below was veiled in a threadbare mist that hovered around the underside of the structure. Rusted ironwork creaked beneath their feet in places. Faded paint peeled away in strips, revealing weathered ironwork underneath. The overhead, thick cables sagged between the towers. The air smelt of damp metal and dirty water. Somewhere in the fog surrounding the bridge, Steve could hear the cries of seagulls.

"I didn't think it would still be here," he said. "Does it open?"

"On occasion," said Hartley. "When those above deem it necessary."

"It could do with a clean," said Steve. "I've seen pictures of what the bridge looked like before the city was rebuilt. Blue and gold paint. Stone towers. It was really impressive."

"It was." Hartley stopped as they reached the centre of the bridge. "It just didn't suit the government's plan for Port London. When they raised the city up, as they did Caercester, the landmarks deemed most important were protected underground and turned into museums. Cathedrals. Palaces. Statue-filled squares." He slapped a hand on the rail of the bridge. "This old gentleman didn't make the cut."

"That's sad," said Steve.

"Of course, by the time the world had solved the environmental problems that had caused the city rebuilds, the workadays had become accustomed to their lofty existence. I doubt the children of today ever give a thought as to what life was like before."

"Hartley, do you know where you are taking us?" said the darkling.

"The captain's message said to travel to Tower Bridge." Hartley turned around in a full circle, hands on his hips. "Maybe if we head to the marina—"

"Hartley." The darkling's voice was urgent. "We have company."

"Helloo," the man called as he walked towards them. "Is it passage you're seeking?"

"That depends on who is asking," said Hartley, raising his fists.

"Ah, Hartley Keg, always the kidder." The man jogged over and dodged a feigned punch from Hartley with a laugh before wrapping his arms around the shopkeeper. "What's the story, my fine fellow?" he said as he released Hartley with a pat on the back.

"You know me, Captain. Never better."

"And you brought family?" The captain had a face that looked as if it had lived an eventful life, maybe several lives. It was battered and carved into deep interlocking lines. He wore a heavy, black duffle coat over a turtle-neck jumper and matching trousers. "I got your message. Did you have any trouble on your travels?"

"Trouble? No, not at all," said Hartley.

"We were followed," said the darkling. "By a Council spy. A grayling."

"Tell-tale," grumbled Hartley.

"I see," said the captain. "Did you leave them dead or alive?"

"Alive of course," said Steve. "And visible."

"Been using your truth-see charms again I see, Hartley," said the captain. "What was it this time? Manacle? Earmuffs?"

"Dog collar," said Steve.

"Classic Hartley Keg." The captain laughed and held out a hand to Steve. "I'm Meeris."

"I'm Steve." He took the captain's hand and gave it a brief shake.

"I can tell," said Meeris. "You have the Haven look about you. I could be speaking to a young Rex Haven his-self. Your uncle was a great friend of mine. He travelled with me on many an adventure. I was sad to hear of his passing. And you are?" said Meeris, looking at the darkling.

"Oh well, this is M—" Hartley began.

"Bodrn," said the darkling.

"Really?" said Steve.

"That is my name," she said. "I am pleased to meet you, Meeris." She took his hand and gave it a firm shake.

"Shall we head over to the marina?" said Hartley, nodding across the bridge in the direction that the captain had come from.

"Why?" said Meeris. "That's a place for the above-ers who don't want people to know what they come down here for. I'm moored over the other side of the bridge on my pier."

"Hartley, you said you knew where we were going," said the darkling.

"My dear, there are limits even to my knowledge."

"But you're Hartley Keg," said Steve with a grin as the captain beckoned them to follow him across the bridge. "I thought you knew everything."

"Where's the fun in that?" said Hartley with a wink. "Not knowing has so much more potential for adventure."

*

"Isn't it a bit small for a sea journey?" said Steve.

"I think the word is modest," said Hartley.

"Don't stand around. Come aboard." The captain ran along a narrow plank that connected the pier to his small, colourful boat.

"Are we sure this is a good idea?" Steve whispered to Hartley.

"Do we have a choice?" Hartley considered the plank. "Do you want to go first?"

"No, no, you go." Steve took a step away from the edge of the pier. "I don't mind."

"I will go first." Bodrn started across the plank. "It is just a bridge over a small stretch of river," she said. "What is the worst that could happen to a human?"

"Exactly," said Hartley. "Steve, you're next."

"Thanks for that." Steve stepped onto the plank with one foot, tested his balance, and then began to make his way across. *Slowly does it,* he thought. *Just a short bridge over a deep river. Nothing to stress about.*

"Onwards!"

Steve was bounced onto the wooden deck of the boat as Hartley bounded onto the plank and wobbled his way across at speed.

"Sorry," said Hartley as he stumbled off the plank with a little jump. "Where did they go?"

The captain and the darkling were nowhere to be seen. The deck of the boat and its small, unroofed cabin were empty of anyone, besides Steve and Hartley. The only thing of any interest was a rope, secured to a heavy, iron ring sunk into the deck. The rope stretched up into the sky and disappeared into a single cloud.

"Maybe…" Steve peered inside the cabin. "Yes, now I get it."

"Get what?" Hartley joined him. "Ah, I see what you mean."

"It must be really cramped down there." Steve stood at the top of the plain wooden steps that led down into the body of the boat. "Hello?" he called down.

"What are you two waiting for?" Steve heard the captain's voice call back up.

"Come along, Steve." Hartley started down the steps. "The man's invited us into his home. It would be rude to keep him waiting."

What should have been five or ten steps turned into twenty

and more, as the simple flight widened into a sweeping, plushly carpeted staircase with a highly polished wooden banister.

"Wow," said Steve as he arrived at the bottom of the staircase.

They stood in a vast room where brown-veined, pale marble pillars rose from a matching marble floor. Chandeliers as large as the footprint of Hartley's kitchen sparkled beneath a ceiling of emerald-green stained glass. Two sweeping staircases to their right travelled to upper landings which split into walkways lining each side of the room.

"Marvellous." Hartley cradled a delicate stemmed glass between his thumb and forefinger. A waiter poured from a bottle of champagne.

"Thank you, Ryder," said Meeris as a second waiter helped him remove his coat and handed him a black velvet jacket. "That's better now." He pulled the garment on in one swift move.

"Where are we?" said Steve.

"You know where we are," said Meeris.

"I know where I thought we were," said Steve. "And this isn't it."

"Is this a protected area?" asked Bodrn.

"Obviously," said Meeris. "Welcome to the *SS Danu*. My home, and yours too until we reach our destination."

The waiter who had served Hartley returned to a polished, wooden bar that ran the length of the room. He immediately began to gather ingredients and splash them into a cocktail mixer, finishing with a squeeze of lime.

Dining tables with high-backed chairs and huddles of leather armchairs sat in islands around the space. Half of the tables and armchairs were filled with well-dressed passengers. Some sat in groups and chatted, while a handful of others were alone, reading or lost in their thoughts.

"I could get used to this," said Hartley.

"I'll message for someone to check on the grayling," said Meeris. "It's no bother," he continued as Hartley began to complain. "My man's a smooth talker. He'll simply find them as he passes by. Or he won't, if the truth-see charm has already been removed."

"If you think that's wise," said Hartley. "And could you put this in safe keeping? The grayling was carrying it to summon the Hidden." Hartley handed the flare charm to Meeris.

"The Hidden?" Meeris held the flare charm at arm's length as if it might explode at any minute. "I'll put it in the lockbox."

"Much appreciated," said Hartley.

"Since you're here, my friend, I was wondering if you could help with a bit of trouble I'm having. Solve a nasty problem for me."

"Problem-solving is my middle name," said Hartley. "Do tell."

"How are you with infestations?" said Meeris.

"Clearing them or causing them?" asked Hartley.

"Clearing them. Boggarts, to be precise. We think a passenger brought them on accidentally. We've got them trapped in the library but they're destructive little hooligans."

"Boggarts. That's nasty," said Hartley. "But completely doable with the right equipment."

"Glad you think so," said Meeris. "Ryder will show you the way to the library."

"Boggarts?" Steve whispered to Hartley. "Should I be worried?"

"No, no, no." Hartley shook his head enthusiastically. "Well, not if they've eaten anyway."

"How will we know if they've eaten?"

"My dear boy, we'll know," said Hartley with a wink. "Come along."

*

"It's a bit dark in here." Steve peered into the shadows of the library. "Can we put the lights on?"

"The boggarts smashed them all," said Ryder, still puffing

from pushing an iron chest that Hartley had commandeered from the captain's cabin into the middle of the room. "I can create a light orb, if that helps."

"Carefully," said Hartley. "We don't want to disturb them." He held a charm he had pulled from his pocket. It was a messy combination of straw, herbs, and red ribbon woven around a rusty old padlock.

Ryder formed a golden light orb in a second and flicked it bobbing towards the centre of the room. The light from the orb revealed torn pages littered around the library. An overturned armchair sagged its stuffing onto the floor. One of its legs was covered with scratches and teeth marks. In the middle of it all sat the iron chest. It was open, its heavy lid hanging back on its hinges.

"That'll do," said Hartley. "Just enough light to reveal the battleground but not so much as to raise alarm."

"I have never seen a boggart." Bodrn peered over Steve's shoulder. "Are they fierce?"

"They're a bloody nuisance," said Ryder. "But yes, fierce. One nearly took my finger off. Teeth like needles and they're always hungry."

"So what now?" said Steve.

"We wait," said Hartley. "Boggarts are like cats. They never can resist an open container, especially when it's loaded up with their favourite food."

"This'd better work," said Ryder. "Those are our last berries."

"Needs must," said Hartley. "It'll be worth it if this goes to plan."

"And if it doesn't?" said Steve.

"You're a fast runner. You'll be fine."

"Will that work?" Ryder nodded to the charm that Hartley held. "It doesn't look much to me."

"Ye of little faith," said Hartley. "Combined with the iron of the chest it should contain the boggarts for a few weeks, long enough to get them off the Danu."

"Look," said Steve as a small hand grasped the edge of one of the bookcases.

The creature that slid around the bookcase was small, around a foot in height, and naked except for a ragged pair of trousers. Its feet were too big for its size, and it was mostly bald except for a bush of hair at the back of its head. Its small facial features were screwed up into an expression of contempt as it sniffed at the chest.

It looked back behind the bookcase and muttered words Steve didn't understand in a voice that sounded like a person gargling. Another boggart rushed out half the distance to the chest and stopped. It squinted up at the orb and pointed, muttering to the first boggart.

There was a sound of scratching and tiny thuds like fingers on a tabletop. With a stench like sweaty feet, a crowd of boggarts rushed into view and descended on the crate, jumping and scrambling inside. The first two boggarts took one last look around the room, their eyes sliding over the humans, and then they too jumped into the crate.

"Now!" said Hartley. The four of them rushed into the library, slamming the chest lid shut.

"They are strong," said Bodrn as the lid of the chest bumped up and down. She sat down heavily on the chest, feet braced on the floor.

"Hold on." Ryder forced the lid down with a grunt. "Hurry up with that charm."

"Just hold it a moment longer," said Hartley as he struggled to tie the charm onto the buckle of the chest.

"What happens if they get out?" Steve pushed all of his weight down onto the lid. He could hear the boggarts' gargling voices and their fists beating on the iron.

"Best not think about that," grunted Ryder. "They already sent our cook to the hospital."

"There, we have it!" Hartley stood back from the chest. "You can get off now. It's perfectly secure."

"Are you sure?" said Ryder. "I can run fast, but I'm not sure you're up to it."

"Rude," said Hartley, holding his hands to his paunch defensively. "And yes, I am sure. Step away."

"On your head be it." Ryder released his hold on the chest and withdrew a few steps.

"You too, Miss D…, I mean, Bodrn," said Hartley. "Off you get. And you, Steve."

"Gladly." She jumped off the chest. Steve held on a second longer before following her. He could see that she was trembling.

"Are you all right?" he asked as she came to his side.

"The iron still scares me." She examined her hands, which looked fine to Steve. "I thought there would be pain, but it did nothing to me."

"That's good, isn't it?" said Steve.

"It is further proof that I am not what I was," she said sadly.

"Seems solid." Ryder kicked the chest. The boggarts inside squealed in response. "Good job."

"Is it at all possible that we could have a bite to eat?" Hartley held a hand to his rumbling stomach. "Now that the infestation is handled. Please?"

"This way," said Ryder, marching past them. "You're dining at the captain's table tonight, so you'd best scrub up a bit first. I've got a cabin ready for you all. Bunking up together, if that's all right?"

"Is it all right, Bodrn?" asked Hartley. "Sharing a room with us boys?"

"It is acceptable," she said with a nod.

"That's agreed then," said Ryder. "This way."

*

Steve 'scrubbed up' his appearance as much as he could, but he still felt under-dressed for the captain's table.

He sat between the darkling and an elderly lady whose

sequinned dress rattled every time she moved. Her arms were sheathed in long gloves up to her elbows, over which she wore several big-jewelled rings. Her hair was piled up around a tiara and her face was covered in more make-up than Steve had ever seen anyone wear.

"I told the Duke," she said, throwing her hands into the air. "I told him that a cruise would be a wonderful distraction, but would he listen?" The captain and the other elderly inhabitants, all dressed in evening wear, laughed politely.

For once, Hartley was on his best behaviour. Sitting on the opposite side of the table to Steve, the shopkeeper hadn't once licked a knife or his plate. He hadn't even reached across the table to grab a bread roll. The seven-course meal had taken a toll on him though, and his eyelids were beginning to droop. Steve was about to call out to his friend when he felt a finger prod his shoulder.

"Who are you?" The elderly lady stared down at him pointing a finger.

"I'm Steve," he said. "Ha—"

"Hailing from the Continent," interrupted Meeris. "He's my nephew, and this is my uncle." He nodded to Hartley.

"And his niece," said the darkling. "Bodrn."

"Don't Continentals dress for dinner?" the elderly lady asked, looking Hartley up and down.

"Our luggage was lost on the way, I'm afraid," said Hartley. "Terribly inconvenient. Attending dinner in these old things." He pulled at the collar of his tweed jacket with a tut. "It's just not done, I know."

"Quite," she said with a blink, and then she returned to telling her yarn about the Duke as if she'd never stopped.

"Steve and Bodrn, why don't you take Uncle for a breath of air?" said Meeris. "I'm sure you have things to discuss."

"What an excellent idea." Hartley pushed his chair back and stood up with a groan. "Back isn't what it was," he said to the guests around the table. "Travelling pains, you know."

"Thanks for the food," said Steve as he stood up.

He wasn't entirely sure what the rules were for leaving the captain's table on a cruise ship hidden under a fishing boat. So he tucked his chair under the table, smiled at the captain, and hurried after Hartley with the darkling at his heels.

"So, are they all magicals?" Steve tried to keep his voice down as they passed other passengers in the hallway. "The guests and the crew?"

"Hard to tell," said Hartley.

"If I was myself, I could read their auras," said Bodrn. "Sorry."

"No matter," said Hartley. "We don't really need to know. And you are as much yourself as you always were, dear girl."

"So what do we do now?" said Steve.

"Well, I don't know about you," said Hartley, "but I could do with hitting the pillow. It's been a long, bumpy day. I don't expect tomorrow to be any less eventful."

Chapter Thirteen

Steve had no idea what time it was when he woke up. He rubbed his eyes and sat up, forgetting that he was on the top bunk of a cramped cabin.

"Ow!" He held a hand to his forehead. "Stupid ceiling."

"Overhead," said Hartley.

"What?"

"On a ship, it's an overhead, not a ceiling. The correct term would be 'stupid overhead'." Hartley stood in the narrow space between the bunk beds and a makeshift single bed that Ryder had set up for the darkling, his hands pressed to the small of his back.

"Whatever." Steve slung his legs over the side of the top bunk. "What time is it?"

"Difficult to tell with no windows."

"Where's the darkling?" said Steve, realising that they were alone.

"You mean, Bodrn," said Hartley.

"It'll take me a bit to get used to that. Where is she?"

"Our friend finds it difficult to sleep unless she is exhausted. I heard her leave the cabin a few hours ago."

"That's worrying." Steve climbed down the rickety ladder that was nailed to the bunks. The metal rungs hurt his feet.

"Bodrn has been looking after herself for a very long time." Hartley straightened his jacket and attempted to run a comb through his hair, which seemed to have developed a white streak down the middle. He failed, tugged the comb from his mane and dropped it back into his pocket. "She'll find us when she's done with her scouting."

"Who are you trying to impress?" said Steve with a grin.

"After last night's comment on our attire, I thought it best to at least try to keep up appearances. Make an effort."

"You've never made an effort before."

"I constantly make an effort," said Hartley, fussing with a handkerchief before stuffing it into the top pocket of his jacket. "See?"

"What's the plan?" Steve pulled on his trainers and grabbed his jacket from the hook on the door. "Don't tell me. Breakfast."

"You read my mind." Hartley's stomach gurgled in agreement. "Hungry is no way to live."

"But then we find Bodrn," said Steve. "I know she can look after herself, but…" He shrugged.

"Of course, dear boy." Hartley's stomach gurgled again. "After breakfast." He pulled the door open with a grunt and gestured for Steve to leave first. "Let's see what delights the ship's cook has to offer this morning."

∗

Bodrn stood on the deck of the *SS Danu*, or rather what appeared to be a small sea vessel suitable for two or three people at most. There was little to suggest this was anything other than a modest ship travelling between continents. That was if you discounted the rope that rose from the deck and disappeared into a small, white cloud in the sky above.

As a darkling, she should have been afraid of the vast, deep ocean, but as a human she found only delight in the ever shifting, sometimes grey, often blue sea. From time to time, a spray of water caressed her face with a scent of salt.

"It's a beauty, isn't it?"

She hadn't heard the captain approach, not a footfall or a deck-board creak. He had changed into the jacket she had first seen him wearing in Port London. He looked exactly as you would expect the captain of a small ship to look.

"Hartley would call it marvellous or wonderful," she said.

"What do you call it?"

"It is…" She searched for the right word. "Impressive," she finished.

"Ironic that you're the one up here," he said. "You being a darkling."

"How did you know?"

"A little gull told me. Well, actually a squirrel." He smiled, deepening the wrinkles in his face. "It also suggested that I make some introductions to ease your passage into Nuova Venezia."

"May I ask who made this suggestion?" She saw no hint in the captain's face as to how he felt about being asked the question. His smile remained in place and continued to shine in his eyes.

"You may not," he said. "Let's just say, they have your best intentions at heart. Now, let's find your friends before Hartley Keg eats me out of ship and berth."

*

Steve waved, as Bodrn and Meeris walked into the breakfast room. It was a long, vast space lined on one side by a painted, underwater vista. Or at least, Steve thought it looked painted but the creatures it contained—turtles, fish, the occasional dolphin—and the variety of waving vegetation moved as if this were a window into the actual ocean. The room was as well lit as if it was open to the elements on a sunny day, and a pleasant breeze caressed Steve's face. The tables were topped with crisp white cloths and all the cutlery and condiments you could wish for.

A handful of smiling waiting staff moved rapidly but deftly between the tables and a pair of white-painted, swinging doors at the back of the room. They delivered plates of food, baskets of bread, and precariously balanced cups of coffee and tea.

"Like I said, ship and berth," said Meeris as he pulled back a chair for Bodrn to sit on.

Hartley's plate was piled with bacon, sausages, eggs cooked in

97

a variety of ways, and a couple of croissants. A white napkin was tucked into his collar, somewhere underneath his beard, and he was slurping a cup of tea.

"Marvellous," he said as he put down his cup. "I don't know why a person would ever leave this place." He stabbed a croissant with a fork and nibbled around its edges.

"Thank you." Bodrn sat down and shuffled her chair forward. Almost immediately, a waiter placed a plate in front of her. It contained a slice of toast topped with ham and a fried egg. Her cup was filled with steaming milk. Finally, the waiter snatched a napkin out of the air with a flourish and laid it across her lap.

"Will there be anything else, miss?" he said.

"No. This is sufficient. Thank you."

The waiter snatched a cup of black coffee from the air, without spilling a drop, and placed it in front of the captain. With a nod and a smile, he moved on to the guests at the next table.

"Is that what you wanted to eat?" said Steve.

"It is now," she said after a mouthful, with a smile. "Is this magic?"

"The choice of food?" said Meeris. "A little magic. A little psychology. I rely on the waiting staff to know exactly what our guests want and need."

Steve pushed his plate away. His stomach was comfortably full of croissants and marmalade. He noticed how crumb-free the table was, and wondered if that was magic too.

"So," said Meeris after a sip of coffee. "Nuova Venezia. Or to be more specific, how we'll get you the blazes in there."

"How do you usually smuggle people into Nuova Venezia?" said Hartley.

"What do you take me for?" said Meeris with a badly hidden smile. "I'm a respectable businessman. I don't smuggle anything."

"Whatever you call it, how's it normally done?" Hartley grinned as a waiter brought him a plate of cold meat, cheese and bread. "Just the thing." He rubbed his hands together and reached for a slice of bread.

"You might have noticed that my passengers are on the wealthy side of society," said Meeris. "They don't need me to get into that place."

"So you can't help us?" said Steve.

"I didn't say that." Meeris drained his cup. "There is someone onboard who'll help. A celebrity."

"Workaday celebrity or our type of celebrity?" Hartley laid alternating slices of meat and cheese onto a slice of bread.

"Both," said Meeris.

"Intriguing," said Hartley. "Do tell."

"She's an old friend of yours," said Meeris. "Mariana."

"*The* Mariana?" said Hartley. "What good fortune. I haven't seen the dear girl since our last Gathering. Do you remember, Steve? She danced for us all."

Steve found the edges of his mouth lift into a smile as he recalled his first and only experience of the dancing enchantress, entertaining the crowds in the woodland area of Darkacre. She had captivated the audience with her performance and her magic, too.

"Officially, she's travelling to Nuova Venezia to perform," said Meeris.

"And unofficially?" said Hartley.

"The usual," said Meeris. "Keeping the peace between the Council and the workadays. Oiling cogs and all that nonsense. Hassan is with her."

"Who is Hassan?" Bodrn had finished her food and was enjoying the warm milk.

"Hassan is Mariana's partner," said Hartley. "Both romantically and in business. He presents himself as her stylist and advisor. Oh, this is going to be fun."

"I've already spoken to her," said Meeris. "We can head over there as soon as you're finished." He frowned as Hartley finished the construction of his sandwich. "Are you eating that now?"

"It won't take a moment," said Hartley.

"It really won't," said Steve as the shopkeeper lifted the

sandwich to his widening mouth. "He has a knack."

"Hartley Keg has lots of knacks," said Meeris. "That's what makes him so useful."

*

"I'm surprised you didn't fill your pockets with food," said Steve.

"I did consider it," said Hartley. "But I'm not sure how the grease and crumbs would affect the other items I carry in my pockets."

"It's not like you to err on the side of caution," said Meeris.

"He is carrying an important item," said Bodrn. "For me."

"I hadn't forgotten." Hartley patted one of his jacket pockets. "Safe as houses."

The captain had led the party of friends to a polished wooden door on one of the sweeping balconies that ran around the grand entrance of the *SS Danu*. At the push of a button, the doors had opened to reveal a lift. It was surprisingly stark compared to the luxurious décor of the ship. The floor appeared to be concrete, and the walls were dull steel. The button that the captain had pushed was right at the top.

When the lift came to a subtle halt with a quiet ping, the doors slid open to reveal a small entrance area. It contained no furniture or ornamentation, but the flooring and the single door were a perfect match for the polished interior of the *SS Danu*.

"Off you go now," said Meeris, holding the doors open.

"Aren't you coming with us?" said Steve.

"No need," said Meeris. "I'd only get in the way of your reunion. Knock on the door, why don't you?"

"Thank you, Meeris," said Hartley, shaking his hand. "You've been a wonderful help." With a nod of his head, the shopkeeper stepped out of the lift and approached the door on the other side of the space.

"Go on then." Meeris pushed Steve and the darkling out of the lift. "It wouldn't be polite to keep her waiting." He pushed one of the buttons and nodded to Steve as the lift doors slid shut.

Almost immediately, the single door in the space opened. Hartley laughed, clapping his hands. "Mariana, my dear. How are you?"

The dancer that Steve had seen at the Gathering in Darkacre greeted them all with a dazzling smile. Steve wondered if she was enchanting them at that moment because he felt his face automatically spring into a grin.

"Come, come." Mariana held the door open for her guests as they entered. She wore a loose dress of gold silk, her dark hair tied back with matching ribbons. "It's so wonderful to see you all."

"If I'd known we were doing formal, I'd have worn a tie." Hartley wrapped his arms around their host and planted a kiss on her cheek. "You look majestic."

"Oh, this old thing?" She hugged him back. "How are you?"

"All the better for seeing you." He released her and stepped back. "Isn't Hassan with you?" he asked as she gestured for them to follow her.

Steve had to stop himself from saying, 'wow', as he stepped into the enchantress's suite. Unlike the vintage glamour of the *SS Danu*, Mariana's quarters were a statement of modernity and opulence.

The marble floors were polished to a shine, reflecting the soft glow of the light from the immense chandelier that hung far above their heads in the centre of the space. A floral aroma hung in the air, coaxing Steve to take a deep breath of the scent. Towering, polished metal columns reached up to the high ceiling, their mirrored surfaces catching softened reflections of the enchantress and her visitors. Beneath the chandelier, and taking centre stage in the suite, was a sumptuous seating arrangement of over-sized sofas, each cushioned seat adorned with intricate patterns.

"Come. Join me." Mariana threw herself onto one of the sofas, patting the cushion next to her.

"This looks remarkably like your house in England, Mariana." Hartley dropped onto the sofa beside her. "By design?"

"I always like to bring a reminder of home with me," she said. "I travel so much. Meeris was happy to oblige me. What do you think, Steve and…?" She raised an elegant eyebrow at the darkling.

"I am called Bodrn," said the darkling as she took a seat.

"I see," said the enchantress with the tiniest of smiles. "Steve?" She turned her attention on him as he sat down beside the darkling.

"It's…" He took in the holographic artworks along the walls. The vibrant images shifted and transformed, moving from vintage landscapes to portraits of well-known figures from the past, and then to abstract designs that appeared to extend out from the screen. Looking up, he could see that the ceiling was adorned with a network of delicate, glowing crystals. "Wow," he finished.

"'Wow' is what I was going for," she said with a smile. "Meeris told me to expect you all, so I arranged a midnight feast." She clapped her hands and a round, low table rose up from the floor between the sofas. "Hassan," she called.

"Yes m'lady." A dark-haired man wearing dress trousers and a loose, grey, silk t-shirt appeared through a doorway at the other end of the room. He carried a large, silver tray that bore a miscellany of food, a silver teapot, and delicate, glass cups. "Hello, Hartley," he said as he carefully lowered the tray onto the table. "One midnight feast, as requested," he said with a grin.

"But it is not midnight," said Bodrn.

"It is whatever time we wish it to be," said Mariana as she began to pour tea into the cups. "Please do help yourselves. There is cinnamon toast and Turkish delight."

"You're spoiling us." Hartley picked up a plate and helped himself to a slice of cinnamon toast which he topped off with three pieces of Turkish delight.

"She likes to entertain." Hassan reclined on an empty sofa,

leaning back into the cushions with one arm laid elegantly across the back of the sofa.

"Don't listen to him." Mariana finished pouring the tea into the cups. "He enjoys company just as much as I do. There is sugar, lemon, honey, and milk. Help yourself."

"Marvellous Turkish delight," said Hartley after a mouthful.

"I'll send you a box," said Mariana. "I only get it in for guests."

"Liar," said Hassan with a grin.

"Don't be bothersome, Hassan," she said, stirring a little honey into her tea.

"This is good," said Bodrn, awkwardly holding her cup of tea. The word 'good' sounded just as awkward too.

"But?" said Hassan.

"We did not come here for a tea party. We need your help."

"Straight down to business," said Hassan. "In certain circles, that would be seen as rude."

"My friend is still developing her social graces," said Hartley.

"Fitting in as a human must be difficult after so long in the shadows," said Mariana. "Of course, I know who you are," she continued. "I was there, at the beginning, when we were all tasked with our quests. This was the form you took back then. It is a shame that our good friend is no longer with us."

"It is," said Bodrn.

"But as you say, you're not here for pleasantries. What is it you need, Hartley?" Mariana raised her cup to her lips as she turned her gaze on the shopkeeper.

"Passage into Nuova Venezia," he said. "I believe there is normally a waiting list but unfortunately our current quest is rather urgent."

"We're looking for my mum," said Steve.

"Urgent and close to your heart, then," said Mariana. "Of course I'll help. Let's see." She placed a long finger on her lips as she thought. "I have just the cover story. You can be my entourage. My cook," she said placing a hand on Hartley's arm. "And my two young proteges," she finished as she looked at

Steve and Bodrn. "Do you dance?"

"I could try," said Steve.

"Stop making them nervous," said Hassan. "It is merely a pretence. Nobody will check."

"When do we arrive in Nuova Venezia?" asked Bodrn.

"In the morning," said Hassan. "So best pack up your things to be ready."

"Easily done." Hartley picked the crumbs from his empty plate. "Seeing as we don't have any things to pack."

"I would expect nothing less from a traveller," said Hassan. "Which begs a question. Why do you need our help?"

"I've never been to Nuova Venezia before," said Hartley. "I can't travel us in there."

"I sense there's something you're not telling us," said Hassan. "The Hartley I know would travel his way onto a flight up to the city. I believe that's possible, yes?"

"In normal circumstances, I can travel into a nearby space that I can see," said Hartley with a frown. "But these are hardly normal circumstances." He sighed and pulled back his sleeves to display the bangles around his wrists. "The Council hampered me."

"Oh Hartley." Mariana took his hands. "How awful."

"That would also explain the grey in your hair and beard," said Hassan. "Or is it a fashion statement?"

"You know me, Hassan. I don't do fashion," said Hartley. "I have my own inimitable style. The grey is an unfortunate side effect." He guzzled down the rest of his tea. "I don't suppose your cook has a fresh shirt, does he?"

"I'm sure it can be arranged," said Mariana. "In fact, all three of you will need to look the part. Hassan?"

"Come with me," he said, leisurely climbing to his feet. "The benefits of having a fashionista for a beau, eh?"

"And a magical one at that," said Hartley as he deposited his empty plate on the table. "Lead on, dear boy. We're in for a treat," he called to Steve and Bodrn as he climbed to his feet.

"You'll like this."

*

"I do not like this." The darkling stared at her reflection. In the mirror, her blouse and trousers had been replaced by a long evening dress with a loose, full skirt. "I cannot fight in this."

"I should hope not," said Hassan. "Other than to fight off suitors."

The dressing room was just as glamorous as the rest of Mariana's apartment, a combination of fashionable form and efficient function. The walls were lined with luminescent glass, which transformed into mirrors at Hassan's touch. With a swipe and a command, Hassan dressed their reflections in new outfits. Steve couldn't tell whether the mirrors were magical or the latest tech.

The room was filled with rows of perfectly spaced, illuminated clothing racks, showcasing an impressive collection of luxury garments. Every fabric offered some form of glimmer, or glitter, or even glowed with a soft, captivating light.

In the centre of the dressing room sat a sleek, minimalist vanity table, which emitted a glow that reminded Steve of autumn sunlight. A holographic display hovered on one side of the table, currently frozen on the image of a simple black dress.

"Do I have to wear a tie?" Steve unconsciously touched a hand to his throat. "Isn't the shirt smart enough?"

"Not for Mariana's entourage, no." Hassan swiped a hand across the mirror and the tie changed from emerald green to a cobalt blue. "This looks good on you. Even the tie."

"I'm not sure white is my colour." In comparison to the formal wear that Steve and Bodrn's reflections had been dressed in, Hartley's reflection wore a chef's uniform. His reflected beard had been trimmed, but the high collar of the jacket still wasn't visible. The double-breasted white jacket sat snug across his rotund middle and the short sleeves showed the bangles on his wrists. "Perhaps a colourful neckerchief to set off my eyes."

"It's only for the journey into Nuova Venezia," said Hassan as he swiped the mirror to lengthen the sleeves. "It's not perfect but it'll do for your purposes. Do you like the cut of the beard? I could go shorter."

"Don't you dare." Hartley's hands leapt to his face. "It's taken me a lifetime to get it into this condition."

"I can tell," said Hassan. "Will you at least let me brush your hair."

"I have a comb," said Hartley. "Thank you very much."

"As for you." Hassan pointed at the darkling. "Shoes."

"I have shoes," she said, looking down at the black plimsolls Hartley had provided from his shop stock.

"Debatable," said Hassan. "I won't force heels on you. No, something flat but chic. I have just the thing. And socks for you." He pointed at Hartley's feet. "Those will never do."

"These are perfectly serviceable," said Hartley. "I've had them for years."

"Again, I can tell," said Hassan. "I'll have your clothes cleaned once you change into your new wardrobe. The jacket—"

"Stays with me," said Hartley.

"Hassan, stop teasing them." Mariana stood at the entrance to the dressing room, leaning against the door frame.

"I'm just having a little fun," he said.

"Fun for you," she said. "There is no need to change your clothes when you have an enchanter to hand."

"At your service." Hassan gave a deep bow. "I wasn't joking about the beard, though. Or the socks."

"Hassan can enchant a veil on your appearances," said Mariana. "That way you'll look the part in Nuova Venezia but hang onto your garments. And pockets," she added, winking at Hartley.

"Unless you want to change your clothes of course," said Hassan.

"I wouldn't say no to a clean shirt," said Hartley. "But only if you're offering."

"And the others?"

"I'm good," said Steve.

"I'm sure you are," said Mariana. "But I think our friend here could do with something more suitable to her skills. Come with me." She drew the darkling to the vanity table. "Sit," she said, tapping on the holographic screen. "This is going to be fun."

Chapter Fourteen

The day had just made itself known as Steve followed the others off the *SS Danu*. The apricot dawn sky was mirrored on the rippling waters of the lagoon, but that wasn't what grabbed his attention.

"I do adore the Venetian lido. So quaint." Mariana was dressed simply in black trousers and a white, silk shirt but she exuded glamour as always. "It's almost a shame to head up to Nuova Venezia."

"Steve, close your mouth," said Hartley. "You'll catch a fly."

"Have you seen these ships?" The modest size and appearance of the *SS Danu* was dwarfed by every one of the yachts that been moored at the lido landing area. The yachts towered above the small vessel with their sleek lines, gleaming hulls, and bright colours that were vibrant even in the delicate morning light.

"This is just a taste of what you can expect in the city above," said Hassan.

"They are only vehicles." The darkling looked more like herself in black trousers, t-shirt, zipped-up jacket, and boots. It was a close match to the clothes Steve had become accustomed to seeing her wear but, coming from Hassan and Mariana's wardrobe, each item was top quality.

"Exactly," said Meeris. "Where's the charm? Where's the tradition? Give me the *Danu* anytime. Eh, Ryder?"

"Yes, Captain." Ryder stood at Meeris' shoulder with his arms folded behind his back.

"Sorry." Steve shrugged. "Your ship is great too. Just in a different way."

"Think nothing of it." Meeris slapped Steve on the shoulder with a grin. "I'm just messing with you." He leant closer and said in a quieter tone, "I know the *Danu* is far superior. Mariana, my lovely." Meeris offered a hand to her. "It has been a pleasure, as always."

"My darling Meeris." She ignored his hand and kissed the captain on both cheeks. "I do enjoy our little jaunts."

Steve was sure that Meeris blushed as Mariana engulfed him in an elegant hug.

"Captain." Hassan shook the man's hand as Mariana stepped back. "I'll arrange for the luggage to be collected."

"Already done," said Meeris with a wink. "If you know what I mean."

"That means with magic," Hartley whispered to Steve.

"Yes, I got that," said Steve.

"Captain." Ryder held out a canvas drawstring bag. "You said to remind you."

"Thank you, Ryder. Yes, before I forget." Meeris nodded for Ryder to hand the bag over to Hartley. "I didn't think you'd want to leave this behind."

"Thank you, my friend." Hartley pulled the bag open and peered inside. "Oh. Are you sure?"

"Am I sure?" said Meeris. "You took that thing off a you-know-what working for the you-know-who. I couldn't be happier to get that particular item off my ship."

"Here you are, Steve. You can carry this."

Hartley handed the bag to Steve. He pulled the drawstrings open and peered into the bag. The flare charm inside gave off the faintest green glow.

"Best keep it out of sight," whispered Hartley. "You never know who might be watching. Put it away."

Steve slid the bag into his pocket, feeling it fall into the magical space within. He considered what would happen if the flare charm went off, picturing a party of Hidden blinking into existence in his pocket.

"So if you're all sorted, I'll be away with no further faff." Meeris clapped his hands together. "Health and wealth to you all now. Stay safe." With that, the captain disappeared into the ship's small cabin.

The landing area for Nuova Venezia was just as impressive as Mariana had suggested, although hardly 'quaint', as she had called it. As a human concierge and his robot assistant escorted Steve and his friends away from the yachts, the sights of the lido laid themselves out in the early morning light.

The lido was constructed of the same materials that Steve was used to seeing back home in Caercester. There was marble, granite, steel, and so much glass, but here these materials were melded into a sophisticated landscape of charm and luxury. There were touches of old Venice in the ornate arches, sleekly crafted balconies, and white marble carvings that adorned the houses. Statues shared the walkway spaces with holographic displays of old Venice.

"If you could wait here, Miss…?" said the concierge, halting at an immense, free-standing stained-glass panel of a winged lion which towered above them all.

"No 'Miss'. Just Mariana," said Mariana.

"Of course, Mariana," said the concierge with a well-practised smile. "I'll confirm the transfer for your party." He instructed his robot assistant with a few hurried phrases in what Steve took to be Italian and left at speed.

"Is it too late to inform everyone that I don't like airplanes?" said Hartley.

"Don't worry," said Hassan. "It's only a brief flight, unless they decide to give us a tour of the ruins."

"Do they have to?" said Hartley. "Isn't there a lift we can ride instead?"

"No, darling Hartley, there is no lift." Mariana took his arm. "If you want to enter Nuova Venezia, it'll have to be by air."

"Unless of course you want to…" Hassan mimed knocking on a door and opening it.

"You know that's not an option." Hartley scowled, grasping the bangles around his wrists.

"Stop teasing him, Hassan," said Mariana.

"Sorry," said Hassan. "I didn't realise the hampering of your powers was such a sore point."

"You're forgiven," said Hartley, his scowl sliding into a grin. "Are you sure your enchantment will work up there?" Hartley pointed to his jacket and trousers.

"It will," said Hassan. "I've had plenty of practice at tweaking my appearance when I haven't had a wardrobe to hand over the years. To the residents and visitors of Nuova Venezia, you will appear as sophisticated and well-cut as would be expected from a member of a global star's entourage."

"Looks like we're up," said Mariana as the concierge returned. "Ready, Hartley?"

"Hartley Keg is always ready," he said but Steve noticed a shake in his friend's voice. "Onwards," he said in a less than enthusiastic tone.

*

As they approached the vehicle that would transfer them to the floating city, the aircraft's wings lifted and rotated to form two rotor blades on top. The now-helicopter was easily big enough to carry twenty passengers split between two rows of seats.

"This is comfy," said Hartley as he settled into a chair at the end of one row. "I don't think I'll need a seat belt. I like to have a wander and—"

"Better safe than sorry." Mariana clicked his seat belt into place. "We don't want to lose you mid-flight."

"Will this take long?" Bodrn had fastened her seat belt as soon as she sat down, pulling it tight across her lap. She gripped the arms of the seat, her fingers digging into the fabric. Her eyes were tightly shut.

"Not long," said the pilot, a young woman dressed in the

same uniform as the concierge. "Visibility is too poor today for a near flyover of old Venice. Apologies."

"Oh, that is a shame," said Hartley. "I was looking forward to it."

"Then you'll be pleased to hear that we have daily flights over the ruins. Just ask your hotel concierge to book it for you."

"Sounds like just the thing, Hartley," said Hassan with a grin.

When the aircraft rotors began to spin, the two rows of seats slowly pivoted and slid into place at the long windows that ran along each side of the vehicle. The aircraft lifted from the platform with the tiniest of judders.

Bodrn's eyes snapped open as she gasped, looking around like a trapped animal.

"It's okay." Steve took her hand. He wasn't sure if she'd slap him or recoil in her current panic, but she didn't. "We're safe."

"If you say so." She sat back in her seat and her breathing slowed. "I have never flown in an aircraft before."

"I'm sure Hartley hasn't either."

"Oh, many times," said Hartley, arms crossed and jaw tense. "Many many many times. I still don't like it. How safe are we?" he called to the pilot.

"Ignore him," said Mariana. "He's just playing to the crowd."

As the aircraft crossed the water, steadily rising towards Nuova Venezia which hung in the air above the ruins of the old city below, the hum of the rotors created a gentle vibration in the vehicle. Steve found it relaxing and, looking at Hartley and Bodrn, it seemed to have the same effect on them. Their tense body language melted away as they stared at the dawn-illuminated vista of the Venetian lagoon. A smattering of rain tapped on the windows, the wet smears making it impossible to see the details of the city ruins.

"We'll be arriving in Nuova Venezia momentarily," said the pilot. "I hope you've enjoyed your flight, and I'd like to wish you an enjoyable visit to our city. Thank you."

The two rows of seats turned and slid back into their original position as the aircraft neared a raised landing platform that was circled by a channel of water.

"That wasn't anywhere near as bad as I'd feared," said Hartley. "No offence," he called to the pilot.

"And I thought I was the dramatic one," said Mariana.

"It's a close battle," said Hassan.

Bodrn grabbed Steve's hand again as the aircraft landed with a jolt. "Sorry," she said, releasing him.

The rotors had barely slowed to a halt before Hartley unfastened his seat belt and sprang to his feet. He patted himself down as if he was checking for broken bones.

"All present and accounted for," he said as he plunged his hands into his jacket pockets. "Everything in its place. Marvellous."

As the doors opened, pivoting upwards like butterfly wings, the full noise and bustle of the floating city descenced on the passengers. Bodrn covered her ears, shrinking into her seat.

"It's loud, I know." The pilot took the empty seat next to the darkling. "But you get used to it after a while."

"Thank you," said Bodrn. "It smells…" She paused. "Dry."

"That's a new one," said the pilot. "I suppose it does. The city sits under a protective dome so the climate can be regulated. Even on a rainy day like today, you don't need an umbrella or a coat in Nuova Venezia."

"That's good," said Steve with what he hoped was an encouraging smile. "Shall we…?" He nodded to the nearest open door.

"The arrivals concierge will arrange transport to your hotel," the pilot told everyone as they began to leave.

"Not another flight?" said Hartley.

"No, just a gondola," said the pilot. "Although there may be a little low-level flight involved, depending on your accommodation."

"Are there lifts?" said Hartley in a hopeful tone.

"Ignore him. The gondola will be fine," said Mariana.

"You look as if you need a little support." Hassan took Bodrn's hand and pulled her to her feet. "Lean on me," he said, tucking her arm through his. "Steve, I think Hartley may need to be reined in a little. Up for the job?"

"I heard that," said Hartley from the platform outside.

"That's what I was hoping for." Hassan winked at Steve.

Steve followed Hassan and Bodrn as they left the aircraft. Hartley and Mariana waited on the platform. Mariana looked to be in her element. Her face, always beautiful, had fallen into a film-star smile as she chatted to another attendant.

"Ready for Nuova Venezia?" said Hassan to Steve. "It's rather a unique experience."

"No," said Bodrn quietly.

"Actually, yes," said Steve. "I know I'm here to find my mum, but this is…" He ran out of words to describe how excited he felt. Maybe it was the buzz of the floating city or perhaps, for just a little while, he had forgotten about all the problems back home.

"This way." Mariana beckoned to the three of them. "Our ride is here."

She took Hartley's arm and pulled him across a walkway that extended over the surrounding band of water. Hassan followed, taking Bodrn with him. Steve went last, looking down at the water as he crossed the walkway.

"That's not water," he said, mainly to himself, as he noticed the tiniest of blurs in the lapping waves.

"It's a hologram," Hassan called back to him. "All part of the illusion."

"Oh," said Steve, feeling a little bit disappointed. "I thought maybe…"

"Careful now, Hartley."

"This isn't as easy as it looks, you know."

Steve's disappointment fell away at the sight of Mariana guiding Hartley onto what appeared to be a floating gondola. Hartley wobbled dramatically with one foot on the vehicle and the other on the pavement.

"And so it begins," said Hassan as he released the darkling's arm. "Excuse me."

"Okay?" said Steve as he joined her. "Bodrn?"

"I am," she said. "As a…" She paused. "Before, I could have hidden myself away, but now…" She shrugged. "How do you humans face such challenges?"

"I'd never thought about it really," said Steve. "We just get on with it, or we run away."

"I think our friend wants to run away from that gondola," said Bodrn.

Hartley stood with both feet planted on the vehicle, arms flailing as Hassan and Mariana joined him.

"Do sit down, Hartley. People are staring," said Mariana.

"I thought you'd appreciate the attention," he said as he dropped onto one of the padded seats.

"Coming?" Mariana called to Steve and the darkling.

"It's up to you, Bodrn," said Steve. "I'm not sure if we can walk to the hotel but I'm willing to give it a try."

She stared at the gondola and its three inhabitants for a moment longer and then she gave a single nod. "Onwards," she said. "Isn't that what Hartley says at the beginning of an adventure?"

"Yeah." Steve chuckled. "And this place is definitely an adventure."

"Don't worry. It's perfectly safe," Hassan called to them. "Even with Hartley on board."

With a last look at the bustle of the city and the floating gondola, Bodrn climbed onto the vehicle in one swift move. Steve followed at a more careful pace and, as he settled into the seat next to Hartley, the gondola set off.

Chapter Fifteen

The journey through Nuova Venezia was taken at a leisurely pace. Steve thought it was probably planned that way, to show off the city sights. The gondola hovered over a holographic representation of a water-filled canal. The water was an appealing turquoise and every so often a dolphin would break the surface—a holographic dolphin, of course—before disappearing into the water again.

If the lido had been an attempt to combine Venetian architecture with the latest technology, then Nuova Venezia took that mission to the extreme. Their canal route led them under ornate bridges that easily allowed for sufficient head height as they passed underneath. The canal was followed on both sides by busy walkways that were lined with carved stone balustrades. Most of the buildings stretched to five or six floors high and were made from a mixture of sleek, polished metal or equally sleek and polished marble. Whatever material they were constructed from, each building had the same jewel-toned doors, arched windows, and intricately crafted metal balconies that looked out onto the canal system below.

From time to time, the canal would pass through wide, open, paved spaces that served as eateries or held immense stone statues, stained glass panels, and holographic projections of the old city. In each open space and along the canal walkways, elegantly dressed figures filed by, chatted and pointed at the sights, or took photographs. Robot assistants—some working in the eateries, others carrying bags—interspersed the human population. Steve reckoned there were almost as many robots as there were people in Nuova Venezia.

The pilot had told them that the city was under a dome but, when Steve looked up, all he could see was a beautiful blue sky. Now and then, he would notice a gondola bearing passengers up to raised platforms that moved between the upper levels of the buildings.

The city was built to be seen and explored on foot or by gondola. It offered a delight around every corner, whether the visual appeal of the architecture, the aromas rising from the eateries, or the holographic information screens that accompanied each bridge. There was just one thing missing.

"There's no advertising," said Steve. "Not on the gondolas or the buildings, or anywhere."

"Nuova Venezia is a very wealthy city," said Hassan. "It doesn't need to make money from advertising. Plus the rich and famous don't come here to be sold to."

"Or at least, not by anyone other than the city itself," said Mariana. "Nuova Venezia offers more than enough for visitors to spend their money on."

"You almost sound as if you don't like the place," said Hartley.

"I like it," she said. "But I'm also realistic. Nuova Venezia may be beautiful but like its holograms, much of the city—its appeal and apparent purpose—is **a façade.** Where better to meet away from the prying eyes of the less wealthy population, than in a destination priced far beyond what most people can afford?"

"So why are you here?" said Bodrn.

"Why, to perform, of course," said Mariana. "What other reasons could I have?" The tone of her voice was as pleasant as always, but her face for once held no smile or hint of playfulness.

The gondola drew into a narrow waterway between two buildings. It was like passing from sunlight into shadow. The waterway below was a subtler shade of the main canal's turquoise. The walls on either side of them were sleek but plain grey marble.

"Where are we going?" asked Bodrn.

"Just our little pied-à-terre," said Mariana. "For when we're visiting Nuova Venezia."

"Or avoiding the press," said Hassan.

The waterway came to an end and the gondola lifted slightly as it moved into a small courtyard. On either side of the space were blank walls of marble. Ahead of them, a pair of peacock green, ornately carved, wooden doors were flanked by two comparatively modest windows. Above the doors, the house extended up a further three floors, each denoted with a sleek metal balcony and arched windows.

"Little?" said Hartley, as the gondola came to a halt.

"Modest," said Mariana. "For me."

"Shall we?" Hassan was already standing on the paved ground, holding out a hand to the enchantress.

"Thank you, darling." Mariana took his hand and elegantly climbed from the gondola. "It's wonderful to be back, isn't it?"

"Always," said Hassan.

"Well, I don't want to be a burden…" Hartley raised his unkempt eyebrows.

"And yet you always are," said Hassan with a grin. "Yes, of course you may stay with us. All of you," he added as Bodrn jumped from the gondola.

"That's a relief." Hartley wobbled out of the vehicle, grabbing the darkling's arm at the last minute. "I may need you to do a little spellw—"

"Of course, you will." Hassan pressed a finger to his lips and nodded to the doors. "Once we're settled."

As Steve climbed out of the gondola, Mariana passed her hands over the surface of the entrance to their house, her long fingers curling and extending into several configurations before she dropped them to her sides.

"Let's talk inside," she said as she pushed on the doors which swung open as if they had no weight to them at all.

The gondola returned to the waterway as Steve and the others followed Mariana into the house.

"What was the…?" Hartley waved his arms around as he followed Mariana and Hassan through the entrance hall into a high-ceilinged room that held an immense glass table with tall-backed chairs. "On the door?"

"I was checking to see if our security had been tampered with," said Mariana. "A necessary precaution to ensure our privacy."

"Nobody can spy on us in here," said Hassan, taking a seat at one end of the table. "They can't overhear us or see us."

"Don't the Council mind that you're using magic here?" said Steve.

"We are subtle with our craft," said Hassan. "We do nothing that would draw unwanted attention. And of course, we're useful."

"You work for the Council," said Bodrn.

"Of course not," said Mariana. "We work for ourselves, but our involvement in the workaday world means that we can carry messages, open discussions, and so on."

"I usually carry out the 'so on'," said Hassan.

"This is hardly welcoming, darling," said Mariana. "Why don't we move into the salon? It's more comfortable and less showy."

The room that she led them into was as sleek and modern as Steve had expected it to be, but modest by comparison to the floating city. The white walls were unadorned except for a large oval mirror whose metallic frame shimmered with undulating shades of green and blue, and a framed map of Nuova Venezia. The flooring was more marble, but white this time with the barest threads of gold. There were no windows or lamps, but the space was flooded with light. The enormous, U-shaped sofa that took up much of the room's floor space was as white as the walls but, when Steve sat, the fabric was soft to the touch.

"So now everyone is comfortable and there's no chance of us

being overheard," said Mariana when everyone had taken a seat. "I want to know the full story."

"The full story?" said Hartley.

"Everything."

"Including why the Council hampered you," said Hassan. "And how did you manage to leave a sealed community? I hear access to Darkacre has been suspended for the time being."

"This might take a while," said Hartley. "I'm sure to get thirsty."

"Hassan, be a darling." said Mariana.

"On it already." Hassan stood with a deep sigh. "I am born to serve."

"Where should I start?" said Hartley as Hassan left the room.

"Jonah Ledwitch," said Steve.

"Good idea," said Hartley. "Well, I'd just returned to my shop…"

*

"Wait! Wait!" Mariana held her hands over the glass tabletop. "Let me get a cloth. I don't want your things chipping the glass."

"I'll be careful." Hartley's hands were full with items he had pulled from his pockets.

"Historically, you don't do careful," said Hassan. He balanced the framed map of Nuova Venezia on one of the chairs. "Do hurry up. This picture is heavy."

"Just a moment, darling." Mariana drew her hands across the tabletop, whispering something under her breath. There was the scent of cinnamon and honey and suddenly the glass table was covered with a silken cloth in a vibrant shade of yellow. "There. Beautiful," she said.

"Yellow?" said Hartley. "For a locator spell? Really, Mariana?"

"But it's such a beautiful shade." She sighed. "Fine." She tapped a finger on the cloth with a whispered word and it turned a subtle shade of brown. "Happy?"

"Divinely," said Hartley. "Hassan, the map, if you don't mind."

"I thought you'd never ask." He picked up the framed map with a grunt and then sidled to the table with it.

"Careful," said Mariana.

"I'm trying to be careful." Hassan flipped the map level and lowered it onto the table. "There," he said, shaking his hands after the weight of the picture frame. "Done."

"I hate to be a bother," said Hartley, tapping a knuckle on the glass panel of the picture frame. "But I don't suppose we could free the map of its prison, could we? The glass may interfere with the spellwork."

"At your command." Hassan pressed an unseen button on the side of the frame and the map slid out on a wooden tray.

"Marvellous." Hartley reached for the map.

"Don't tear it." Mariana stood with one hand to her mouth. "It's one of a kind, created by a dear friend when the city was first constructed."

"I'll lay it out." Hassan gently lifted the map from the wooden tray. "Could someone remove the frame? You'll see why we needed such a long table in a minute," he said as Steve picked up the frame, struggled a little with its weight, and then leant it against the nearest wall.

"This map portrays each and every level of Nuova Venezia," said Mariana as Hassan unfolded and unfolded and unfolded and finally unfolded the map a fourth time, laying its length along the table. "My friend has an eye for detail, as you can see."

"Almost each and every level," said Hassan. "Since this was drawn, a lot of the buildings have been extended upwards. Progress and all that."

The intricate map was drawn in black ink and painted in many of the colours that Steve had seen in the city: turquoise, grey-blue, white, and grey. Each panel of the map portrayed a different level of Nuova Venezia. The panel with the greatest detail was the level they were on now.

"The city is massive," he said, tracing their canal route on the map with his eyes. "There's so much we haven't seen yet."

"Which is why we need a little help to discover where your mother is in Nuova Venezia." Hartley dropped the items he held onto the map.

"Hartley, please. You're giving me heart palpitations," said Mariana.

"Sorry." Hartley picked up the items again. "My dear?" He beckoned to Bodrn. "If you'd be so kind."

"Very well." She held out her hands.

"Everything we need. One. Two. Three." Hartley counted the items into her hands. There was a small horse-shoe shaped magnet, a length of string, a scrap of paper, and a short stub of a pencil.

"That's four," said Steve.

"Pedantic," said Hartley. "The pencil is simply to write on the paper, speaking of which…" He held the pencil and paper out to Steve.

"What do you want me to write?"

"Your mother's name. We don't have anything of hers to hand, except for you."

"Right." Steve took the pencil and paper. The pencil was so short that he could barely write with it but after a couple of fumbles, he handed the paper back.

"Mary Tesha Haven. Perfect." Hartley wrapped the scrap of paper around the magnet and secured it with one end of the piece of string.

"Will this find her?" said Bodrn.

"If she's here, with any luck." Hartley suspended the magnet over the nearest panel of the map. "That'll be the purpose of the first sweep. If that doesn't work, we'll try again to see where she last visited in Nuova Venezia."

"Aren't you forgetting something?" said Hassan with a smirk.

"Am I? Oh yes." Hartley took the magnet in one hand and held it out to Hassan. "May I borrow your magic? Please?"

"If I must," said Hassan with rolled eyes. He took the combined magnet, paper, and string in one cupped hand and blew on it gently. Then, he turned his back to the others and whispered a couple of words to it. "There you are, Hartley. That should do the trick."

Steve crossed his fingers behind his back as Hartley began the first pass of the dangling magnet over the five panels of the map. It was something his mum had always done when looking for her bag or her wrap-phone or anything that his father had mislaid. It seemed like the right thing to do in this moment.

"No," said Hartley as he eventually finished the first pass. "I don't think she's in the city."

"Try again," said Steve. "Please. Maybe you missed a bit."

"I didn't miss any fragment of the map," said Hartley. "I made sure of that. Even if she were in one of the renovated buildings with extra floors, the magnet would have informed me."

Steve uncrossed his fingers and plunged his hands into his pockets. "So now what?"

"I conduct a second sweep so we can find out which part of the city she last walked. Eleanor said that your mother travelled here. Well, you don't simply travel to somewhere like Nuova Venezia. You investigate. You explore. She must have walked here."

"In between gondola rides," said Hassan. "Sorry, that's not helpful, is it?"

"Why in between gondola rides?" asked Bodrn.

"What Hassan's getting at," said Hartley, "is that this spell can only trace where Steve's mother physically walked. If she was carried or rode on a gondola, I won't be able to trace that."

"Why would she be carried?" said Steve.

"Just an example," said Hartley, offering the magnet to Hassan again. "New spell please."

"At your command." Hassan repeated the breath and whispered words.

The second sweep seemed to take even longer than the first as

Hartley scanned the first panel of the map.

"Not here," he said.

"She must have walked there," said Bodrn. "How else would she have entered the city?"

"I'm sure she did walk there," said Hartley, moving the magnet to the second panel of the map. "But it wasn't where she walked most recently, which is odd."

"Why is it odd?" said Steve.

"Because how else would she have left Nuova Venezia?" said Hassan.

"Now we're talking." The magnet began to swing in Hartley's grasp, back and forth in one repeated motion. "Let's test this out."

Hartley moved the magnet to another part of that panel of the map. The magnet instantly ceased in its movement. He moved the magnet around the remainder of the panel, but to no effect. It wasn't until he returned the magnet to where it had first reacted that it began to swing again.

"She walked this path," said Hartley, moving the magnet up and down the route. "That's for sure."

"Where does it go?" said Steve.

"I can tell you where it starts," said Mariana, placing an elegant finger at one end of the path. "The *Soggiorno dell'Esploratore*. It's a hostel for academic visitors to the city who can't afford the more popular accommodation." She shrugged. "It's perfectly acceptable if you don't mind minimal."

"What she means is if you don't mind sleeping pods and shared eating facilities," said Hassan. "Visiting the city as an academic is the only way to avoid joining the waiting list for Nuova Venezia."

"Where does her route end?" said Bodrn.

"That's a boarding platform," said Hassan. "You can ride a gondola from there to the other city levels."

"Well, it wasn't the first level," said Hartley. "We know that much. Let's investigate the next level up."

Hartley's sweep of the third level was a failure, as was his sweep of the fourth. Steve's fingers were crossed again as he waited for the magnet to react.

"And we have a result!" boomed Hartley.

"Where does that lead?" asked Steve as Hartley moved the swinging magnet along a path on the fifth panel of the map.

"The *Biblioteca Serenissima*," said Mariana. "The city's library and archive. I suppose it would make sense for an academic to go there. Would you consider your mother an academic, Steve?"

"She's an archaeologist, like Dad," he said. "So, yeah, I suppose so. But hang on, she came here to find him, not to look at books."

"Knowing your mother," Hartley began. "Well, knowing what a mother who created someone like you would be like," he spluttered, "I'm sure she had a very good reason to visit the library."

"Why not start at the beginning?" said Hassan. "Ask about her at the hostel. They'll be able to tell you when she booked out at the very least."

"That's actually a very good idea," said Hartley. "Mariana, would it be a terrible imposition to leave the map like this? Just in case."

"I suppose not," she said. "But only for a little while."

"I'm sure a little while is all we'll need." Hartley rolled the string around the magnet and popped it back into his pocket. "Who's up for a stroll?"

"Not me," said Hassan. "I need a rest after all this excitement."

"And I need to get ready for tonight," said Mariana.

"What happens tonight?" said Bodrn.

"Tonight, darling girl, I dance." Mariana span a skilful pirouette. "Now, off you go. I have people to speak to and costumes to prepare."

"I think we've been dismissed," said Hartley as the couple linked arms and left the room. "Shall we?"

"Can you remember how to get to the hostel?" said Steve as

Hartley dashed off in the other direction.

"Have faith. I'm sure we'll find our way."

"I have memorised the route," said Bodrn.

"See?" called Hartley from the entrance hallway. "There's absolutely nothing to worry about. Come on."

I hate it when he says that, thought Steve as he and Bodrn rushed after the old shopkeeper. *Because there always is something to worry about, and it's usually Hartley Keg.*

Chapter Sixteen

The hostel for academic visitors wasn't quite as minimal as Mariana had suggested it would be. Accessed via a simple door from a narrow side-street, the interior was practical and comfortable. The lobby's walls were adorned with photographs, paintings, and sketches that depicted the city's canals, gondolas, and walkways, along with framed photographs of some very serious looking people. Steve didn't recognise any of them.

A small gathering of comfortable sofas and armchairs sat to one side of the lobby, while a series of check-in kiosks with touch screen displays lined the other side. Central to it all was a simple reception desk that seemed to be made from the same polished wood as the gondolas. Behind the desk stood an elderly man in a suit that had probably been pressed too many times. It hung stiffly on the man's thin frame and, in one or two places, the fabric took on a threadbare sheen.

"Welcome to the *Soggiorno dell'Esploratore*," he said in a tired but welcoming voice. "Do you have a reservation?"

"Helloo," called Hartley as he crossed the lobby at speed. "I wonder if you can help us. We're looking for a friend who stayed here."

"You don't have a reservation then." The man stopped smiling. In fact, he looked decidedly disappointed.

"Not technically," said Hartley.

"No," said Steve as he and Bodrn joined Hartley at the reception desk.

"Then I can't help you," said the man. "I'm not permitted to give out information about guests."

"But it's my mum," said Steve. "I think she stayed here. We need to find her. Mary Haven. If you could just—"

"It's hostel policy. I can tell you nothing."

"My dear fellow." Hartley laid a hand on the reception desk and graced the man with a wide, toothy smile. "The boy has travelled all the way here to find his mother. Are you sure you can't help us? Just a tad?"

"No," said the man. "At the *Soggiorno dell'Esploratore*, we pride ourselves on the privacy and protection we offer to our guests. I can't tell you anything about Mrs Haven."

"So you remember her?" said Hartley.

"Of course," said the man. "I remember everyone who stays here."

"Is there anything you *can* tell us?" said Steve. "Please?"

"Good morning, Enzo."

"Good morning, Mrs Frum." The man's smile returned as he nodded to the elderly lady who approached the reception desk. She was dressed in at least four layers of clothing, despite the pleasantly warm temperature. "Can I be of help?"

"Actually," she said. "I'm still having problems with the light in my sleeping pod."

"Still?" said Enzo, his smile slipping away.

"Still," she said. "Could you get it sorted and save an old woman's eyes?" She blinked at him. "Please?"

"Not a problem, Mrs Frum," said Enzo although the expression on his face told a different story. "I'll mend it straightaway." He gave Hartley one more stern look, nodded to the elderly woman, and left.

"Poor Enzo. All this running around at his age," said Mrs Frum. "Still, at least he won't have to mend anything."

"He will not?" said Bodrn.

"No. The light is working perfectly well," said Mrs Frum. "Now, did I hear you say Mary Haven?"

"You did," said Hartley. "Hartley Keg." He held out his hand to her. "Pleased to meet you."

"Antonia Frum. No need for formalities," she said staring at his hand. "You must be Steve," she said. "Mary told me about her son, and she didn't mention any other children, so I assume you're he."

"I am," said Steve.

"Good, good. Now, let's take this out of here," she said. "I don't think Enzo will be very happy when he returns, poor man. Shall we?"

Hartley dashed across the lobby and opened the door to the street with a flourish. "After you, dear lady."

"Is he always as enthusiastic as this?" Mrs Frum asked Steve as they crossed the lobby.

"Most of the time," said Steve.

"How tiring," said Mrs Frum. "I know a wonderful little eatery close by. We can talk there."

"Did I hear you say 'eatery'?" asked Hartley as he closed the door behind them. Bodrn waited ahead, where the narrow side street met the main walkway.

"You did," said Mrs Frum. "I'll take you to *Gusto's*."

"Perfect," said Hartley. "Lead on, my dear lady."

"I am," she called back to him. "And drop the lady. I haven't been one of those since my husband died."

*

Gusto's, as Mrs Frum had called it, was a small café that sat on a canal-side square only a few minutes' walk from the *Soggiorno dell'Esploratore*. *Gusto's* was short for *Gusto Cucina Casalinga*. The eatery's name was displayed on what looked like hand-painted signage which was built into the arched doorway. On either side of the door hung wrought iron lanterns and below the lanterns, wooden troughs overflowed with vibrant flowers. An almost white canopy extended out from the building to cover the ten or so wooden tables—with surprisingly comfortable chairs, Hartley commented—that fronted the eatery. The tables and chairs sat on a floor of faded tiles that had once been painted with ornate and colourful designs. Or maybe it was simply made to look that way, Steve thought as they sat at one of the tables. Unlike the eateries that he had seen so far in the city, *Gusto's* seemed a little worn, not overly high-tech, and the perfect place to chat with friends. He could see why Mrs Frum liked it.

"*Grazie*, Marc," said Mrs Frum as the waiter led them to a table.

"*Prego*, Signora Frum," said Marc with a smile and a nod to the others.

"You seem to be a regular," said Hartley, tapping his fingers on the tabletop. His stomach was making hungry noises again.

"I've been visiting *Gusto's* since Nuova Venezia first opened to the public. Of course, my husband was alive back then, and it was Marc's father who ran the place." She took a sip of the small black coffee that Marc brought for her the moment that they had sat at the table. "You can't get a better coffee anywhere in the city than here, and I can't be doing with all those drone-waiters and holograms. Give me down-to-earth reality any time."

"Here, here. I couldn't agree more," said Hartley.

"So, about my mum." Steve couldn't hold the question in any longer. "Where did she go?"

"Straight to the point," said Mrs Frum. "Just like your mother."

Marc appeared at the door to the eatery, pushing a trolley that jiggled its contents over the tiled floor.

"*Grazie*, Marc," said Mrs Frum as the waiter transferred plates of cured meats, cheese, olives, and crusty bread slices onto the table, along with a jug of water, glasses, and more of the small coffee cups that Mrs Frum drank from. With a flourish, Marc poured from a large coffee pot into each of the cups. He finished by refilling Mrs Frum's cup.

"He's a good boy," she said as Marc trundled off with his trolley again. "Always knows the right thing to serve without a word of instruction. Magical."

"Do you think?" said Hartley and then, "What?" as Steve elbowed him in the ribs.

"What are you waiting for?" asked Mrs Frum. "Dig in."

"I was waiting for you to start," said Hartley. His stomach was insistent now, burbling almost as loudly as his voice.

"Oh, I don't eat here," she said. "I just come for the coffee and ambience. This is all for you three. It'll keep you quiet while I tell you what happened to Mary Haven."

"What did happen to my mum?" said Steve.

"Load up your plate, young man. All of you. This may take a while."

"Well, just to please you, Mrs Frum." Hartley picked up a plate of cheese. "I wouldn't want to seem ungrateful."

*

"Over the years, the clientele of the *Soggiorno dell'Esploratore* has aged," said Mrs Frum. "Or that's how it appears to me, anyway. I visit every year and stay there, and each time I find myself surrounded by elderly brains and aging bones. Quite tedious." She took a sip of her coffee and pressed her lips together, deep in thought.

"Mrs Frum?" said Steve after a moment. "You were telling us about my mum."

"I know what I was telling you about, young man. Now where was I?"

"Aging bones," said Bodrn.

"Absolutely," said Mrs Frum. "That's why your mother stood out. A breath of fresh air. Much to the annoyance of Enzo."

"Why?" said Steve.

"She hadn't made a reservation. I first came across her interrogating the man for the whereabouts of her husband. As you know, Enzo is a stickler for guest privacy. He was having none of it. So she did the only thing she could do."

"She hit him," said Hartley.

"No, not at all," said Mrs Frum, looking the shopkeeper up and down. "She made a reservation."

"That makes much more sense," said Hartley as he manhandled a chunk of cheese and a slab of meat between two slices of bread.

"I liked her tenacity, so I introduced myself. And as a long-time visitor to the city, I offered to show her around. We became rather pally. I told her about my late husband, and she told me about her search for your father, Steve."

"She needed to tell him that my uncle Rex died."

"Now I understand," said Mrs Frum. "There was an urgency about her. I take it your father travels abroad a lot?"

"You could say that." Steve nodded. "He's an archaeologist. They both are. They go away a lot."

"She didn't strike me as the archaeologist type. Still, maybe these modern times call for a different type of archaeologist."

"You said you'd tell us what happened to her."

"And I will," said Mrs Frum. "But allow me the enjoyment of spinning my tale. And eat something."

Hartley brushed breadcrumbs from his beard with one hand while balancing a small coffee cup in the other. Bodrn bit down on an olive and smiled at the taste. She had already piled up her plate with cheese.

"Okay." Steve reached for the plate of bread. "But please, tell us everything you can. I need to find my mum quickly. She'll know what to do."

"I'm sure she will. Marc!"

The waiter appeared at the door to Gusto's. "*Si*, Signora Frum?"

"Could you fetch a coffee carafe?"

"Of course," he said with a nod as he disappeared back into the café.

"Now this is one kind of technology that I do like," she said. "A carafe of coffee that keeps itself warm and texts Marc when it's empty. Genius."

Steve made himself a sandwich of the cheese and meat as the carafe arrived with a smile from Marc, and Mrs Frum continued to enthuse about the delights of her self-heating carafe. Of course, it wasn't anything new—the carafe—but he was glad it pleased her so much. There was a sadness about Mrs Frum, despite her sensible enthusiasm, that made him think she was probably a little bit lonely.

"It was actually here at *Gusto's* that your mother spilled the beans about her search for your father. She was quite distraught, you know, but I instantly knew what to suggest." She looked at them all with a bright smile.

"What was that?" asked Bodrn when Mrs Frum didn't continue.

"A little, old-fashioned detective work," said Mrs Frum, pouring herself another cup of coffee. "You may or may not have noticed that there is a guest book in the lobby of the *Soggiorno dell'Esploratore*. Not an actual book, of course, but a screen that you can write on nonetheless to leave your thanks or complaints about your stay. An entry is added automatically when a guest arrives with their name and the number of their sleeping pod. Any guest can access it."

Mrs Frum paused as a well-dressed couple passed their table to take a seat near the entrance to *Gusto's*.

"Thankfully, the pod that your father had used was vacant," Mrs Frum continued in a quieter voice. "It had been thoroughly cleaned in readiness for the next guest. It's the only task that Enzo allows the robots to do in the hostel. I didn't think there'd be any trace of your father, but I was wrong."

"What did you find?" asked Steve.

"A ticket for the *Biblioteca Serenissima*. The kind of thing you're given if you want to view an item from the library archives. You pay for a set number of visits," she said. "A lot of the guests at the hostel sell their tickets to other academics if they haven't used up their visits before they leave. This one was stuffed down under the mattress."

"So Mum visited the archives?"

"She did."

"And?" said Steve.

"Maybe it's best you see for yourself." Mrs Frum unzipped a pocket on the gilet she was wearing and drew out a plastic card. "There's one visit left on it. Hand it over to the clerk at the *Biblioteca Serenissima* and they'll let you access all the documents and books that your parents requested."

"Aren't you coming with us?" said Steve taking the card from her.

"I can't. It's time to pack my things and go home. Hence the unnecessary layering." She tugged at the jacket she wore over her gilet. "One word of warning, though. I'm not sure what your mother discovered in the archives. She said she wanted to investigate on her own. Something about not wanting to put me in danger. She left the ticket with me, but I'm afraid I never saw her again."

"Dear lady, you have been a great help," said Hartley. "And an excellent dinner host."

"None of that," said Mrs Frum. "Mary Haven was a good sort. Is a good sort," she corrected herself. "I do hope you find her, Steve. And your father."

"Me too," said Steve.

"One more thing." She leaned a little closer. "When I came down to breakfast the day after we visited the library, I saw Enzo deep in discussion with two men. Maybe 'discussion' is the wrong word. He looked like a schoolboy being reprimanded. Anyway, when I went back to my pod after I'd eaten, the same two men were clearing out Mary's pod. They took her belongings away with them."

"Did you recognise them?" asked Bodrn. "What did they look like?"

"Thugs, by the way they intimidated poor Enzo. Smart. The suits they wore looked expensive," she said. "Not the kind of people you'd want to annoy."

"Thank you, Mrs Frum." Steve pushed back his chair. "Shall we walk you back to the hostel?"

"What do I look like? An old lady?" said Mrs Frum with a stern folding of her lips. Then she laughed and slapped the table with one hand. "I'm joking. No, I'm more than capable of looking after myself. Have been for years. You three get along to the *Biblioteca Serenissima*. No time like the present."

The card felt heavy in Steve's hand as his friends said goodbye to Mrs Frum. This was his first real clue as to where his parents had been all this time. It was exciting and scary, all rolled into one. He had so many questions and plenty of worries too. But all of those would have to wait.

Chapter Seventeen

"Do you have any bags?" The well-dressed woman who sat at the reception booth of the *Biblioteca Serenissima* looked them up and down.

"Nothing to declare," said Hartley, holding his arms away from his body and doing a slow turn. "Just that we are delighted to be visiting your captivating establishment."

"In that case, you may enter the *Biblioteca Serenissima*. Should you need guidance…"

Steve didn't hear what she said next. He was far too interested in what was happening above his head. At first glance, the arched ceiling of the entrance lobby was home to a gallery of paintings that appeared to hover inches off the ceiling. There were scenes of actual gondolas (not the high-tech ones they had travelled in) gliding along busy waterways which were lined with impressive, ornately adorned houses. Figures in elaborate masks danced across painted skies. Women clothed in long, pastel-coloured dresses knelt in front of a winged lion. Steve had only just taken in each painted image on the ceiling when they shifted and evolved into scenes of bustling street markets, the rising sun warming the Venetian cityscape, and a sea of people moving along narrow, canal-lined pathways.

"Steve, do we need help?"

"What?" He felt a tug on his arm.

"Steve?" Bodrn looked at him with a tilted head and a raised eyebrow. "Do we need help to find where we are going?" The woman at the reception booth stared at him as if he was an annoyance to be dismissed.

"Yes," he said, holding up the ticket that Mrs Frum had given to him. "We need to use this."

"That ticket is for the archives," said the woman. 'Scan it on the other side of the archway and you'll be guided to a station. Thank you for visiting today." She gave them a quick smile that didn't reach her eyes before turning to the next person in the queue.

Hartley bounded ahead through the archway. Steve and the darkling followed close behind, so close that when Hartley stopped with a cry of "How wonderful!", they knocked into the elderly shopkeeper.

"Sorry, sorry," said Hartley. "But look at this. What a sight."

The *Biblioteca Serenissima* was indeed wonderful. Vast, circular, and filled with the hushed buzz of voices, footsteps, and pages being turned, the library was flooded with light that spilled down from the glass domed roof above. The flooring looked like highly polished marble, but channels of blue and green light ran across the surface, guiding visitors throughout the library. Towering bookcases lined the walls, and an army of small robots travelled up and down ladders to retrieve books from the shelves. Clusters of seating and tables were scattered throughout the space. Most of them were already taken.

"Wow. There are so many books," said Steve.

"While this building is beyond impressive, books are just books," said Hartley. "I have plenty of them in my shop, you know."

"But I don't think I've ever seen so many real books in one place." Steve stared around the immense space. "At home, everything is online. We read books on a tablet," he continued as Hartley frowned at him. "Or a holographic display. Nothing like this." He shook his head. "This is—"

"May I scan your ticket?" said one of the robots as it extended a limb towards them. The limb ended in a small, illuminated screen that was just a little larger than the ticket Steve held.

"Okay." Steve held the ticket to the screen which blinked

green in response.

"A path will guide you to an allotted archival chamber," said the robot. "Enjoy your visit to the *Biblioteca Serenissima*."

"Is this what it means?" said Hartley, staring down at his feet.

On the floor, a circle of blue light blinked around the three friends. After three or four pulses, the light travelled in a straight line out into the main body of the library. Once it had advanced only a couple of feet, it stopped.

"Must be," said Steve. "I think it's waiting for us."

"Fascinating," said Hartley as he set off at a swift pace with Bodrn on his heels.

It wasn't until Steve followed that the line continued its journey, travelling in an almost straight route with the occasional diversion around a seating area or a stationary visitor. After the first couple of enthusiastic *helloo's* and the resulting glares and shushes, Hartley got the message. He didn't say another word until the line finally blinked out of sight at a pair of clear glass doors.

"We appear to have arrived," he said as the glass doors parted. "After you, Steve."

The archival chamber was one glass cubicle in a row of many. As Steve stepped through the doors, the chamber illuminated to something close to sunlight. In the centre of the room was a simple glass table and a cushioned chair. There was nothing else.

"This is hardly private," said Hartley as he and Bodrn followed Steve inside. "Anyone can see what's going on in here."

As if the chamber had heard him speak, the doors closed behind them and the glass in the door and the walls frosted over, obscuring the view beyond.

"Ah," said Hartley. "Now that makes more sense. But it's a tad sparse in here, don't you think?"

"This is all we need."

Steve sat on the chair and tucked himself under the glass table. At his touch, a computer interface popped into view. A holographic orb of swirling, blue light lifted from the table and came to rest at Steve's shoulder.

"Welcome to the archives of the *Biblioteca Serenissima*. I am the interface." The light and colours of the orb pulsated along with the voice. "Before we begin, may I confirm your name and place of origin."

"Steve Haven. Caercester, UK."

"Steve Haven," the voice continued. "Only son of Elijah and Mary Haven. Welcome, Steve. Would you like to continue your parents' search?"

"Absolutely," said Hartley.

"I think Steve must do the talking," said Bodrn.

"Sorry." Hartley mimed the turning of a key on his lips then folded his hands in front of him.

"Yes, please," said Steve. "Can you show me what my parents were doing here?"

"Your parents investigated a number of documents from the library's archives. Your father accessed twenty-four archived documents." The screen display on the tabletop filled with a list of reference numbers and accompanying thumbnails. "Would you like to view any of these documents today?"

"Not yet," said Steve. "What did my mum look at? Mary Haven."

"Mary Haven accessed only one document," said the interface. "This document was also accessed by your father."

"What is it?" said Steve. "Can I see it?"

"Document MAP-2089-1004. Would you like to access the document as a flat display on the screen or as a 3D holographic view?"

"What is 3D?" asked Hartley.

"I'll show you," said Steve. "Interface, show me the document in 3D please."

"An excellent choice. Initiating 3D holographic rendering."

The image that appeared on the glass tabletop was a standard flat map coloured in shades of aqua, green, and grey. Labelled 'Venice' in the bottom left corner, the map showed the city adrift in the lagoon except for a single road that connected Venice to the Italian mainland.

"What are these symbols?" said Steve pointing to five points on the edge of the city, where white circles pulsed on and off. Each bore a different design of lines and curves.

"They're runes," said Hartley. He scratched his beard for a second. "Of course! They're all aspects," he said. "Fire. Wood. Metal. Earth. Water. But what—…?"

Before he could finish, the map jumped off the tabletop, coming to rest a few inches above the glass surface. As they watched, the symbols slowly raised up from the flat map. Each circle transformed into an orb that took on the colour of its respective element: crimson for fire, blue for water, green for wood, silver for metal, and brown for earth. As the packed buildings of the city rose from the map, the symbol orbs climbed above the holographic roofs, each tethered in place by a thread of light that descended to the map's surface.

"As I was saying," said Hartley. "What is that?" He pointed to a sixth orb that hung over the centre of the map. This orb was white and joined to each of the others by a thick, white thread of light which pulsated and fizzed.

"It contains another symbol," said Bodrn.

"I know that one too," said Hartley. "It stands for many things. Strength. Potential. But in this context, I think it means power. As in a power source for the other whatever they are." He waved a hand at the surrounding orbs.

"Interface, where is this symbol located?" Steve pointed to the central orb.

"Thank you for your question. The location is the Doge's Palace, St Mark's Square, Venice."

"Interface, what are we looking at?" said Steve.

"A schematic for a barrier illusion over Venice," said the interface.

"Pardon?" said Hartley.

"A schematic for—" Steve began.

"No, I heard the first time," said Hartley. "I'm just startled that a workaday gadget would know about magic. I'm not sure the Council would approve."

"What's a barrier illusion?" said Steve.

"Just as it sounds," said Hartley. "It provides both a barrier to prevent specific people from leaving a place and an illusion to conceal what the contained area looks like."

"So there's one of these barrier illusions over the ruins of old Venice?"

"The map would suggest that," said Bodrn. "And both of your parents discovered this."

"Or they knew about it already," said Steve. "You don't think they went down there, do you?"

"It's one possibility," said Hartley. "They are archaeologists after all. Investigating old ruins is what they do. Of course, the situation appears a little more complicated knowing that this—"

He touched a finger to the holographic orb in the centre of the map. With a fizz, the orb, its companions, and the 3D view of the map disappeared. All that remained was a plain, single screen on the glass tabletop.

"I think you broke it," said Bodrn.

"I'm not always to blame," said Hartley. "Sometimes, but not always."

"Incoming message," said the interface. "Will you accept, Steve Haven?"

"Yes?" said Steve, looking at his friends for confirmation.

"It can't do any harm," said Hartley with a shrug. "Can it?"

"Who is the message from?" said Steve.

"Identity withheld," said the interface. "Do you wish to continue?"

"Yes," he said. "Yes, please, interface."

With a blip, a flashing, red cursor appeared at the top left-hand corner and three words typed out one letter at a time.

'Who are you?'

"That's odd," said Hartley.

"Interface, how do I reply?" said Steve.

A flat keyboard appeared in the glass tabletop. Steve thought for a moment and then he typed, *Tell me who you are first*.

The cursor flashed a couple more times, and then the same three words appeared again—'*Who are you?*'—but this time they continued.

'*Why are you interested in Venice? We don't have long. They are watching.*'

"Who is watching?" said Hartley. "Ask them."

"Okay." Steve typed the question.

'*No time to explain. What do you want?*'

Tell them, his mind nagged.

But what if it's a trick? I don't want to give too much away.

What choice do you have?

Steve nodded to himself and then he typed, *I'm looking for Mary and Elijah Haven. Am I on the right path?*.

"Who is watching?" said Hartley again, looking around the room. "Steve, maybe it's wise to finish up here."

"Wait," said Steve. "They're going to answer. I know they are."

Instead of the response he wanted, two words appeared on the screen.

'*Get out.*'

"Message ends," said the interface as the screen and keyboard disappeared from the glass tabletop. "Can I help you with anything else today?"

"Come on." Hartley pulled Steve to his feet. "Whoever our mysterious friend was, I think we should take their warning seriously. Let's go."

"But what about…?" Steve protested as Hartley took him by the arm. "Wait."

"We need to leave," said Bodrn. "We can ask Mariana about—"

Before she could finish, the glass walls returned to their transparent state as the doors opened. Two suited men walked into the room. They might have been twins or brothers because they looked almost alike: the same slicked hair, the same square jaws, and the same cold look in their eyes.

"You should come with us." One of them reached for Steve.

"Leave him alone." Bodrn stepped between them, pushing Steve back a few steps.

"Move out of the way, little girl," said the man.

"I am not a little girl." She raised both fists.

"Really?" He swatted a hand at her as if she was an annoying insect.

"You have no idea," said Hartley as Bodrn blocked the man's attack with her forearm and jabbed him in the ribs.

"You'll regret that," said the man as he lurched towards them.

"Stop it." The second man grabbed his companion's arm. "We're not here for a fight."

"That's a shame," said the first man.

"Steve, Hartley, and..?" said the second man as he looked at Bodrn. She didn't answer. "That's fine. You can be mysterious if you like. I'm Miles."

"Why'd you reveal your name? We're not here to make friends," said the other man.

"We're not here to draw attention to our actions either, Troi," Miles told his companion. "Let's keep this peaceful."

"Fine," said Troi.

"What do you want?" said Steve.

"We want you," said Miles. "But your companions can come with us too. Don't worry. You're all perfectly safe."

"Unfortunately, we have no way of confirming that," said Hartley, his hand sliding into his pocket.

"Careful now," said Miles. "I know what you are, Hartley Keg, and what you're capable of. I suggest you keep your hands where I can see them. My colleague here can be a little trigger-happy."

"As you wish." Hartley raised his empty hands.

"You will not take him," said Bodrn.

"Face it. You can't stop us," said Troi.

"Maybe this will help." Miles pulled back his jacket sleeve and held his arm out to them. On the bared skin of his inner wrist was a tattoo Steve had seen before.

"You're with Parity," said Steve.

"Got it in one," said Miles. "Our superior wants to have a chat with you all."

"And who exactly is your superior?" asked Hartley.

"People like you know her as the Auditor," said Miles. "She wants to meet you, Steve. I think you'll be interested in what she has to say."

"Why?" said Steve.

"Because she can tell you where your parents are. That is why you're here, isn't it?"

"This is taking too long," said Troi. "Decide for yourself or—"

"I'll go with you," said Steve.

"*We'll* go with you," said Hartley, placing a hand on Steve's shoulder. "All three of us."

"Good choice," said Miles. "You won't regret it."

Steve wanted that to be true, for there to be an easy answer to his search for his parents, so why did he feel as if he was leading his friends into more trouble?

"After you," said Troi, stepping back as Bodrn approached. "We won't be leaving through the main library, so don't think you can call for help."

"Don't be like that. They've already agreed," said Miles. "Haven't you?" he asked Steve.

"It's okay." Steve took Bodrn's hand. "I want to do this. If the Auditor can tell me where my parents are."

"Smart decision," said Troi. "Follow me. It isn't far."

Chapter Eighteen

Troi had been truthful when he said it wasn't far. Their route from the *Biblioteca Serenissima* wasn't out so much as down. The lift door was discreetly set into the wall of a nearby corridor, the same shade as the marble walls and of a standard size. The interior was quite standard too. It might have been a staff lift in a shopping mall. Unlike the rest of the floating city, it wasn't designed for aesthetic impact.

"Where exactly are we?" said Steve as the lift door opened onto a cold, metal corridor.

"Officially," said Miles, stepping out from the lift. "This is the Subterranean Infrastructure Complex. Unofficially, it's the underneath of the city where you'll find everything that makes Nuova Venezia work."

"Fascinating." Hartley had followed the Parity operative out of the lift and stood looking first one way and then the other down the stark corridor that stretched away into the distance. "The gubbings of the machine."

"That's one way of putting it," said Miles.

"Time we were moving." Troi gestured for Steve and Bodrn to follow their friend. "Please," he said when the darkling didn't move.

"It's okay." Steve pulled her after him as he stepped out of the lift. "I want to be here."

"There's really no reason to be scared," said Miles. "The Auditor just wants to talk."

"I am not scared," said Bodrn.

"Quite right," said Hartley. "None of us are scared. We are

simply wary, given your companion's actions."

"Whatever." Troi set off down the corridor. "The Auditor doesn't like to wait."

"He's right," said Miles. "Best we get on. After you."

Walking between the two Parity operatives, Steve and his friends followed Troi's brisk pace through the underbelly of Nuova Venezia. Their route took them past a series of open doorways, all of which revealed glimpses of the city's inner workings. Staff dressed in a variety of uniforms bustled about, focused on their tasks and assisted by just as many robots. Conduits and pipelines snaked along the walls and, above their heads, carrying power and fluids to different parts of the city. At every junction they encountered, they saw signs that indicated the function of each area, with phrases like *'Power Generation'* and *'Environmental Control'*. Computer screens accompanied some of the entrances, featuring lists of staff names, daily schedules, or schematics.

"Stop." Troi held up a hand and jerked his head to a door very like all the other doors they had seen in the underneath. The only differences were the small screen, camera, and keypad set into the wall beside the door.

Troi pressed his palm on the central screen, which emitted a bar of blue light running from top to bottom. When he took his hand away, the screen displayed a message, *'Welcome, Troi. Please proceed to the next step.'* He looked up at the camera which blinked with the same blue light. The screen showed another message, *'Identity confirmed. Please enter the code.'* He typed a six-digit code on the keypad. The screen flashed green and a voice said, "Code accepted. Access granted." As the door slid open, Troi gestured for Steve and his friends to follow him inside.

"That was thorough," said Hartley.

"It's how she likes it," said Troi.

The corridor they found themselves in was different to the extensive network that existed below the floating city. It could almost have been a hotel corridor in Nuova Venezia. Their shoes tapped on the marble floor. The white walls, polished to a metallic sheen, featured digital panels of abstract artwork. The lighting was soft, not the glaring illumination they had left behind.

Ahead, Steve could see the entrance to a room and already hear people talking.

"Are we sure we want them to see this?" Troi called back to Miles.

"What do you suggest? Hoods over their heads? That's a bit extreme."

"I was thinking we'd drug them," said Troi.

"He's joking," said Miles as Bodrn planted her feet and raised her fists.

The room they stepped into was circular, compact, and dominated by a holographic centrepiece which shifted between intricate schematics, maps, and camera views of the city above. Around the holographic projection, a small team of individuals worked with an air of focused determination. Three robots mirrored the actions of the humans. Steve was pleased to see no sign of the hound robots that he'd encountered during his last interaction with Parity.

"I take it she's in?" said Troi, patting one of the operatives on the shoulder.

"Where else would she be?" said the woman.

"True that," said Troi.

Three softly-lit corridors branched off the control room. Troi led Steve and his friends down the central corridor, which ended after only four or five paces.

"Now, behave," he told them although his eyes rested mostly on Bodrn. "She won't take no nonsense or backchat."

"We'll behave," said Steve.

"Absolutely," said Hartley.

Bodrn said nothing.

"You'd better." Troi knocked on the door. "Ma'am?" he said as he opened the door a crack. "Your guests are here."

Guests? thought Steve. *This doesn't feel like a 'guest' situation.*

"Bring them in." The woman's voice was authoritative but tired.

"After you." Troi opened the door wide. "She doesn't bite," he added when none of them moved. "Not often."

"Do stop worrying them." The woman in the room beckoned with one hand. "Come in, Steve. Please. And bring your friends with you."

Steve looked at Hartley, who nodded in response. "Right." He took a deep breath and stepped through the doorway. He heard Hartley and Bodrn follow and then the door closed behind them.

"My name is Vigila," said the woman, leaving her chair to walk around the desk. "I'm the Auditor."

"Parity," said Steve.

"Yes." She tilted her head as she stared at him, her eyes never leaving his own. "I can see that you're nervous of me, of us."

"The boy hasn't had the best introduction to your organisation," said Hartley. "None of us have."

"Yes, well, Elrick Olen and his team were hardly a fair representation. They were a rogue operation." She said 'rogue' as if the concept was distasteful. "That situation has been handled."

By us, Steve thought, but he didn't say anything.

Dressed in a pristine white shirt and navy loose-legged trousers, Vigila moved with an efficient and considered manner that matched the way she spoke. She looked to be in her late forties or early fifties. Her long blonde hair, pulled into a low-slung bunch, showed patches of grey. She wore the barest traces of make-up, enough to keep up appearances but not so much as to appear feminine.

Her office was a continuation of the room they had walked through. The walls, in the same metallic white as the corridor, featured subtle geometric artwork. Against one wall, a large, high-resolution screen stretched from ceiling to floor, displaying the sparkling skyline of Nuova Venezia stretched out beneath the transparent glass dome. It could have been mistaken for a piece of art if it wasn't for the gondolas and people that moved across the panorama.

The large desk that Vigila stood before was placed in the centre of the room. On its surface, a holographic display projected a plan of the city that reminded Steve of the map Mariana had shown to them. A line of three chairs broke the distance between the desk and Steve and his friends. The room held only a few personal touches: a single, carefully potted plant, a collection of awards and commendations mounted on one wall, and an accompanying photograph of a younger Vigila with a group of older suited individuals.

"You are a conundrum, Steve Haven," she said. 'As far as I know, you are currently at school in England. So how is it you are also here?"

"The boy—" Hartley began to answer but Vigila cut him off with a raised hand.

"I'm sure Steve can speak for himself."

"That isn't me," said Steve. "At school. He just looks like me. It's a favour."

"Aren't you the lucky one?" Her lips lifted into an almost smile, then her eyes fell on Bodrn who waited at the door. "Sorry, I don't think we've been introduced."

"My name is Bodrn." The darkling stepped forward to stand at Steve's side.

"Bodrn." Vigila nodded to herself. "I'll remember that."

"What do you want?" said Steve. "Why are we here?"

"I'm sure my operatives have filled you in." Vigila returned to the chair behind her desk and sat down. "You want to find your parents. I know where they are. You want information. I want assistance. It strikes me as a win-win situation. Sit please."

Steve didn't ask for reassurance from Hartley this time. The thought of finally locating his parents was too tempting a prospect.

"Or don't," said Vigila as Steve and Hartley sat down but Bodrn remained by the door. "Whatever is more comfortable."

"You know where my parents are?" said Steve.

"I have a good idea," said Vigila. "Mainly because I sent them there. First, your father, and then your mother."

"When?" said Steve. "Why?" He had so many questions that he didn't know where to start.

"Why don't we start with 'where'?" she said. "That's the simplest question to answer."

"Okay," said Steve. "Where did you send them?"

"I sent your parents to the ruined city of Venice below us. The 'why' is rather complicated. Have you heard of a man called Xav Mallorick?"

"We have," said Hartley.

"Good," she said. "What do you know about Mallorick?"

"A bit," said Steve, looking at Hartley. "He was a magical who broke the Council's rules."

"That's putting it lightly," said Hartley.

"I agree," said Vigila. "Mallorick is a highly dangerous individual, regardless of his magical abilities. The Council call him a mind flayer."

"Like Blaike Harn," said Steve.

"The head of the Council? I always wondered if that was the case." Vigila nodded. "He has a way of getting into your head, influencing people. He can be especially convincing when he speaks."

"So why not hamper his magic?" asked Bodrn. "Parity have the ability, the equipment."

"We did," said Vigila. "And it worked, for a while. He was imprisoned in Venice. It was already a safe harbour for your kind, Hartley," she said.

"You do realise that my kind is still human?" he said.

"It was the perfect place to site our prison." She ignored Hartley's comment, concentrating on Steve. "With the help of the Council of course. We conveyed Mallorick there, hampered," she added, her eyes darting to Bodrn. "Unfortunately, the man is as canny as he is dangerous. He somehow managed to disable his collar. And then he took over the minds of his jailers. That was over twenty years ago."

"So what's that got to do with my mum and dad?" said Steve.

"Your father came to Nuova Venezia to find a way into old Venice. You've seen the documents he accessed at the *Biblioteca Serenissima*, including the schematic for the illusion barrier. We always knew that if anyone went looking for that particular document, they likely knew about the prison."

"So you set an alarm on it," said Steve.

"We did and just like you, when your father activated that alarm, he was escorted here. He wasn't happy about our intervention, but we did reach an understanding in the end."

"You sent him into Venice to stop Xav Mallorick," said Bodrn.

"Yes," said Vigila. "He wanted information from Mallorick. Elijah agreed that once he had that, he would help me. That was the last time I saw him."

"But that didn't stop you from sending Steve's mother down there as well," said Hartley. "Or am I missing something? Do tell."

"Elijah and Mary knew the risks they were taking when they accepted my terms. Elijah was insistent that only Mallorick could provide the answers he wanted. Mary was equally insistent that she find her husband."

"So where are they now?" The hope that Steve had hung onto was slowly beginning to dim, like a flame running out of oxygen.

"I'm sorry, Steve." Vigila's expression softened for the first time since they had entered the room. "I truly am. I can only assume that they fell under the influence of Mallorick."

"Which means they're still in Venice." The failing light of Steve's hope that he would find his parents flickered back into life. "We can rescue them."

"If they are still alive," she said, "I believe they are in Venice. But as for rescuing them, I'm not sure a boy of your age can succeed where so many adults have failed."

"Failed to rescue my parents?"

"Fail to put an end to Xav Mallorick's rule," she said, her expression returning to its initial cool watchfulness.

"She means that she won't allow you to go down there to rescue your parents unless you agree to work against Xav Mallorick. Did I get that right?" said Hartley.

"You did." She leaned back in her chair, looking at each of the three friends in turn before she spoke. "I'm sorry, Steve. You may have got the better of the Council, of Winters, even of Elrick Olen, but this is one quest you can't achieve on your own."

"But he is not alone," said Bodrn. "He has us."

"A hampered traveller and a teenage girl?" said Vigila. "The three of you are hardly an elite taskforce."

"Ah, you know about that," said Hartley, looking down at the bangles around his wrists. "Still, I find your comment rather insulting. The girl, as you call her, is an expert fighter with an in-depth understanding of magic and its applications. Steve has the heart of a lion and the questioning mind of any top professor."

"And what about you?" said Vigila.

"I am Hartley Keg," he said. "Do I need to say more?"

"Modest to the very end," she said with no trace of a smile. "But yes, I am aware of your reputation. You have a knack for getting into trouble."

"I'd like to think that I have a greater knack for getting out of trouble," he said.

"If I did send you in. *If*," she added as Steve opened his mouth to speak. "There would be next to no chance of rescue. You do understand that?"

"That's okay," said Steve.

"No, it isn't," said Vigila. "Adults taking that risk is one thing. But you're a child."

"I'm a teenager," he said.

"And that would be your only advantage. It seems that Xav Mallorick can't influence young minds. Not with his magic anyway."

"So that's decided," said Steve. "You can send us down there, just like you did my parents."

"You make it sound so simple, Steve."

"Because it is!"

"Not if…" She stopped and turned to Hartley. "Could I speak to the boy alone please? Just for a moment. He'll be perfectly safe," she added when Bodrn started to complain.

"If it's acceptable to Steve," said Hartley. "Is it, Steve?"

"Yes. Of course it is." If this was what it took to convince Vigila, he was more than willing to speak to her alone, however scary that felt.

Hartley looked at Bodrn, shrugged, and nodded to the way out. Vigila remained silent until the door had closed behind them.

"You think you know what you're walking into." She opened a drawer and withdrew something that she cupped in her hand. "But you have to understand the insidious powers that Mallorick has over people, including your parents."

"I get it," he said. "He's a mind flayer. I've faced one of those before."

"This isn't about you though." She walked around her desk and took the seat that Hartley had just vacated. "It's about how he'll affect the people around you. Not just your parents, but Hartley and maybe Bodrn too. She looks like a teenager, but her eyes tell a different story. I assume she's much older than she appears."

"Maybe." Steve shrugged. "But that doesn't change things."

"It might," she said, "if Mallorick gets his claws into them. They could turn on you in an instant. They could betray you. You may only have yourself to rely on. Have you thought about that?"

Part of him wanted to say that of course his friends wouldn't do that, but he knew she was right, so he just nodded. "I still want to go."

"You're a very stubborn individual," she said in a way that suggested it wasn't a judgement or a criticism, merely a fact.

"Just like your parents."

"I am," he said. "Can we go now?"

"Not without this." She offered him a small, clear plastic sachet. Inside was a white tablet. "This will stop Mallorick in his tracks."

"Will it kill him?"

"Not at all. We don't want him dead. It'll just knock him out for a few hours. Once he's unconscious, his influence over our operatives and anyone else he controls should cease. Drop it in his drink and his digestive system will do the rest."

"Right." He took the sachet from her and quickly dropped it into his pocket where it magically disappeared from his grasp, for now. "Let's go."

"Steve, you can't tell your friends about this." She grabbed his wrist as he started to stand. "This has to be our secret."

"Okay." He nodded, aware of how firm her grasp was on his wrist. "I won't tell them."

"Good." She released him. "As long as we understand each other."

"I think that's long enough." The door opened and Hartley peered through. "Have we reached a decision?"

"We have." Vigila returned to the chair behind her desk. "Troi will take you where you need to go. Goodbye, Steve. I hope I'll see you again."

"Me too." Steve said the words automatically, but he knew they were a lie. The last thing he wanted was to face the head of Parity ever again.

Chapter Nineteen

"This is Ruslo." Troi nodded to a skinny man with a heavily freckled face and dark hair pulled back into a messy pigtail. "He'll get you into Venice."

"Hi," said Steve. "I'm—"

"No names," said Ruslo. "I don't need to know." The man kept his eyes downcast, hardly moving his lips to speak.

Once he'd said goodbye to the Auditor, Steve had expected the Parity agents to take them straight into the ruins of old Venice. Instead, a rapid journey by helicopter had brought them back to the Venetian Lido, but further north than the landing area where they'd left the captain. The pavements here gleamed with the same polished stone, but the waterfront was lined with buildings that looked as if they'd been boarded up for years. A single covered jetty waited for them with a sleek, metallic grey boat. The vehicle was partially roofed, with dark shaded windows running around three sides of the cabin and a matching, sloped windscreen at the front of the boat.

"This way," said Ruslo, heading towards the jetty.

"We need to tell Mariana that we're leaving," said Steve.

"No time for that," said Troi. "And I'm not your messenger, so don't ask."

"Mariana will understand." Hartley steered Steve in the direction of the jetty. "She's used to my ways. Coming?" he asked Bodrn when she didn't follow.

"Can we trust him?" she said in a low voice. "The driver?"

"Who knows?" said Hartley. "But isn't that the fun of the matter? Finding out?"

"Perhaps," she said as she fell in step with her two friends.

"Wait." Steve stopped as his heart raced. "Are we doing the right thing? We don't know what will happen when we get in there and…" He felt breathless and off balance. His chest was tight and his mouth was dry. "I want to find Mum and Dad, but we don't know they're still there. Not really. And if Xav Mallorick can control people and—"

"What can you see?"

"What?"

"What can you see?" Ruslo held Steve's hands in his own. Now that Steve could see the man's eyes, he was surprised by how dark they were, black but with specks of gold. "Tell me."

"I see you," said Steve. "And my friends."

"What do you hear?"

"I hear…" Steve listened for a moment. "I hear the water moving against the jetty."

"And what can you smell?"

"The lagoon. And Hartley." Steve smiled. His chest wasn't tight anymore. "Sorry, Hartley, but your jacket always smells of cabbage and coffee."

"Apology accepted, dear boy," said his friend. "Just this once."

"A bit of panic," said Ruslo, releasing Steve and taking a step back. "Happens to the best of us."

"Better?" said Hartley as Ruslo walked off.

"Yeah, better," said Steve. "We're doing this."

"Good to hear." Hartley patted Steve on the back. "And as far as the right thing is concerned, there's really no way to tell. All you can ever do is take a deep breath and dive in."

"Hartley Keg style," said Steve.

"Absolutely." Hartley gave him a wink. "Hold up, my dear," he called as Bodrn climbed aboard the boat where Ruslo was now waiting.

As Steve watched Hartley noisily struggle onto the boat, with a lot of help from Bodrn and Ruslo, he took a deep, steadying breath. On the one hand, he might finally find out where his parents had been all this time. On the other… *They might not be there. Xav Mallorick may take over the minds of my friends. Venice could end up being my prison too.*

"Steve, there are comfy seats." Hartley waved at him. "It's all very luxurious. Come on."

Comfy seats, thought Steve. *Trust Hartley to concentrate on that.* But his friend's words were reassuring as he headed towards the boat. After all, if you had to travel into danger, you might as well do it in style.

"Best buckle up," Hartley said as Steve took the seat next to him. "These water taxi journeys can be a little bouncy."

"That must have been a long time ago, old man," said Ruslo. "This water taxi isn't bouncy at all."

With Ruslo at the controls at the front and no engine noise at all, the boat rose up in the water, and set off from the jetty.

Hartley twisted in the restraints of his seat belt and pressed his face to the window. "We're flying," he said. "Is this magic?"

"Electricity and hydrofoils," said Ruslo. "Makes for a quiet and smooth ride. It's what people expect these days. Most people anyway."

"Haven't you seen a hydrofoil before?" said Steve, as if he'd seen lots of them himself. Of course, he hadn't. Until recently, he'd spent his whole life in the city of Caercester.

"Hydrofoil." Hartley tried the word out. "How fascinating. Don't you think?" he asked Bodrn.

"It is a vehicle." She shrugged. "I only care that it gets us where we want to go." She shrugged again and looked out across the water to the distant city ruins that sat in the shadow of Nuova Venezia floating above.

The journey continued at near-silent speed, with no vibration or sense of their movement across the lagoon, for only a few minutes. As they reached what Steve judged was around halfway, Ruslo halted the boat. It sank back into the water. It was only now that Steve could feel the effect of the waves.

Ahead of them, the old city of Venice sat in a state of

dilapidation. Waterfront walkways had collapsed into the lagoon in places. Many of the grand buildings lay open to the elements, their roofs having fallen in on themselves. A handful of towers stood out above the rest of the city, but even more of these towers were partly collapsed and without their spires.

"I assume you know what you're getting yourselves into," said Ruslo.

"Parity have filled us in," said Hartley.

"We know about the illusion, and the prison," said Steve.

"Not much then," said Ruslo. "This is Xav Mallorick's city now. You can't trust anyone here because he's probably in their heads. Or at least, he can be if it serves him. That goes for you too."

"I hardly think—" said Hartley.

"Everyone takes it for granted that they'll be able to resist his control, but he has his charms. He'll talk his way into your head and you won't even notice."

"Does he control you?" said Bodrn.

"He has," said Ruslo. "Other times he's just delved into my mind to get the information he needs. You can't keep him out."

"So how do we beat him?" she said.

"Beat him?" Ruslo looked as if he was about to laugh but it didn't happen. "You don't beat him. You survive. Be pleasant. Tell the truth."

"Like slaves."

"Telling the truth doesn't have to be about giving in," said Ruslo. "Be clever about which truth you tell him, or how much of that truth. I've taken people in there before, knowing full well that once we're past the barrier they'll change. I've never taken a child in before, though. That's the only reason I'm warning you. Any more questions?"

"Why didn't Parity fly us straight into old Venice?" said Steve. "Why back to the Lido and take a boat?"

"Officially, entry to the old city is banned because the ruins aren't safe," said Ruslo. "Unofficially, the powers-that-be don't want the public to know the truth. A flight into the old city might raise suspicions or give wealthy tourists a reason to demand a closer look. That place up there," he said, pointing at the high-tech city that hung in the sky above its ruined predecessor, "is run on ignorance. Best leave it that way."

"Thank you, Ruslo," said Steve.

"Don't thank me yet." Ruslo returned to the boat's controls and the vessel raised up out of the water. "We're about to pass the barrier."

*

Logically, Steve knew that they had simply passed a little further across the lagoon, but his body and his senses told him a different story. As the boat passed through the invisible barrier, Steve's stomach lurched as if he was on the jerkiest rollercoaster ride he had ever experienced. At the same time, the scent of the lagoon—fresh and a little salty—filled with other aromas. He smelt fish, mud, and flowers. The quiet of the lagoon was replaced with many voices and the creaking of boats.

The biggest change by far was what Steve and his friends could see. The waterside walkways were intact. The buildings were well kept, each with a complete roof. What had seemingly been a ruined and abandoned city was suddenly filled with people. People in gondolas and fishing boats on the water. People selling at stalls in the streets. People simply going about their lives.

Three uniformed men stood at the waterfront where a series of short jetties with ornate lamps jutted out into the lagoon. The men were dressed in black but appeared to be unarmed.

"Is that our reception party?" asked Hartley.

"No, not them. They're sentries. They keep an eye on the barrier." Ruslo waved to one of them. "They work for Mallorick."

"Are they Parity operatives?" said Bodrn.

"They were. It's like I said." Ruslo tapped a finger on the side of his head. "He gets into your mind."

Behind the men, an immense open area was bordered on three sides by ornate buildings of pale stone with intricate tiling, arched windows, and flat roofs adorned with statues and pointed merlons. It looked just as Steve had expected Venice would be. It was only when he looked up that he noticed the absence of the natural sky. It was as if someone had cut out the vibrant city and placed it on a plain, white bed sheet.

"Now we've been seen, we'll have to keep to the Grand Canal," said Ruslo as he turned the boat away from the jetties and headed towards a wide waterway that cut into the city. "Prefer the narrower canals myself, but needs must."

"You know this place well," said Bodrn.

"I grew up here. My people came to Venice when, well, you know," he said, turning to Hartley. "This place has always been very accepting of my kind."

"Your kind?" she said.

"Yes." He removed one hand from the controls, clicked his fingers, and opened his hand. "My kind." A whirlwind of dust and light span on his outheld palm.

"You're a wind whisperer," said Hartley.

He nodded and closed his hand, extinguishing the whirlwind. "The workadays accepted us. Helped keep our secret. We had a good life here."

"Until Xav Mallorick," said Bodrn.

"Until the Council decided that Venice was the ideal place to imprison him. I don't blame Mallorick. I blame them."

"But why here?" said Steve. "Venice isn't like Darkacre. It's a workaday city."

"It is quite a conundrum," said Hartley. "Why use Venice as a prison when they could easily have created a protected area to imprison Xav Mallorick?"

"To extinguish two flames with one breath," said Ruslo.

"How do you mean?" asked Hartley.

"Like I said, Venice always accepted us. Don't get me wrong. Some happily took advantage of our skills but most just saw us as people. And they didn't understand why we would hide those skills. Some of us didn't either."

He stopped speaking as a gondola approached, filled with loaded sacks. He nodded to the gondolier, who responded with a brief greeting. It wasn't until there was a distance between the two boats that Ruslo continued.

"There was a plan, a workaday plan, to quietly spread the word to other cities. They reckoned it would make it easier for us. It was a nice idea, but it didn't take long for the Council to get wind of the fact."

"Extinguish two flames." Hartley nodded. "That does sound like something the Council would do. And Parity?"

"They insisted that a force of Hidden wouldn't work as both jailers and enforcers. Instead, they installed their own forces. Idiots."

"But the people here," said Bodrn. "They are also prisoners."

"Yes," said Ruslo. "That's the price they paid for being good to magicals. Most of them accepted it. A few pushed back. They were the ones who disappeared."

None of them said another word as they travelled down the Grand Canal. The waterway grew busier the further they went. The hubbub of the people working and walking on either side of the canal gave the impression that the citizens of Venice had taken the best aspects of their fate and found a way to live here, regardless of their constraints. Two or three looked up as the water taxi travelled past and Steve wondered if they were under the control of Xav Mallorick. Did he know they were on their way to see him?

"Here we are." Ruslo finally broke the silence as he manoeuvred the water taxi alongside a jetty. "This is as far as I can take you. They'll see to you now."

As the water taxi lowered to the surface of the water, two Parity operatives left their posts in front of a canal-side building. It didn't look like a prison to Steve. It looked like a rather pleasant hotel with its modest double doors topped off by a pristine, white canopy, arched windows, and flower-box laden balconies.

"Is this it?" he asked as the uniformed men waved to Ruslo.

"Don't be fooled," said Ruslo in a low voice. "You're about to enter the lion's den. Remember what I said." He threw a rope around one of the jetty upright posts and tied it into a secure knot.

"We were expecting you," said one of the men. "Mr Mallorick is waiting."

Steve watched as Bodrn jumped from the boat, avoiding the hand offered by one of the guards. Hartley made a show of needing help, almost pulling the two men off-balance.

"I'll get a message to your friends up top." Ruslo kept his back to the men as he spoke to Steve. "Not that they can help."

"Come on, boy." One of the guards reached out to Steve. "Mr Mallorick is a busy man."

Steve took the man's hand and allowed himself to be hauled off the boat. He looked back at Ruslo, but the man was busy readying the water taxi to leave.

"Eyes front, Steve," said Hartley. "There's no turning back now."

Chapter Twenty

"There really is no need for this indignity" Hartley complained as one of the guards patted him down, spinning the shopkeeper around, and even rifling through his unruly beard. "I'm unarmed."

"Here." The guard handed Hartley's jacket back. 'Nothing," he told his companion. "He's clear."

"Just the boy then," said the second guard. His face still bore a red weal where Bodrn had slapped him when he'd attempted to search her. She'd finally relented but the guard hadn't dared touch her again.

"Jacket off," said the first guard.

"I'll take that," said Hartley.

"No, you won't," said the guard. "Hand it over."

"Okay." Steve slipped his jacket off and let the guard snatch it. Theoretically, the magically-imbued pocket in his jacket should conceal the pill that Vigila had given to him, but the tailor had warned them the pocket might not last. It had been a rush job, after all.

"Here." The guard handed it to his companion who delved into the pockets and patted the rest of the jacket. "Nothing."

"Nothing here either," said the first guard as he finished searching Steve.

"Best take them inside," said the other, handing the jacket back to Steve. "Mr Mallorick doesn't like to be kept waiting."

"You heard him." The guard jerked his head towards the doors as his companion opened one of them.

"Thanks," said Steve, pulling his jacket on. If what Vigila had told him was true, these Parity operatives were under the control of Xav Mallorick so they could be excused for their treatment of the three friends. *Or maybe they're like Troi, and idiots anyway*, he thought.

Inside, the hotel lobby was spacious and elegant. There was a high ceiling with white walls and a marble floor that reflected the natural light coming from the large windows.

"Mr Mallorick is waiting for you." Another uniformed guard stood at the highly-polished wooden reception desk. He briefly pointed towards a square archway with a glazed smile.

"Well, this is rather pleasant," said Hartley as they entered what appeared to be a bar with cosy seating and tables, each of which was cloaked with a luxurious tablecloth.

"There you are. Welcome. Welcome."

After all that he had heard about Xav Mallorick and his powers, Steve expected the man to be intimidating, or hardened, or grim. What he didn't expect was a short man with thinning blond hair dressed in a silk, paisley dressing gown over shirt and trousers, all topped off with a ruby red cravat.

Xav Mallorick sat on a tall stool, a cocktail in his hand, and an immense, leather tome of a book open on the bar beside him. His slippered feet barely reached the stool's footrest. Paying close attention to him, a Parity operative waited behind the bar with the same odd smile as the guard at the reception desk. A third guard played a calming but complicated melody on the baby grand piano at the other end of the bar.

"This does not look like a prison," Bodrn whispered to Steve.

"Speak up," said Xav. "Share your thoughts with the class, why don't you?"

"This does not look like a prison," she repeated.

"This old place?" said Xav. "Bit of a doer-upper, but it suits me. For now."

"You appear to have done rather well for yourself." Hartley edged a couple of paces ahead of his friends. "For a jailed felon."

"Needs must," said Xav. "Please, Hartley. Introduce your

friends."

"My young companion here is Steve Haven. And this," he said looking at the darkling.

"I am called Bodrn."

"Interesting," said Xav, narrowing his eyes a little. "Not quite human. Something else. Don't tell me. I'll get it in time. Drink?" He drained his glass and handed it to the guard behind the bar who immediately set about making another.

"This isn't a social visit," said Hartley. "The boy has questions."

"You're not normally such a killjoy, Hartley. Drinks all round," Xav told the guard.

"No, thank you," said Hartley. "As I said—"

"Stop." Xav's command wasn't loud, or even authoritative, but Hartley fell silent immediately. "You will have a drink with me, Hartley. Just like old times. I insist."

"Of course, Xav." Hartley's face contorted into a beaming smile and his feet shuffled forward, the soles dragging across the marble floor. A rumble that began in his throat worked itself into a growl, and with a lopsided shake of his head, Hartley shouted, "Stop that!" His smile disappeared but his feet continued to edge forward.

"Spoilsport." As Xav turned to take the refreshed drink from the guard behind the bar, Hartley slumped to his knees with a noisy exhalation of breath.

"Never do that again!" Hartley climbed to his feet, shook himself like a dog that had come in from a rain shower, and staggered back a pace. "I'm all right," he said as Steve and Bodrn took his arms. "I just don't appreciate other people interfering with my mind."

"You're no entertainment at all," said Xav. "Maybe one of the others—"

"I'm looking for my mum and dad." Steve stepped in front of his friends. "I know they came here."

"Steve Haven." Xav took a sip from his drink, keeping his eyes on Steve all the while. "I remember you. You were a sullen baby. Cried a lot. I never saw the appeal, but your Uncle Rex thought you were worth the time and expense."

"I don't understand," said Steve.

"Of course, you don't." Xav looked him up and down. "Well, if none of you are going to partake." He grabbed one of the three cocktails that the guard had lined up on the bar. "Bottoms up!"

Steve looked at Hartley, who simply shook his head. He looked at Bodrn. She seemed confused by the jailed magical's behaviour.

"Let me get this right," said Xav as he finished the first cocktail and grabbed the second. "The Auditor once again sends in a panel of assassins to, what do they call it, take me out? But this time, she sends a boy, an elderly wizard, and a, a, well, whatever you are. The woman shows no imagination."

"We're not assassins," said Steve. "We're telling the truth."

"Oh, I know you are. You told me as much yourself in the library."

"In the library?" said Steve. "That was you talking to us through the computer?"

"Just my little game." Xav drained another cocktail. "I have to amuse myself somehow. The Auditor got to you though, obviously. I know Ruslo works for her. Thankfully, he works for me too."

"Okay, yes. She did send us here, but I don't care about that. I just want to find my parents."

"I see." Xav toyed with the drink in his hand, swirling it around the glass. "It seems the Haven family just can't do without me. First, Rex, then your father, your mother, and now you. It's flattering, sometimes useful, but generally rather annoying."

"So you know where they are?" Steve tried to restrain his hopes of a 'yes'. He knew by now that life was rarely that straightforward.

"Yes and no."

"Stop being so obstructive, Xav." Hartley touched a hand to Steve's shoulder. "The boy's come a long way to find his parents.

He deserves an answer."

"*Deserves*, is it?" Xav slammed down his glass, spilling some of the drink on his hand. "You overstep, Hartley. Remember where you are."

The guard behind the bar instantly grabbed a cloth and began to dab at Xav's hand and sleeve cuff.

"Get off me!" Xav batted the man away.

"Yes, Mr Mallorick." The guard backed off, the smile on his face a curious combination with the fear in his eyes.

"Your father did visit me." There was no pleasantry in the tone of Xav's voice now. "He wanted answers, about you, Steve."

"Me?" Hartley's grasp on Steve's shoulder tightened.

"I was stupidly generous at the time, of course." Xav leant back on the bar in a relaxed fashion, but his eyes were narrowed like a cat about to pounce. "I said he could leave in return for news from the outside world." He ran a finger through the puddle of spilled drink on the bar. "I knew letting him go would annoy the Auditor. Foil her plans, if you will."

"And Mum?" said Steve. "Did she leave too?"

"Oh no," said Xav. "Your mother is a delightful woman. I couldn't possibly let her escape. She's around here somewhere."

"Where?" Steve's heart was suddenly in his throat, beating fast and pulling up all the hopes he had tried to keep down. "Can I see her?"

"Eventually." Xav grabbed the cloth that the guard had dropped and wiped his hands. "But for now, let's get you all settled. There are plenty of rooms here."

"Rooms or cells?" said Hartley.

"You know me, Hartley," said Xav. "I have no real need for cells." He clicked his fingers at the guard playing the piano. "Find a room for my guests. Somewhere large enough for three. The family room. How lovely," he said. "Will that be acceptable?"

"Do we have a choice?" said Bodrn.

"Not at all."

"Yes, Mr Mallorick," said the guard, with that same displaced smile as the other Parity operatives. "This way, please." He gestured for Steve and the others to follow him back into the lobby. "Welcome to the Mallorick Hotel. I do hope you'll enjoy your stay."

Chapter Twenty-One

"I don't think 'lovely' is quite the word I would use," said Hartley as the door closed behind them, followed by the click of a key in the lock.

The room had at one point been a luxurious place to rest your head. There were three beds—one double and two singles—a burgundy and gold floral carpet, ornate glass ceiling lights, and elegantly carved wooden furniture. But the carpet was faded, the furniture was velvety with dust, and the gold-flocked wallpaper was peeling away in places. There was an unpleasant smell of decay in the air.

"We do have a view, thankfully." Hartley pulled back the long, heavy curtains, coughed at the storm of disturbed dust, and charged out onto a modest balcony that overlooked the Grand Canal.

"Not too far to jump," said Bodrn as she leaned over the rail.

"For you maybe," said Hartley, grabbing her sleeve. "Best not trust the balustrade. It hardly looks as if the place has been maintained over the years."

"You are right." She dropped her hands from the rail but didn't step back. "If I could change into shadow…" She sighed.

"And if I could travel us out through a door back to Caercester." Hartley shrugged. "Wishing won't make it happen, so there's no point in beating ourselves about the noggin. Steve?" He turned around, peering through the open balcony doors. "Are you all right?"

"She's here." Steve sat on the end of one of the single beds. "I should be happy about that." Instead, his hopes had dived into a knotted, anxious pit in his stomach. "Why aren't I happy about that?"

"You will be." Hartley marched into the room and perched on the other single bed. "Once you see her again."

"But Dad's gone, and Mum..." Steve shook his head. "What if she's under Xav Mallorick's control?"

"She probably is," said Bodrn.

"Your honesty isn't at all helpful." Hartley scowled at her.

"Sorry." She dropped into a cross-legged position on the floor. "She might not be."

"No, you're right," said Steve. "That must be how he made her stay. Mum wouldn't give up looking for Dad." He shook his head again. "I just have to make her understand. Talk her round."

"We can worry about navigating that particular bridge when we have to." Hartley reached across to pat Steve's hand. "For now, let's investigate."

"Investigate what?" said Steve. "We're locked in."

"That way is locked, and most likely guarded," said Hartley, nodding to the door they'd entered through. "But what about that one?"

Beyond the three beds and between two impressive, oversized wardrobes, was a single, modest door. There was no key in the lock and the dusty carpet in front of the door spoke of how little the entrance had been used recently.

"Do you think it's open?" said Steve.

"Shall we find—"

Bodrn reached the door and turned its handle before Hartley had a chance to finish his sentence. "It is locked."

"Well, it's lucky that I brought these in that case." Hartley pulled a ring of rusty keys from his pocket. "I may not be able to travel us out of here, but I still have my uses. Now then." He ran a hand over the keyhole, grunted to himself, and then he licked his forefinger and thumb.

"Can you open it?" said Steve.

"Can I open it?" said Hartley. "Have I ever failed you before?"

"I'm not answering that," said Steve.

Hartley separated one of the rust-encrusted keys from the others and slid his finger and thumb down its length. When Steve had seen Hartley use the magical keys in the past, the rust had fallen away to reveal a polished, silver key that was perfect for its intended lock. This time around, nothing happened.

"Bother," said Hartley with a scowl. "Non-magical solution it is then."

He dropped the keys back into his pocket and pulled out a small leather wallet. Turning back the flap of the wallet, Hartley pursed his lips in thought as he touched each of the revealed metal tools in turn. After a moment, he pulled out a tool that ended in a hook and another that was flat and shaped like a 'Z'.

"Will those work?" said Bodrn, tilting her head.

"Will they work?" Hartley squinted as he inserted the tools into the door lock. He grunted to himself as he jiggled, pushed, and pulled the tools. "Absolutely," he announced as they heard a decisive click. "The deed is done."

Two things happened in a very short period of time. First, Hartley pulled the door open and charged into the space beyond. Second, a figure in the other room lunged at the elderly shopkeeper, swinging a bronze statuette and a pillow.

"Stop that at once!" Hartley ducked, evading the statuette, but as he straightened up he took the full force of the pillow on his face.

Bodrn darted through into the second room and disarmed the attacker, pinning the woman's arms behind her back. The statuette thumped onto the carpeted floor.

"Calm down," Bodrn snarled into her ear. "We do not want to hurt you."

"Too late," said the struggling woman. "Get off me!"

"Mum?"

"Steve?" The woman continued to struggle but the anger fell from her face.

"You can let her go," said Hartley. "She's no threat to us now."

As Bodrn released her, Mary Haven staggered forward a step. She looked tired and thinner than when she had left Steve at school, but the smile on her face was the best thing he had seen in a long time.

The two of them rushed into each other's arms with such force that their heads butted. Both clasped hands to their heads, laughed, and then wrapped the other one in a heartfelt hug.

"How are you here?" Mary was the first one to draw back, grabbing Steve by the shoulders. "Is your father with you?"

"No. Just me." Hartley stood with his hands behind his back. "And our young friend here." He smiled at Bodrn.

"But if he didn't send you, how…?" She stopped, her face hardening as she broke away from Steve. "Hartley Keg, what have you got my son into?"

"It wasn't my idea," said Hartley. "Well, only a very little bit," he said, showing how little with his forefinger and thumb.

"It was my idea," said Steve. "I said we had to find you and Dad."

"But how do you two even know each other?" said Mary. "And who is she?" She pointed to Bodrn.

"It's a really long story," said Steve.

Before he could say more, the door to the hallway was flung open and two guards burst into the room. One of them carried a dress on a hanger and a pair of high-heeled shoes.

"I told you I heard voices," said the other to his companion. "You shouldn't be in here. Get back in your room."

"We're not children to be ordered around," said Mary, pushing Steve behind her. "You can't tell us what to do."

"Maybe we can't, but you know that Mr Mallorick can. Leave them on the bed," he told the other guard. "Watch yourself. She's quick."

"I won't wear that," she said as the guard carefully laid the dress out.

"And we're not going back to our room." Steve hoped he

sounded as confident and defiant as his mum.

"Leave them," said the guard as he dropped the shoes on the floor. "What harm can they do, locked away in here? It's not like they can escape Mr Mallorick."

"True," said the other guard. "Fine. I'll let you all stay together, for now."

The two guards backed towards the open door, and left without another word.

*

The telling of Steve's adventures to his mum didn't go quite as expected. Everyone he or Hartley had told the story to in the past had stayed quiet until they were finished. Mary Haven was anything but quiet. She interrupted every few minutes, made comments on their adversaries, and regularly blamed Hartley for the scenarios Steve found himself in. What she didn't appear to be was surprised.

"This is why I tried to keep you out of it," she said, pacing around the room. "I didn't want this kind of life for you."

"What does that mean?" said Steve.

"I'm sure your mother is simply worried about you," said Hartley.

"Oh, so you pulled my son into all kinds of danger and trauma, but you didn't think to tell him about us?" She spread her hands wide at Hartley, and when he only blinked in response, she said, "Really? Nothing to say? How convenient."

"What do you mean 'us'?" Steve looked from Hartley to his mum.

"I just didn't think it was necessary," said Hartley. "I didn't want to alarm the boy."

"Well, you did a terrible job at that, didn't you?" Mary's face was growing redder by the minute and her voice was increasing in volume.

"Mum, calm down."

"Calm down? How can I…?" She stopped, breathing heavily with her shoulders hunched up to her ears. For a moment, Steve didn't know if she was going to hit Hartley or scream. Instead, she let out a long, slow breath, her shoulders lowered to their rightful place, and she sat down on the double bed in her room.

"It's all right, Mum. We're here." Steve sat down beside her and took her hand.

"That's what I'm worried about," she said. "Sorry, that came out wrong." She released his hand and put her arm around his shoulders. "I didn't want you to be in danger, that's all. I thought a normal life would be safer."

"It's too late for that," said Steve.

"It is." She nodded. "Hartley, I'm sorry. In your own chaotic way, I'm sure you thought you were acting for the best."

"I did," said Hartley. "Although truth be told, I have enjoyed the adventure."

"I'm sure you have." She smiled and shook her head. "I suppose I would have too."

"So this 'us'?" said Steve. "What's that about?"

"Us," she said. "Hartley, Blessing, your father, and me. We were quite a team when Elijah and I were your age."

"I think we know different Blessings," said Steve. "She's only…" He glanced at Hartley as the elderly shopkeeper lowered himself onto a small sofa by the window. "She was only my age."

"One more thing that Hartley didn't think to explain," said his mum. "Let's put that to one side. When I was your age, I ran away from home. I won't go into it now," she said when Steve opened his mouth to ask why. "That's a whole other miserable story. I had it in my head that I could just walk out, get on a train, and find somewhere better to live. Anywhere had to be an improvement. I got as far as the nearest underground station before Maeve Kendra and her son cornered me. You've met Braeden already."

"Unfortunately," said Bodrn.

"We can agree on that," said Mary. "Maeve had a way of

convincing kids. Nothing magical, just a motherly veneer that made you think she was a safe person to be around."

"She always had a keen mind for discovering how to control young people," said Hartley. "I can attest to that."

"But I didn't trust her," Mary said. "On the other hand, I couldn't see any way out of the situation either. When you're that age, it often feels like you have to do what adults tell you. I was thinking about going with her when—"

"I arrived," said Hartley with a raised finger.

"Actually, your father arrived," Mary told Steve. She chuckled. "You should have seen the look on Maeve's face when the door of a seemingly normal janitor cupboard flew open, knocking Braeden to the floor. She was furious. Her caring act disappeared. She shouted at her son to get me. Your father said…" She chuckled again. "Come with me if you want to live. I mean, can you imagine? What a cliché."

"It did the job though," said Hartley.

"I grabbed Elijah's hand, still wondering why we were jumping into a cupboard, and ran."

"And never stopped," said Hartley. "Until now."

"Until now," she agreed. "So believe me, I understand the allure and excitement of adventures with Hartley Keg." She gave Steve a hug. "It's good to see you."

"You too," he said. "Now, we just have to find Dad."

"He's not here," she said sadly. "Mallorick is a horrible man, but he rarely lies. He's too arrogant for that."

"But he must know." Steve pulled away a little so he could look at his mum face-to-face. "Did he tell you where Dad went?"

"Did he tell me?" For a second, she looked at Steve as if he had asked the most ridiculous question. The love drained from her face and the edges of her mouth twitched up into an almost smile. "I don't think we have to worry about that at the moment," she said.

"I'd like to know," said Steve.

"What did the Auditor tell you to do?" she asked. "Did she

give you anything?"

"No." The woman at his side looked like his mum, but it was as if she had stepped out for a moment and someone else had stepped into her body. "She probably told me what she told you."

"That's odd." His mum tilted her head, or whatever was in there did. "I thought she would have given you a plan to follow."

"Are you feeling all right, Mary?" Hartley stood up and moved closer.

"I'm fine." She turned to face the elderly shopkeeper with a bright smile. "Thanks for asking, Hartley. If you don't mind, I'd like to get changed before we meet with Xav. He chose a beautiful dress for me."

"Of course, Mary. Come along, Steve. Bodrn."

"But can't we—" Steve began.

"Come along now." Hartley pulled Steve to his feet, grabbed his shoulders, and steered him to the door to their room. "Your mother needs some privacy."

It wasn't until Bodrn closed the interconnecting door behind them that Steve had the chance to speak again.

"What are you doing?" He pulled himself free of Hartley's grasp. "We've only just found her and—"

"Xav is using her," said Hartley. "Why else do you think we were put in the room next to hers? Didn't it occur to you that it was just a little too easy to find her?"

"Her voice changed," said Bodrn. "And her body language. You must have noticed."

"Yes," Steve admitted. "But that's my mum."

"Undoubtedly, that is Mary Haven," said Hartley. "But Xav is in her mind. If we're to rectify that, we have to tread carefully. For now."

"But—" Steve started to protest but then he remembered the Auditor's warning.

They could turn on you in an instant. They could betray you. You may only have yourself to rely on.

He looked at his friends. Both of them looked back with expressions of concern, and support, and all the strengths he had seen in them over the last few months. But if Xav could control his mum, how easy would it be for him to control Hartley and the darkling too?

"You're right." He nodded, watching how the others responded. "Careful it is."

"Good boy," said Hartley, pressing a hand to his stomach. "I wonder if they'll feed us."

Steve smiled. Hartley was still Hartley, for now.

Chapter Twenty-Two

"Glorious view, isn't it?"

Xav Mallorick sat at the head of a long table on the rooftop terrace of the hotel. He had swapped his dressing gown for an emerald green velvet jacket and his slippers for smart, black leather brogues.

"If you like that kind of thing."

Mary Haven sat on Xav's right hand side. She wore the long, red dress that the guards had brought for her but once she was on the roof terrace and no longer under Xav's influence, she had kicked off the high-heeled shoes and complained that she was cold. One of the guards had brought her a shawl and her own shoes. She had wrapped the shawl so completely around her that the dress could barely be seen.

"It's a beautiful city. There's no denying that." Hartley sat beside Mary, a glass of red wine in his hand. "But we didn't come here to sightsee."

"Are you okay, Mum?" Xav had insisted that Steve took the chair to his left. Bodrn sat upright and cautious beside Steve.

"I'm fine," she said with a brief smile. "Now that I'm dressed for the temperature."

Xav wasn't wrong in his description of the rooftop view. In the dying daylight, the city of Venice displayed its faded grandeur. Steve could see verdigris domed roofs, buildings fronted with white stone pillars, and the Grand Canal stretching out of view in both directions. A handful of people walked alongside the canal and crossed the small bridge nearby. Warm light filled ground and first floor windows, and waterside lamplights blinked into life. The only detail that seemed out of place was the sky, or rather the lack of it. All that could be seen was a sheet of grey.

"You've had quite an adventure, Steve," said Xav as two guards set down plates of steaming food in front of each person at the table. "Winters. Braeden Kendra. Magical devices. Darklings," he said, looking at Bodrn with a knowing smile. "Fighting the Council. Defeating Parity. That must have annoyed Vigila no end."

"How do you know about that?" said Steve.

"He was listening," said Mary. "Through me. Sorry."

"Nothing to be sorry about, my dear." Hartley patted her hand. "It's what he does." Hartley looked at his plate of food, breathing in the aroma, but for once he held back from eating.

"You do realise that Parity can't be trusted," said Xav. "They always act in their own best interests. Take Elrick Olen and his crew."

"They were rogue agents," said Bodrn. "They did not act on the Auditor's commands."

"Well, she would say that." Xav picked up his knife and fork. "Gods forbid that she would associate herself with any failed operation. Dig in." He cut a sliver from the large fish on his plate.

"You might as well," said Mary, picking up her own cutlery. "The prison food here is good and you all need to keep your strength up."

"Only because you insist," said Hartley. He picked up his fork and jabbed at the fish. "I can't remember the last time I ate sea bass." He moved the fish around his plate, disrupting its bed of lemon slices and herbs.

"It isn't poisoned, if that's what you're thinking, Hartley," said Xav. "Although I can have my men take it away if you're not hungry."

"I didn't say that I wasn't hungry." Hartley cut into the sea bass and placed a chunk of fish in his mouth. He chewed slowly, messy eyebrows knitted together, and then he smiled. "Delicious," he said. "And I'm still alive, which is always a bonus."

"See?" said Xav. "I may be a criminal, in the eyes of the Council, but one crime I would never lower myself to is the despoiling of perfectly good food."

When his mum began to eat, Steve picked up his own fork. Bodrn wasted no time in following his example, stabbing the fish with knife and fork, demolishing it into pieces, and devouring the plateful at speed.

"I suppose there's no need for darklings to learn table manners." Xav watched her, wide-eyed and lips pulled back into a look of distaste. "Still." He shook his head and returned to eating at a more leisurely pace.

"Food is fuel," she said. Her plate was empty, so she licked the tines of her fork and the blade of her knife.

"So Steve," said Xav after two more mouthfuls of food. "Do you know why your father visited me here in Venice?"

"I don't think Steve has any—" Mary began to speak but as Xav raised his hand, she stopped. Her lips clamped shut. She glared at him, clutching her knife like she wanted to stab him with it.

"I asked Steve the question, not you, Mary," said Xav.

"I don't know," said Steve. "Something to do with his work?"

"His work," said Xav. "Do you know what type of work your father does, Steve?"

"Stop playing with the boy." Hartley put down his cutlery with a thud. "He just wants to find Elijah. Perfectly reasonable, now that he's reunited with his mother."

"You can shut up too." Xav pointed his fork at Hartley.

"Of course, Xav." Hartley nodded, mimed zipping his mouth shut, and sat back. His eyes had glazed over and his eyelids dipped. It looked as if he was about to fall asleep.

Mary hit her fork on the table—bang, bang, bang.

"I will not be interrupted or chastised at my own dinner table." Xav placed his knife and fork on his plate and dabbed at his mouth with his cotton napkin.

"Please don't hurt them," said Steve, watching as Hartley swayed back and forth in his seat.

"I'm not," said Xav. "I've just silenced them so we can have a proper chat. They're perfectly fine."

"I think Hartley and Mary would disagree," said Bodrn. Her fork lay on the tablecloth, but the knife remained in her hand.

"It's a shame I can't silence you too, darkling." Xav looked her up and down. "I have tried. I'll figure it out eventually." He clicked his fingers at the guards. "Take Mary, the old wizard, and the girl to their rooms."

"Yes, sir." One of the guards reached for Bodrn. He wasn't quick enough to avoid the knife that she slashed at him. It sliced across the top of his hand, drawing blood.

"You can stop that, thank you very much." Xav clicked his fingers at Mary. In a second, she pressed her knife against Hartley's hand, cutting down on his little finger. "Unless you want Mary to do something she'll regret."

"I will stop." Bodrn dropped the knife on the table and spread her open hands wide.

"That's better. Thank you, Mary. You can put down the knife."

Scowling at him and complaining as best she could from behind her closed lips, Mary threw the knife onto the tablecloth and lunged at Xav. The nearest guard stepped between them, grabbing her shoulders, and pushing her away.

"Let's have a little chat, Steve." Xav picked up his glass of wine as the guards led the drowsy Hartley, complaining Mary, and silent darkling back down the stairs into the hotel. "I think it's time we got to know each other," he said as they were left alone on the roof terrace. "I have so much information to share."

*

The non-sky above them had darkened over the course of their meal, and now it was completely black. The city beyond was illuminated by streetlights, lamps on the boats that passed along the canal, and the windows of occupied houses. If it hadn't been for the situation that Steve found himself in, he thought he could have enjoyed a visit to Venice.

"Now that we've got rid of the rabble, we can have a civilised chat." Xav leaned back in his chair, his refilled glass in his hand. "Just us two boys."

"Okay," said Steve. His throat was dry under Xav's gaze, but he felt too self-conscious to take a sip of his glass of water. "What do you want to talk about?"

"Don't you have any questions for me, Steve?"

"You know I do. I want to know where my dad is."

"But don't you care why he came here?"

"I suppose." Steve swallowed, eyeing his glass of water. "Does it matter?"

"It might." Xav breathed in the scent of his wine, his eyes ever watchful of Steve. "Would it interest you to know that your father came here because of you?"

"Me?" said Steve. "Why me?"

"You have no idea, do you?" Xav stood up and wandered to the balustrade that ran around the roof terrace. His wine glass remained on the table. "Your parents kept you totally in the dark. I find that very revealing. I mean, don't get me wrong. A visit to such a beautiful city like Venice has to be a pull for a young man of your age but still…"

With Xav's back turned, Steve took the opportunity to feel in his pocket for the pill that Vigila had given him. It came to his fingers immediately. If he could just drop the pill in his captor's wine, this would all be over in no time at all. With the pill in his grasp, he reached for Xav's glass.

"I honestly assumed that you'd come here for answers about yourself, not your parents." Xav turned back to face him. Steve closed his hand around the pill and dropped his elbow to the tabletop, hoping that he looked relaxed.

"No," said Steve. "I just came here to find Mum and Dad."

"Really?" Xav returned to the table, retrieving his glass. "You didn't yearn for adventure and danger?"

"I've had lots of adventure and danger already, thanks." Now, Steve did grab his glass of water, taking a large, noisy gulp. "I just want my family back."

"How tedious." Xav sat down and took a deep drink of wine. "I had hoped that you'd be more amusing than your parents."

"Look, I'm not here to entertain you." Whether it was his nerves, thoughts of how his mother had been treated, or just the frustration of finding her and not being able to leave, Steve was angry. "I just want to take Mum out of here and go find my dad."

"Feisty. I like it," said Xav. "I can see why Elijah came to me. It's like watching a captured wolf throw itself against the bars of its prison."

"What are you talking about?" said Steve. He desperately wanted to leave, run, go find his friends, and escape Venice. The hairs at the back of his neck bristled upright. Anxious energy buzzed just under his skin. His hands were clenched shut.

"You hate me right now, don't you, Steve? I can see it in your eyes. You'd happily topple me off this roof. And it isn't even because of your mum, not entirely. It's that beast inside you, that monster clawing to get out." He slammed a hand down on the table, startling Steve so much that he almost spilled his drink. "And the best part is that you don't even know that you have powers. I'm so good at what I do."

"Powers?" said Steve. "I don't have magical powers."

"You're right. You don't." Xav was watching him intently, eyes wide and a mad grin slashed across his face. "You're much more dangerous than that. That's why Rex brought you to me."

"Rex?" Steve struggled to speak as his thoughts scattered in confusion. "When…? I don't understand."

"Rex asked me to bind your powers when you were a baby. I told him that it would only work for so long. Teen years would probably be the trigger. How old are you, Steve?"

"Thirteen."

"Exactly." Xav sat back with a smug smile. "I called it."

"But I don't have powers. I'm just me, normal."

"By workaday standards, there is nothing normal about you, Steve Haven. Elijah knew that. He wanted me to keep your powers hidden. Bind them all over again."

"What powers?" Steve all but shouted the words. He could barely stay in his seat. His legs jumped with nervous energy. There was a low hum in his ears. "Tell me."

"In time." Xav gestured to one of the guards. "Take Steve to join the others."

"No!" Now, Steve did stand up, banging his thighs on the underside of the table as he charged to his feet. "Tell me the truth!"

The guard reached for the gun in his belt. Xav raised a hand, and the guard froze in place. Xav's grin had melted away and been replaced by wide-eyed fear.

"Now, now, Steve," he said. "I'll tell you, but first I want you to answer a question. Have you noticed anything strange happening to your magical friends, or even enemies, when you get angry?" His eyes narrowed as he waited for Steve's reply. "To be more exact, have you noticed a weakening of their magic?"

"No." Steve's breathing slowed as he thought back over the last few weeks. Yes, said the voice in his mind.

"You have noticed it, haven't you?" said Xav, his smile returning.

"When the Council tried to measure Blessing's magic, their device wouldn't work properly until I moved away from it."

"And?" said Xav.

"When Jonah Ledwitch tried to bind Hartley's magic…" Steve shook his head. "That isn't right. I didn't do anything."

"Not consciously," said Xav. "But somewhere deep, you willed that to happen."

Steve sat down with an 'oh' and stared into space as Xav gestured to the frozen guard. The man immediately released a breath, turned on his heel, and returned to his post.

"Dad knew," said Steve.

"Elijah did, yes. And Mary."

"They didn't tell me."

"Hardly surprising," said Xav. "How do you explain to a teenage boy who isn't even aware of the existence of magic that he's, well, you?"

"Hartley would say something like 'carefully'," said Steve.

"Of course that buffoon old wizard would try to make a joke out of the situation. He has no sense of decorum. Just like Elijah."

"Where is Dad?"

"When I couldn't help him, he left. Rather rude, if you ask me."

"But where did he go?"

"How should I know? For a workaday, your father has a knack for making his thoughts difficult to read. All I got was 'the middle of nowhere'. Absolute nonsense of course."

The two of them sat in silence for what felt like an awkward moment to Steve. He didn't know what to say. And not because he had nothing to say. That was the problem. He had far too many questions to ask.

"If I don't have magic," he finally said, "what do I have? What am I?"

"An exceptional question," said Xav. "But that's enough chatter for now. I'm exhausted with all this drama. Go back to your room, Steve. We'll talk about this tomorrow."

"But…" Steve wanted to protest but suddenly he didn't have the strength. The nervous energy that had surged through his body was gone. Without it, he simply felt empty.

"You'll have outbursts like this," said Xav. "Times when the binding will weaken because of stress or anger. I could remove the spell altogether, but you need to be prepared for that. We'll talk about it in the morning."

As one of the guards grabbed his arm and urged him to his feet, Steve dropped the pill that Vigila had given him back into his pocket. At this moment in time, defeating Xav Mallorick was the last thing on his mind.

Chapter Twenty-Three

Bodrn stood on the balcony. It was early. The absence that denoted the sky had changed from a deep blue to a delicate grey, then shades of lilac and apricot. She shivered in the morning chill, even though she had wrapped the quilt from her bed around her body.

In the room behind her, the mood was equally cold. When Steve finally returned after his time alone with Xav Mallorick, his mum and Hartley had been asleep. Bodrn was sure that Mallorick had forced this on them. She had seen how much Mary cared for Steve. The woman would never have slept without knowing he was safe.

Still, in Steve's eyes it must have looked as if neither adult was concerned about him. When Bodrn had asked if he was all right, he had simply shrugged and climbed into bed, turning his back on her. She saw his shoulders shake and assumed he was crying. Unsure of how to comfort him, she had gone to sleep.

This morning, the tension between Steve and the two adults was tangible. Steve sat on his bed, with his head lowered and his hands in his pockets. He'd hardly said a word since waking, other than to snap at the others.

By comparison, Mary hadn't stopped talking as she paced around the room, flinging her arms wide to strengthen her sentiments.

Hartley interjected from time to time, trying to draw Steve into the conversation in a jovial fashion, but the man's usual liveliness was gone. Overnight, his beard had turned completely white. His hair was a mixture of chestnut and grey. His cheeks appeared to have sunk in slightly too. Every so often, he would close his eyes and rub at his forehead as if to rid himself of a headache.

"I should have stopped your dad from going alone. If I'd known what he was planning…" Mary shook her head. "Elijah has always been impulsive. I told him so many times that he had to think of the family. He's a parent, he—"

"He was thinking of the family," said Steve. "He came here because of me."

"Is that what Xav said?" Mary stopped pacing, clasping and unclasping her hands. "That man's an expert manipulator. You shouldn't listen to him."

"You said he doesn't lie," said Steve.

"Yes, but he twists things." She put her hand on Steve's shoulder, but he pulled away from her. "Steve."

"None of this is your mother's fault," said Hartley. "Whatever Elijah's reason for coming here was—"

"It was me!" said Steve. "He wanted Xav Mallorick to fix me."

"Fix you?" Mary looked at Hartley, who simply shrugged, and then back at Steve. "You don't need fixing."

"Don't lie. Xav told me that you know all about it."

"I honestly have no idea what…" She stopped, eyes widening. "He told you about Rex. Oh." She sank down onto one of the beds.

"What about Rex?" said Hartley.

"Steve, I didn't want you to find out like this. I told your father that we should sit you down and explain the whole story. It just never seemed to be the right time."

"Because you were always away travelling," said Steve.

"No," she said. "Well, yes. That did get in the way. But what age is the right age to tell a child that…" She stopped, pressing her lips together. "That they're—"

"A monster," said Steve.

"A what?" Mary's eyes widened. "What are you talking about?"

"That's what Xav Mallorick called me. And dangerous," said Steve. "Dad came here to ask him to bind my powers, again."

"Powers?" she said. "But you don't have magical powers. You're a workaday like me."

"Stop lying!" The words started as a shout but ended in tears as Steve's face crumpled. "You're lying," he sobbed.

Bodrn was quicker than Mary. She darted to his side and wrapped her arms around the weeping teenager before his mother had a chance to react.

"Steve?" said Mary as he buried his face in the darkling's shoulder. "I don't understand what that man told you. I…" She hesitated, reaching for him and then pulling back her hand. "There's something I need to tell you. Something else. But I don't know how to begin."

Bodrn felt Steve's sobbing stop. He pushed her away and turned his tear-streaked face to his mum. "What?" he croaked.

"I thought Xav Mallorick had told you…" She paused again and then her words came out in a hurry as if they frightened her. "Steve, you're adopted."

*

Adopted. The word hit Steve like a physical blow. The news about his powers had shocked and upset him, but this was different. He felt the air leave his lungs as if he'd been punched. He wanted to react, but all he could do was stare at his mother, or the woman he had always thought was his mother.

"Steve?" His mum stood up and stepped a little closer. "Say something."

He blinked and coughed to clear his throat. "No." He shook his head. "No, that can't be true."

"I'm sorry we didn't tell you." Mary reached for his hand, but he flinched away from her.

"Who am I?" he whispered. "If you're not my mum, who is?"

"I am your mum, Steve," she said. "Maybe not by blood, but

in every way that matters. I love you just as much as—"

"As what?" he snapped. "As much as if you'd had a child of your own?"

"Steve, please."

"Did you know?" he snapped at Hartley. "You've known them all these years and didn't tell me." He said the word 'them' as if it was an insult. "Did you know I was adopted too?"

"No, my boy, no," said Hartley. "I had no idea. Please believe me, but as your mother says—"

"She's not my mother!" Steve could feel his face reddening as he spat out the words. His hands buzzed with energy and his head hurt. "She's someone else," he said more quietly.

"Steve, you must calm down," said Bodrn. "Mary is trying to explain. This is difficult for her."

"For her?" said Steve.

"For both of you," she said. "Please listen to her."

"But…" He shook his head. "I'm too angry to listen."

"Try," said Bodrn. "This is family."

"We're not family. Not now."

"Family is more than blood connections," she said. "Look at us. A magical, a darkling, and you. Blessing too. I see you all as my family."

"I suppose," he said with a reluctant shrug. He looked at Mary for the briefest of moments. "Okay. Go on."

"I wanted us to tell you together," said Mary. "So we could say that we loved you, that in our hearts you were as much our boy as if…" She stopped, swallowing back her emotion. "Rex brought you to us when you were a baby. He said that you needed a loving home because your parents couldn't keep you. They wanted something better for you. And he told us your name."

"What else did he tell you?" said Steve.

"Nothing until much later, and then only to your dad. Whatever it was, I think that's why he and Rex fell out."

"Dad must have known, or he wouldn't have come looking

for Xav."

"Steve, what did Xav tell you?" said Hartley. "What exactly are these powers?"

"He said that Rex brought me to him when I was a baby to bind my powers. Not magical powers. Something else."

"And your father wanted Xav to bind your powers again?"

"Yes." Steve nodded, rubbing the tears from his face. "The binding isn't working any more. That's what he said anyway."

"But that doesn't make sense," said Mary. "What powers are there apart from magic?"

"Teenage years," said Hartley. "All those raging new hormones. It would be the perfect scenario to weaken a binding spell."

"It doesn't feel perfect," said Steve. He looked at his hands as if seeing them for the first time. He wondered what they were capable of.

"I had no idea," said Mary. "I'm so sorry. For all of this."

"Can Mallorick bind powers?" asked Bodrn. "Is that possible?"

"In theory," said Hartley. "It would have to be different to his usual mind slaying techniques. Knowing his inability to control the minds of youngsters, it would be more of an enchantment."

"When I first saw Steve, his aura was wrong." Bodrn shook her head. "Not wrong. Empty. There were no colours, just a hard line around his shape."

"That's it," said Hartley. "Xav placed an enchantment on Steve's aura, blocking it off from the world, and the magic, around him. That would work."

"Steve, what did Vigila tell you to do?" said Mary. "No, don't tell me. Mallorick might be listening. Whatever it is, Steve, do it. I don't like that woman, but she's a lesser evil at the moment."

"I agree," said Hartley. "Let's fight one battle at a time."

"Good idea," said Mary.

"Oh, I'm full of those," he said with a grin. "Now, next steps—"

A heavy knock at the door ended their conversation. Bodrn

raised her fists.

"No need for that," said Hartley as the door opened and one of the guards stepped inside. "Is it breakfast time, my dear fellow?" Hartley held a hand to his paunch. "Maybe you heard my rumbling stomach out in the hallway."

The guard beckoned with one hand, his gun outheld in the other. He backed out of the room, keeping his eyes on Bodrn and Mary the whole time.

"Onwards," said Hartley, although in a quieter voice than usual. "Let's see what the day has in store for us, shall we?"

*

Hartley picked crumbs from his beard as the gondola he sat in moved along the Grand Canal. Breakfast had been a luxurious spread that the elderly shopkeeper had taken full advantage of.

Bodrn rubbed at a growing point of pain above her right eyebrow. She and Mary rode in the same gondola as Hartley, accompanied by the gondolier who propelled the boat and two armed Parity agents.

In the gondola ahead, she could see Steve's discomfort at being separated from them. He nodded in response to Xav's incessant speech but would look back at the other gondola every few minutes.

"Headache?" said Mary.

"Yes," said Bodrn. "Is this normal for a human?"

"Sometimes," said Mary. "Has this never happened to you before?"

"No." Bodrn squeezed her eyes shut against the glare of the morning light. "It feels as if something is drilling into my brain."

"Or someone?" said Hartley with a raised, messy eyebrow. "What do you think, Mary?"

"That's how it started with me," said Mary with a nod. "Headaches. Then drowsiness. Blurred vision."

"What are you talking about?" said Bodrn, opening her eyes

just a little.

"Xav is doing his best to access your mind," said Hartley. "You must be stronger than most people for it to take this long."

"I am not people," she said. "I am a darkling."

"Not right now," said Hartley. "Until you can recover the power to change into a shadow, you are just as human as the rest of us."

"You don't have to rub it in, Hartley," said Mary. "I'm sure she's perfectly aware of her situation."

"Apologies, Bodrn." Hartley sighed, knitting his eyebrows into a miserable frown. "Our predicament has me at a loss. I feel redundant without my magic."

"Welcome to my world," said Mary.

Bodrn shook her head in an attempt to get rid of the pain, clicking her neck and blinking her eyes wide open.

"Good girl," said Mary. "Don't let that horrid man beat you."

"You know," said Hartley, looking from one side of the canal to the other. "I've seen plenty of adults since we arrived, but I haven't seen any children. Not even a teenager."

"I noticed that too," said Mary. "Maybe their parents are keeping them indoors. Or Xav doesn't like children."

"Or he cannot control them," said Bodrn. "That is what the head of Parity told us."

"Steve's one advantage over us grown-ups," said Hartley. "Even you, Bodrn."

The journey along the Grand Canal continued in silence. The darkling resisted the temptation to rub at the pain in her forehead. Instead, she tried to distract herself by taking in the city.

This was a reverse route of their journey with Ruslo, but a more leisurely one. The response of the Venetian people was different this time. On their way to the hotel, they had passed with little reaction from the city's inhabitants. Travelling with Xav Mallorick in the gondola ahead of them, the people they encountered reacted in one of two ways. Most people quickly vacated the canal-side, moving indoors or retreating down alleyways. Only a handful remained, staring blankly at the passing gondolas, their lips drawn into a strange, tense smile.

"How does Mallorick control a whole city?" said Bodrn. "There must be hundreds of people in Venice."

"Thousands, more like," said Hartley. "Quite a trick, isn't it?"

"Trick?" said Mary. "That's a bit of an understatement."

"Maybe 'trick' is the wrong word to use," he said. "But Xav isn't all-seeing. He's powerful, yes, but he relies on the cumulative effect of his presence. How do I explain this?" He patted his pockets, gave up, and then looked around. "Let me put it like this. Without wanting to make him sound any more grandiose than he already believes himself to be, Xav Mallorick is like the Grand Canal."

"Wet and smelly?" said Mary.

"Very funny," said Hartley. "But you're spoiling my metaphor."

"Sorry."

"Xav likes to give the impression of power and glamour. But just as the effectiveness of the Grand Canal is reliant on the smaller waterways that feed into it, so is Xav's control over people's minds reliant on small actions and suggestions. He is like a silent gondolier travelling along those narrow, unnoticed canals to reach deeper into the minds of his victims."

"That just sounds creepy," said Mary.

"Granted," said Hartley. "But effective. And the longer he's in your proximity, the greater his influence becomes. Hence his ability to control the Parity agents and Venetian citizens even when he's asleep."

He pressed a hand to his mouth as he coughed, his face growing red and his eyes watery. When the coughing stopped and he dropped his hand, a few strands of his beard dropped to his lap.

"The bangles are really taking it out of you, aren't they?" said Mary.

"Yes," he wheezed. "I doubt Jonah Ledwitch had any idea

how much the hampering would affect me."

"You are aging," said Bodrn.

"And you have a knack for stating the obvious, my dear," he said.

"Sorry."

"It isn't just that I can't perform magic, or that the bangles are draining that precious commodity out of me. They've also put a stop to a spell that was cast on me so that I could safeguard Blessing, an age-lengthening spell. Without its effect, I'm slowly reverting to the age I should be."

"Not so slowly," said Mary.

"I think we have Xav's influence on me to blame for that," he said. "His magic most likely triggered the bangles to drain me at a speedier rate."

"We will fix this," said Bodrn.

"Of course we will. There's no doubt in my mind, none at all." He nodded and smiled, but it was a pale imitation of his usual enthusiasm.

Chapter Twenty-Four

On their journey into Venice, Steve had only been able to view the sights of the city from a distance. As he left the gondola at the city waterfront, hurried by Xav Mallorick's insistence, he had a chance to see the city up close.

The building that Xav had announced as the Doge's Palace was beyond impressive with its ornate archways, pale carved columns, and alternating white and red brickwork. Steve could have stood there for hours, or at least minutes longer than Xav allowed him.

"This way." Xav rushed ahead as one of the guards pushed Steve after him.

"What about the others?" Steve resisted the guard's shove, turning around to face the man. At the waterfront, he could see his mum and friends leaving another gondola and stepping onto one of the jetties.

"They'll catch up." The guard shoved Steve again, spinning him around to face the open doorway that Xav had disappeared into.

Steve wanted to dig his heels in and insist that he wait, but he had to admit that he was curious to see inside the palace. He took one last look at the others and then allowed the guard to steer him into the doorway.

He expected to enter a grand room with high ceilings, its walls decked with classical paintings, and the space populated by statues. Instead, he found himself in a long, open courtyard. Rows of white stone archways ran along each length of the courtyard to his right and his left, with more archways or windows above.

Within the paved space, two ornate bronze bowls sat on stepped, stone pedestals. There were more archways, statues, a clock, and a grand staircase at the other end of the courtyard. Beyond all of that were a cluster of towering domed roofs, topped with intricate crosses.

Normally, he would have been in awe of the courtyard itself, but what really grabbed his attention was something else altogether. In the centre of the space, a towering column of light surged skywards from a base of rough stone that looked out of place in the elegant courtyard. The air hummed with a deep, deep note that Steve could feel in his chest.

"Quite monstrous, isn't it?" Xav stood a few feet away from the column of light, almost in the shadow of one of the archways.

"I think it's beautiful," said Steve, stepping closer to it.

"Steve, here you are."

He turned to see the others enter the courtyard. Mary was intent on Steve, but Hartley and Bodrn stared at the column of light as they followed her.

"Are you all right?" She took his hand. "Did he hurt you?"

"I have no reason to harm the boy," said Xav. "He's going to help me. Aren't you, Steve?"

"Am I?" said Steve, letting go of her hand. "I'm fine." He almost said 'Mum' but stopped himself. The morning's revelation still felt too raw.

"Sorry." She took a step back but kept her eyes on his face.

"What is that?" said Bodrn.

"If I'm not mistaken," said Hartley, "this is the power source we saw on the map in the library."

"Well done." Xav clapped his hands in mock applause. He moved closer but still kept his distance from the column of light. "This powers the illusion that conceals Venice. It also prevents me from leaving the city. That buzzing that you can hear is perfectly attuned to my essence. If I attempt to step outside the barrier…" He shook his head. "That's why I need you, Steve."

"The boy can't help with this." Hartley planted a hand on

Steve's shoulder. "If the Council created the spell—"

"I disagree," said Xav. "Steve is powerful. Much more powerful than any of you. That's why Rex and Elijah wanted me to bind him."

"I'm sure they had good reason," said Hartley. "Don't listen to him, Steve."

"They're afraid of you, you know?" said Xav. "All of them. But Steve, you're better than that. I say you should embrace who you are. Help me. Set me free, and then you and your friends can leave."

"Don't listen to him," said Mary. "He's lying to you."

"Like you lied, Mary?" said Xav. "When you didn't tell Steve that he was adopted? When you didn't tell him about his powers?"

"That's not the same," she said. "I just wanted him to have a normal life. I wanted to be a good mum. I didn't know about any powers. Honestly, Steve, I didn't."

"What would you do, Xav?" Hartley stepped closer to the mind flayer, the darkling at his shoulder. "If you left Venice. What have you got planned?"

"You know the answer to that," said Xav. "The world deserves to know about the existence of magic. And we deserve the chance to live freely and without constraint."

"You haven't changed," said Hartley. "This is all about your ego and nothing to do with anyone else's rights or freedoms. I may not agree with the Council on most grounds, but the sudden revelation of magic to the world would be like putting a flame to a powder keg."

"And what would you suggest? Sit down and have a nice chat with the workadays? Have a cup of tea and oh, by the way, magic exists!"

"It needs to be handled with care."

"By who? You? The Council? Despite all you've seen and gone through, Hartley, you're still a naive do-gooder."

"Naïve?" Hartley snarled the word. "I'm being realistic.

What happened when your own community was revealed to the locals—the riots, the violence—is testament to the fact that the public aren't ready to know about magic yet."

"The Council overreacted." Xav dismissed Hartley's concerns with a flap of his hand. "There was no need to isolate Wynhelm and seal it off like that. The locals could have been reasoned with. And as for Parity—"

"Parity cleaned up your mess," snapped Hartley. "And you should be glad they did."

"Mass hysteria caused by a chemical leak." Xav tutted and rolled his eyes. "How pedestrian."

"People died, Xav. On both sides. Imagine that tenfold, a hundredfold. And this time there would be no chance to convince the world that it was simply a misunderstanding." Hartley shook his head and released a long sigh. "The world has changed while you've been shut away in Venice. Governments are more technologically advanced than ever. They'd scramble to control and weaponise magic. Big business would find ways to exploit us for profit. Our entire culture, our way of life, would be under threat."

"Maybe it should be," said Xav. "That would grab the Council's attention and shine a very bright light on their shortcomings. It's time for Blaike Harn and her cronies to hand back our freedoms."

"What you're proposing isn't freedom. It's chaos."

"In your opinion," said Xav. "As usual, we disagree. Be silent now."

As Hartley's lips clamped shut and he staggered to his knees, Bodrn dashed towards Xav, her hands clamped into fists. The mind flayer dodged away, clicking his fingers at two of the Parity guards. As they charged towards her, she dropped to the ground, sweeping her leg in a motion that toppled both men off their feet.

"Stop her!" Xav called to the other two guards in the courtyard as he backed away from the advancing darkling.

Mary bashed into one of the guards, hardly affecting his momentum, but distracting the man enough to stop him in his tracks.

The toppled guards had recovered themselves. Joining the third guard, they circled Bodrn, fending off her punches and kicks.

Hartley reached into his jacket pocket, pulling out the hockey stick that Steve had seen him use before. Digging it into the paved floor, Hartley pushed himself to his feet.

Mary struggled with the fourth guard, pulling on his arm as he tried to prise himself from her grip.

Steve watched, torn between helping his friends and his eagerness to learn about his new powers. The hum created by the column of light still vibrated in his chest but now it was accompanied by a rising surge of energy in his stomach.

"Stop it," he said in a voice too quiet to be heard above the fight.

They're not listening to me, he thought. *Why do adults never listen?*

The sensation in his chest and the energy in his stomach had merged into one. His limbs felt heavy. His head hurt. He couldn't feel the ground beneath his feet. This time, the voice he used came from deep inside and yet detached from the Steve he had always thought he was.

"Stop this now!"

His words had the effect of a gale force wind. Each person in the courtyard staggered to their knees, pressing their hands to their ears. Xav clung to one of the archways. For the first time since Steve had met him, the man looked utterly helpless.

The guards were the first to recover, jumping to their feet and drawing truncheons from their belts. Without a word, they advanced on Steve.

He tried to find that voice again. "Stop," he said, but the guards didn't listen. "Stop!" He held out his hands in an attempt to muster up the power he'd felt before.

The guards were within an arm's length, close enough to grab his outstretched hands. Steve stumbled backwards as one snatched at him.

"No!"

Steve thought he'd shouted the word himself, until he heard it again.

"No!" Xav held out both splayed hands as he repeated his command. "Get away from the boy."

The guards froze in place and then, moving like stiff-limbed dolls, they backed away.

"It's all right, Steve." Xav's voice was full of concern now. "This was always going to happen." He crept closer, his open hands raised. "But I can help you control your powers. I promise."

"For a price." Hartley helped Mary to her feet. "Steve, don't listen to him. This is a trap."

Steve knew that Hartley was telling the truth. He knew that his mum loved him, even if she wasn't his birth mother. And he knew that he couldn't trust Xav Mallorick. The mind flayer's motives for helping Steve were too self-serving. But these new powers—whatever they were—terrified him. He didn't want to hurt anyone. There was only one voice he felt he could rely on in that moment.

"Bodrn, what do I do?"

Xav threw his hands in the air and then planted them on his hips. Mary sighed and gave a nod.

"I think," Bodrn said as she went to Steve's side, "that we need to know what choices you have."

"That is an excellent idea," said Hartley. "I heartily agree."

"There are no choices," said Xav.

"There are always choices," she said. "However ill-advised they may be."

"Fine," said Xav. "One." He began to count on his fingers. "Steve does nothing, loses control, and causes all kind of catastrophes."

"What else?" said Steve.

"Two." Xav tapped a second finger. "I try to bind his powers again."

"Would that work?" said Mary.

"Unlikely," said Xav. "Failure would have the same consequences as option one. Three—"

"I know what this is going to be," said Hartley.

"What we've just witnessed is the destruction of the binding spell. But I can show Steve what he's capable of. I reached into his mind when he was a baby. I saw what skills he would develop in time. None of you can say the same. Steve, I'm the only person here who can train you to control your powers."

"I don't want to hurt anyone," said Steve. "I don't want to cause catastrophes. And I'm not sure that I want these powers."

"Two out of three will have to suffice," said Xav. "Your powers are as much a part of you as the colour of your eyes or your ability at sport. They cannot be denied."

Steve watched the others. Hartley's eyes moved from Steve to Xav and back again. Mary looked as if she wanted to run to Steve and make the decision for him. Xav tapped his foot on the ground. Only Bodrn appeared to be calm.

"Okay," said Steve. "You can show me how to control whatever this is."

"And you'll help me escape," said Xav. "Help all of us," he added.

"Steve, are you sure?" Mary crossed the space to stand in front of him. Her face had been bruised in the struggle with the guard.

"I'm as sure as I can be," he told her. "I've never had powers before. So, yeah." He let her brush the hair off his face and then he said, "So when do we start?"

"Right now." Xav rubbed his hands together enthusiastically. "I've some people for you to meet. Bring them and follow me," he told the guards. "Quickly now, before anyone changes their mind."

Chapter Twenty-Five

At the far end of the courtyard, an ornate, white stone wall reached part of the way across the space. A clock guarded by two classical statues sat atop an upper floor walkway. Below this, three archways led into darkness. Xav Mallorick, happily humming to himself, walked through the central arch and disappeared from view. Steve didn't have a chance to look back at his friends before he and they were pushed through the archway.

He blinked as the daylight of the courtyard was replaced by a stark, cold light. The entire interior of the space that he found himself in was constructed of a dull, grey metal that refused to come into focus. The cold light glared from the walls, ceiling, and floor of a long, wide corridor. It was lined on one side by a series of blank, metal doors and ceiling-to-floor glass windows.

"Where are we?" he asked as the guard pushed him onwards.

"The prison facility created by the Council," said Xav. "Holding cells for newly-arrived prisoners."

"In the Doge's Palace?" said Hartley. "How did they fit all of this in here?"

"Obviously, they didn't," said Xav. "It's a protected area. A pocket universe attached to the city," he told Steve. "As if the barrier illusion wasn't sufficient." He tutted.

Beyond each window, Steve could see a barely-furnished room, with beds, tables and chairs, and a door at the far side. Within each room, three or four children or teenagers watched Steve and the adults as they passed by.

"Why are these children here?" Steve heard his mum's voice behind him. "Is this the Council's doing?"

"They wouldn't," said Hartley. "They may make some ridiculous decisions, but this isn't one of them. I take it this was your prison, Xav."

"Why do you continue to support those pompous fools?" said Xav. "After all the trouble and heartache the Council has caused. Look at you." Xav turned on his heel and pointed at Hartley. "They've bound you. Before that they chased you, imprisoned you, and so often took away the people that you care for. What more must the Council do before you realise that they must be stopped?" He lowered his hand with a grunt. "And yes, this was my prison, when I first came to Venice. Now, it serves my purposes."

"You did this?" said Mary. "Why imprison these kids? They couldn't hurt you."

"They get in the way," said Xav. "Like noisy, stinking vermin."

"You can't get into their heads," said Hartley. "That's the real reason they're here, isn't it? You can't be sure that they won't spoil your plans. Even with the adults controlled, these young minds still pose a threat, however minimal. So you lock them away for your own peace of mind."

"You're a monster," said Mary.

"I'm realistic," said Xav, turning his back on them all to set off again. "The children are well fed, clothed. They lack for nothing."

"Except freedom," said Bodrn as Xav turned on his heel and continued down the corridor.

She snatched her arm away as one of the guards grabbed her. Hartley shook his head and placed a hand on her shoulder. He gestured to Mary and the three of them followed the mind flayer. Steve trailed behind a little, watching the children, who in return watched him back as he passed by.

"Here we are," said Xav as the corridor opened out into a wider, circular space.

On the far side of the room were three of the blank doors that Steve had seen in the corridor and a tall wide archway. Above each of the doors was a wall-mounted screen. At the side of each door hovered an orb but unlike the light orbs that Steve had seen his friends create, these orbs were grey and metallic and constantly shifting.

"Time for a little practice, I think." Xav thrust his hand into the orb that hovered beside the middle door. Immediately, the screen above it blinked into life and Steve could see the room beyond. The door opened inwards, just enough to reveal a strip of light and movement within but no more. "In you go, Steve," said Xav.

"I'll be right behind you," said Hartley.

"Just Steve," said Xav. "This is his lesson, not yours."

"Leave him alone." Steve heard his mum's footsteps as she ran to his side, only to be grabbed by one of the guards. "Don't you hurt him. Don't you dare. I'll…"

"Contain yourself, Mary." At Xav's words, her lips clamped shut but she continued to struggle in the grasp of the guard. "Let me make myself clear. If Steve can't help me escape Venice, then I really have no reason to keep any of you alive. It was fun having Mary here for a while, but I'm tired of her rebellion. Hartley, you're only of use to me as a hostage because of the boy's attachment to you. Other than that, I have so many reasons to wish you dead. The darkling may be a fascination for a while. I've never had the chance to examine the inner workings of a fae mind before, but I grow bored very quickly."

Steve looked at his companions. His mum had given up struggling but she glared at Xav and looked ready to pounce. Bodrn was obviously assessing how easy it would be to disarm the guards, her eyes flicking between them and her hands drawn into fists. Only Hartley looked back at him, miserably, helplessly.

"I'll do it," said Steve.

His mum mumbled through her closed lips, pulling towards him as much as she could in the guard's grasp. Steve wanted to tell her that it was all right, that there was no need to struggle, but he knew his words would never convince her. Instead, he turned away and walked to the open door.

*

The ceiling, walls and floor of the room were lined with a white, padded material. The only break in the fabric was the door that Steve had entered through. In the centre of the room was a glass case. It was the kind of container that Steve had seen in museums to house exhibits that weren't to be touched. Inside this one, however, something was alive.

The fire imp looked very like the one that Steve had encountered in Hartley's shop. Its orange fur seethed like hot coals in a fire. The occasional spark pinged off the creature's body, to hit the cold glass with a sputter. The fire imp crouched in the centre of the case, arms wrapped around its body. It peered over its knees at him.

On the floor next to the case was a doll. It looked very old, its porcelain face dulled and faded by age. Its hair was all but gone. The clothes it wore were obvious replacements because they hung loose on its body. The eyes of the doll looked out of place too. Steve assumed that a doll of this age would have glass eyes, but these looked almost human.

Curled into a corner of the room, a child whimpered. Maybe four or five years old, the dark-haired girl wore an over-sized sweater and a pair of patched-up leggings. Her feet were bare.

"It's okay." He took a step towards her. "I'm Steve."

"Can you hear me?" Xav's voice sounded crackly and seemed to come from every surface in the room.

The child hid her face in her hands with a sob and a yelp. She pushed herself further into the corner. The fire imp simply turned his back, muttering 'stupid' and 'useless' and other words that Steve couldn't make out.

"Yes, I can hear you," said Steve. "Why is there a child in here?"

"To help you hone your powers."

"I'm not hurting anyone."

206

"Of course not," said Xav. "This is simply a test of your focus. It shouldn't hurt them at all."

"What do I do?" said Steve.

"Think back to when you used your powers in the past," said Xav. "How did you feel?"

"I didn't use them," said Steve. "It just happened."

"But how did you feel?"

Steve thought about when the Council had tested Blessing's magic, and more recently to Jonah Ledwitch's binding of Hartley's travelling skills. "Protective," he said.

"And?" said Xav. "Anything else?"

Go on, said the voice in his head. *Tell him how you really felt.*

"Angry," said Steve. "I felt angry."

"Good. Now I want you to take those feelings and use them."

"How?"

"In exactly the same way as you used them before. Concentrate, Steve. Find those emotions. Own them."

Steve had no idea what 'own them' meant. He thought back to when he'd stood at Blessing's side in the Council chambers. He had felt protective of his friend, and angry at the Council members. But had there been anything else?

He closed his eyes to better remember. There were those emotions, tugging at him to stay by his friend's side and make the Council stop hurting the people he cared about. He remembered how the light of the Omnometer had swelled as Blessing touched it, and the alarm in her face. He remembered how smug Jonah Ledwitch had looked, and the panic in Hartley's eyes.

Finally, he remembered the surge of energy that had started in his stomach. Maybe 'surge' was the wrong word. It was more of a tension, the kind of tension you feel in your muscles when holding them in place. Whatever it was, surge or tension, it had radiated out to his chest, and then his shoulders, reaching as far as the top of his head. He opened his eyes, unsure whether he was actually feeling that tension now or just remembering.

The child had crawled out of the corner to watch him, but

she scooted back across the floor as Steve looked at her.

"Xav!" he called out. "I need to know what my powers will do to the child and the imp and the doll."

As the microphone turned on, Steve could hear Hartley and his mum's voices arguing with the mind flayer.

"Don't do it!" That was his mum.

"Let the boy go. He doesn't know how to control—" Hartley's demand was cut short as the microphone was switched off. It seemed like a long moment before Steve heard Xav's voice again.

"Sorry about that interruption. Now, where were we?"

"I won't hurt the child or the imp," said Steve.

"Of course not," said Xav. "Your power doesn't injure. It simply removes magic."

"Imp am magic." The fire imp pressed itself against the glass, blinking at Steve. "No remove imp. Imp be good, promise."

The child had curled up in the corner again, weeping uncontrollably with her arms wrapped around her head.

"What about the doll?" said Steve.

"Interesting choice," said Xav. "The doll is cursed or possessed. Nobody really knows. I would be intrigued to see what effect your powers have on it. Go ahead. Try it out."

Cursed or possessed, thought Steve. *Not at all scary.*

"Do you know anything about the doll?" he asked the imp.

"Nasty vibes." The fire imp had settled down into a crouch again. "It's the eyes. Follow, follow. Where-ev's you go."

"Bad doll," said the child. Her sobs had settled into sniffs. "Scary."

Okay, he thought. *So what's the harm in removing the magic from a nasty, bad, scary doll that may be cursed or possessed? That has to be a good thing, hasn't it?*

He closed his eyes to check that the tension was still there. It was, and he was definitely feeling protective of his own life at that moment. Two out of three would have to do.

When he opened his eyes, both the child and the fire imp were watching him. The child wiped her dripping nose on her sleeve, while the imp scratched at its furry top knot.

"Right," said Steve with a nod. "Right," he said again as he sat down in front of the doll. *How bad can this be?* he thought. *It's not alive. It's just a doll.*

He nudged it with a finger. The fire imp drew in its breath and shook its head, but the doll didn't do anything. Steve picked up the doll. Beyond its state of disrepair, it didn't look scary or nasty, just in need of some care. Steve brought it closer to his face.

That's when the eyes moved. And now he was close up, he could definitely see that they were human eyes, filled with hatred and madness.

The porcelain brow of the doll impossibly wrinkled into a frown and the painted mouth snarled. Steve threw the doll onto the floor and pushed himself away from it, sliding back on his bottom across the padded floor.

"Told you," said the imp. "Nasty."

"Fascinating," came Xav's voice. "Although of course, you don't have to touch the doll to affect it. Best keep your distance."

"Right," said Steve as the fire imp sniggered. *Don't touch it. Keep your distance. Use your powers,* he thought. *He makes it sound so easy.*

Steve climbed to his feet, took a deep breath, and closed his eyes. That tension was still pulling at his stomach and his chest. He breathed out, testing whether the feeling would melt away. When it didn't, he opened his eyes.

He looked at the child and the imp. His instinct was to protect the child, maybe the imp too, rescue them, and get them out of there. Burning beneath this emotion was a growing anger at their captor.

Without knowing why, Steve raised his hands and reached towards the doll. It was as if his body knew exactly what to do, had always known, and he was simply watching. He wasn't sure what he expected using his new-found powers to feel like. If he was taking away the magic in the doll, did that mean he would absorb it into himself? Would he be filled with whatever haunted the doll? Would he still be himself? Would he…?

The doll flipped itself onto its knees, its face contorting into an expression of rage. It clicked its neck to one side and then it began to crawl towards him, all the time growling and muttering.

"You've angered it," said Xav. "Best act quickly."

"Not good," said the fire imp with a *tut-tut-tut*.

Steve wanted to run away, even though he was locked in the room and had nowhere to run to. Instead, he found himself rooted to the spot, hands outheld, intent on the monstrosity scrabbling towards him. *Too close, too close*, he panicked in his mind. But his body remained calm, and his heartbeat and breathing steady.

With a final snarl, the doll launched itself from the padded floor.

Steve wanted to close his eyes as the doll flew through the short distance of air between them. He wanted to jump out of the way. He wanted to shout to Xav to open the door and let him out. None of those things happened.

As the doll came within reach of him, the tension in his chest took on a different quality. It felt cold, and solid, as if he was suddenly encased in metal which was chill against his skin. He felt his chest inhale, the breath expanding his diaphragm, and then with a rumbling note that began deep in his throat, he released the breath like a war cry.

The snarl fell from the doll's face. With a final gasp, it collided with Steve's chest. He heard the porcelain face shatter, and then the doll fell to the floor.

All at once the tension and the imagined armour disappeared. Steve lurched away from the doll at his feet, falling back onto the padded wall.

"Bravo! Bravo!" came Xav's voice.

The fire imp let out a low whistle and gave Steve a double thumbs up with a guttural snigger.

"How did you do that?" The child crawled out of the corner.

"Are you a serf?"

"I don't know what that is." Now that he had control over his body again, Steve felt sick. He clamped a hand over his mouth and ran to the door, hammering on it with his free hand.

When the door opened and he rushed out to hopefully not vomit, the first voice he heard was his mum's. She tried to reach him but was pulled back by a guard who held a knife to her rib cage.

"Are you all right, Steve?"

"No," he said. "I think I'm going to be…"

"An understandable reaction," said Xav as Steve' stomach contents spilled out onto the floor. "Don't worry about the mess."

"I wasn't." Steve stayed bent over, just in case his stomach wasn't empty. "That doll. It almost killed me."

"I knew your powers would kick in. You were perfectly safe."

"Perfectly safe?" Mary struggled with the guard again.

"Hush and stand still," said Xav.

Immediately, her lips clamped shut and she froze in place. Only her eyes moved.

When Steve straightened up, carefully, he saw that Mary wasn't the only one pinned by a guard. Another held a knife to Hartley's throat. Bodrn stood apart from her friends, arms loose at her sides. Her jaw was bruised and cut, as if she'd been punched. Her eyes told the full story of how she felt—angry and trapped—but her lips were lifted into a disconcerting smile. A third guard watched her with his gun lowered.

"Just a little safeguarding," said Xav as he watched Steve. "In case you decided to turn your new-found skills on me. My hold over the Parity operatives is entrenched. Should you incapacitate me, they'll continue to act on my orders for the time being."

"What are you going to do with the child?" Steve could feel his powers responding to Xav's threat, but he pushed them down and clenched his fists. "And the fire imp?"

"The child can go back to her cell," said Xav. "And I'm sure I can find some use for the imp. Nothing for you to worry about."

But Steve was worried: about his friends, about all of the imprisoned children, and about exactly what Xav Mallorick had in mind for them all. "What now?" he asked.

"Now?" said Xav with a smug grin. "Personally, I'm exhausted. Why don't we return to the hotel for a spot of lunch? Yes?"

Steve allowed himself to be steered out of the room by one of the guards. This wasn't the time for a fight; but soon, he promised himself and his seething powers, soon it would be.

Chapter Twenty-Six

"Damn that man." Hartley sat on one of the beds in their hotel room, a trembling hand clamped to the back of his skull. "I hate it when Xav drills down into my brain like that."

"At least you haven't been stuck with that man in your head for weeks." Mary pressed a damp flannel to Bodrn's jaw. "Is it feeling any better?"

"Yes, thank you." The darkling took the flannel from Mary. "It does not hurt as much now." Her face was bruised and cut, and her bottom lip was swollen.

"Isn't it enough that he can control our minds?" Hartley continued his rant. "Was it really necessary to set his guards on us too?"

"Xav is nothing if not thorough." Mary sat down beside him, tilted his bearded chin down to his chest, and examined the back of his skull and his neck. "There's no damage that I can see."

"There is in here." He rapped his knuckles on the side of his head. "I hoped that I'd seen the last of Xav Mallorick when the Hidden carted him off. I've always believed in giving people the benefit of the doubt, second chances and all that. But that man." He grunted. "There's no excuse."

Steve stood on the balcony, listening to the others and taking in the busy traffic of the Grand Canal. He hadn't said a word since the guards had locked the door of their hotel room. He still wore his jacket, his hands stuffed into the pockets. The memory of the cursed doll crawling towards him as it snarled and muttered kept pushing its way back into his mind's eye.

He tried to distract himself by listing what was stored in the magically-enhanced pocket of his jacket. Each item came to his touch as he named it in his mind.

"Are you all right?" Mary called across to him. "Steve?"

"I'm fine." He answered her but he didn't turn around. "Just thinking."

"About what?" she asked as she went to the open balcony doors. "Anything you can let us in on? Can I help?"

"Just stuff." He shrugged. He wanted to tell her, but he didn't know if Xav was listening in, through her or Hartley, or even Bodrn. "Nothing important."

"Well, if you need me." Mary sounded sad. "I'm always here." He heard her walk back across the room.

Steve thought back to the children imprisoned in the holding cells, how watchful their scared eyes had been, how desperate they'd looked, and how powerless he had felt as he could only walk past them. He wondered what had happened to the child in the padded room. He didn't even know her name.

"I have a question." The sudden words—so close to him on the balcony—made Steve jump. "Sorry." Bodrn retreated a little at his reaction. "I did not mean to startle you."

"What's your question?" he asked, trying to concentrate on her eyes and not the injuries on her face.

"Mary, Hartley, and I have all been affected by Mallorick's magic. He has read our thoughts and controlled us. What about you?"

"No." Steve shook his head. "His magic hasn't affected me."

"So Vigila was right," she said. "He can't control young minds, including the imprisoned children."

"Those poor kids," said Mary. "Their poor parents too."

"At the risk of sounding cruel," said Hartley. "That could be to our advantage."

"What? An army of children against a city of adult mind zombies?" said Mary.

"I've been thinking the same," said Steve. "What Hartley

said. Sorry."

He wanted to say more and put a plan together of how to rescue the children, but he couldn't be sure that Xav wasn't listening. So he kept the thought to himself and changed the subject.

"The child in the testing room asked me if I was a serf," he said.

"I have not heard that title in a very long time," said Bodrn.

"I did wonder," said Hartley. "I suspected when I saw what you could do."

"Suspected what?" said Steve. "What is a serf?"

"But it shouldn't be possible," said Hartley. "They'd never send one of their children out into the world alone."

"Unless they were not alone," said Bodrn. "Unless Rex took that child."

"For what reason?" said Hartley. "The serfs may be regimented, but they're not unkind. They can even be reasoned with, on occasion."

"But who are they?" said Steve. "Who am I?"

Before Hartley or Bodrn could answer, one of the guards opened the door and peered through at them. He seemed especially keen to locate Bodrn. He kept an eye on her as he spoke.

"Mr Mallorick says you've had long enough to rest. He asks that you clean yourselves up and meet him in the hotel foyer."

"Is that an order or a request?" said Mary, crossing her arms.

"It's, er, a party invite," said the guard.

He hovered on the threshold for a moment longer and then he pulled the door closed after him. There was no sound of a key turning in the lock.

"Well, if he expects us to dress up…" Mary rolled her eyes.

"Let's look at this as an opportunity," said Hartley, "to gather information and get the lay of the land."

"With Xav poking about in our minds?" said Mary.

"Nothing ventured, nothing grabbed by the bootstraps."

Hartley rubbed his hands together with a grin. "Do you think there'll be food at this party?"

"Do you ever stop thinking about your stomach, Hartley Keg?"

Steve watched his mum and his friend as they pulled on their shoes and coats. With their joking and banter, he could almost pretend that this was a normal family holiday. Almost.

"Ready?" said Hartley, planting a hand on his shoulder.

No, he thought. *Not even close.* "Yeah," he said. "I mean, it's only a party."

"And we're together," said Mary, joining them. "That's what counts."

*

"When the guard said 'party', I envisioned something a tad more intimate," said Hartley.

"Really?" said Mary. "With Xav Mallorick in charge?"

"Fair point," said Hartley.

An orb-lit evening walk through the streets of Venice should have been a pleasant experience. Instead, Steve and the others had been jostled along by the guards. At the head of their procession, Xav had been accompanied by a band of magicals who bore the grim smile that Steve had seen on so many faces in Venice. It was these magicals who created and controlled the light orbs that bobbed above the procession. All the doors they passed were closed and the windows shuttered or barred by heavy curtains. It seemed to take an eternity to reach their destination, the *Palazzo Mallorick*, renamed just as the hotel had been.

Candlelight and music spilled from the many arched windows of the tall, pale stone building. Masked entertainers juggled and performed acrobatics close to the entrance, accompanied by pipes and drums. The musicians danced as they played, twirling and swaying to the melody. If it hadn't been for the guards stationed at the doors, the palazzo would have been a welcoming sight.

As it was, Steve and the others were pushed into the imposing building without a word from the guards or Xav Mallorick.

"Well, at least we didn't have to dress up," said Hartley, his voice muffled behind the mask he wore.

The ballroom of the palazzo matched the grandness of its exterior. The walls and ceiling were painted with classical scenes. A series of ornate chandeliers that looked to be as tall as Steve hung from the ceiling, adding a warm illumination. Filling the largest part of the room, a sea of masked, dancing couples circled the space in time to the music which hung in the air with no trace of a source.

"I suppose I can cope with a mask and a cloak." Mary's mask only covered the top half of her face. She pulled the long, sapphire blue cloak around her like a cocoon.

"Now what?" said Steve. His mask felt scratchy on his skin and his cloak was too long, pooling around his feet.

"There you are."

Xav stepped out from the mass of dancing couples. He was dressed in a costume that reminded Steve of a fairytale prince, or maybe a villain pretending to be a fairytale prince. Xav wore a deep red frock coat trimmed with gold thread over an even more ornate waistcoat. Under that, his white shirt finished in a series of frills tied at Xav's throat. The man's thinning hair was hidden beneath a white, piled-up wig and his face was powdered pale. In his hand, he carried a mask painted in shades of gold.

"If you're expecting us to dance—" Mary began.

"I could make you," said Xav. "But maybe I won't. I'm feeling charitable tonight."

"Charitable?" blurted Mary.

"We must be thankful for small blessings." Hartley stepped between Mary and the mind flayer. Steve wondered whether his friend wanted to protect his mum or stop her from attacking Xav.

"Why are we here?" said Steve.

"To celebrate, of course!" With a smug grin, Xav slid on his mask and grabbed Bodrn's hand. "Dance with me."

Steve watched as the darkling's stance switched from retreat to obedience. There was no way of telling under her full-face, white mask, but he imagined her lips curling into an unnatural smile as Xav danced her away into the crowd.

*

Bodrn felt a moment of panic as her body refused to do what she wanted it to do. Under the control of the mind flayer, she found herself gracefully in step with her dancing partner. She deftly swirled her long cloak as she moved, avoiding the danger of tripping herself up or becoming entangled in the velvet lengths. She looked around for her friends, but the dancing couples blocked her view as they closed in around her.

"Quite the spectacle, isn't it? Venice does know how to celebrate." Xav danced on his tiptoes in an attempt to match Bodrn's height.

"What are you celebrating?" She was glad that her mask hid the discomfort she felt.

"My imminent departure, of course." He twirled her around before clasping an arm around her waist again.

"With Steve's help."

"The boy has been invaluable. An absolute gem. However, even gems are useless without a master artificer."

"And that is you?"

"Why, thank you." She imagined his smug smile under the mask.

"And all these people are here to applaud you?"

"They're here because I willed it. Some came through fear, but most are my marionettes. I control them."

"You make them dance."

"It's quite a feat, I know," he said. "But I wanted to test my limits before I face the outside world."

"That is impressive." She said the words before she realised

218

that Xav had impelled her to speak.

"I am," he said. "You know, you have a fascinating mind. I've never encountered a darkling that I could read before, let alone control. Even in this human form, your mindscape is completely different. I could explore it for days and not get bored."

She could feel his presence in her mind. It was an uncomfortable sensation, much like being forced to dance with a man she considered to be her enemy.

*

Only minutes after Xav Mallorick danced the darkling away, Steve noticed a change in Hartley's stance. It was as if someone had grabbed the shopkeeper by his tweed collar and pulled him upright. At the same time, Mary's lips lifted into that puppet-like smile that Steve was now familiar with. With a nod, Hartley placed an arm around Mary's waist and grabbed her hand. Then they had danced into the crowd, stiff-limbed and silent.

Steve stood alone at the edge of the room, his mask pushed up and arms crossed under the folds of his cloak. His mum and friends were nowhere to be seen. He felt like he should be doing something, but he had no idea what that something could be.

His cloak pulled back over his shoulder as a hand grabbed his upper arm and the cold edge of a blade touched the base of his neck.

"Quiet," a voice rasped in his ear. "Do not turn. Do not react."

"You've got the wrong person," said Steve as a second unseen assailant pulled his hands behind him and held them in place.

"I said 'quiet'. You come with us now. No trouble."

Steve tried to find his friends in the mass of dancers as he was pulled away. The knife nicked his skin as he turned his head to see who held the weapon.

"Do not look round," said the voice at his ear. "Keep your eyes front."

"Okay," said Steve as the knife was removed and he was pulled away from the crowds. "But I really think…"

As the door shut behind them, Steve was released and pushed further into the room beyond. It was a smaller, empty space with plain, plastered walls, illuminated by a single glass chandelier.

"Who are you?" Steve span around to find that he was alone. There was nobody else in the room so why did he feel as if he was being watched?

"Hey!" Hands clapped close to his right ear and another pair pulled at his clothes, making him stumble backwards. The lengths of his cloak tangled in his legs, and he began to fall.

"Stop it, Argi." Unseen hands grabbed Steve by the shoulders, setting him back on his feet. "Excuse my brother. He thinks he is funny."

"Who's there?" Steve called into the seemingly empty space.

There was a whistle to his left and a clap. "Over here, *pataca*."

As Steve turned, there was a glint in mid-air as if the light had found a floating diamond. First one, then four more figures appeared. The three boys were the eldest. They all looked older than Steve, but still teenagers. One girl was probably a few years younger than him, and the other could only have been around six years old. She was giggling and pointing at Steve. None of them looked as if they had washed in a while.

"What is so funny, Solana?" asked one of the boys.

"*Pataca*," the youngest girl giggled, still pointing at Steve.

"What?" said Steve.

"My brother Argi called you a potato. It's an insult for outsiders," said the tallest boy. "Solana, you should not point. It is rude."

"*Pataca*," said Steve.

"*Pataca!*" Solana erupted into another burst of giggles. "Funny."

"Stop laughing." Another of the boys held the knife that Steve had felt on his neck. He berated the girl in words that Steve didn't understand. "Not funny," he said finally.

Solana's bottom lip trembled as she wiped a tear from her eye. The other girl put an arm around her and pushed the boy away.

"I'm Steve," said Steve.

"We know who you are," said the boy with the knife.

"Faro, calm," said the tallest boy. "Sorry," he told Steve. "We do not talk to many outsiders." The other boys nodded. "The mind flayer sits in their heads."

The boy with the knife muttered something to him.

"Not sits. He gets into their heads. That is better, yes?"

"Yes," said Steve.

"I am Lucian," said the tallest boy. "These are my brothers and sisters. Faro," he pointed to the boy with the knife. "Argi." The third boy nodded to Steve. "And my sisters are Chiara and Solana."

"What are you?" said Steve. "Your magic, I mean.'

"We are luminants," said Lucian. "Our magic is tied to light."

"And you can go invisible?"

"We can…" Lucian brought his hands together as if he was holding and turning a ball. "We can shape the light to hide us. Hide other things also."

"So could you hide other people?" said Steve.

"Of course," said Lucian as if hiding someone with magic was the most natural and easy thing to do. "But we must ask for your help. The mind flayer has our friends."

"Xav Mallorick has my friends too," said Steve. "He controls them. I don't know how much I can help you."

"You have to," said Argi. "You are a serf. Serfs always help."

"I'm not a serf," said Steve. "I don't even know what that is. I'm just me."

"I saw you. In the palace," said Faro, pointing at Steve with his knife. "Why do you refuse us?"

"The mind flayer says you are a serf. I heard him say so." Lucian tilted his head as he looked Steve up and down. "This is new for you?"

"*So* new," said Steve. "I didn't know until I came to Venice. I still don't really know."

"You will not help?" said Chiara.

"I don't know if…" Steve looked at the five. Their clothes were as dirty as their faces and torn in places. "What do you want me to do?"

"Our friends," said Lucian. "You saw them in the prison. We must free them."

"How?" said Steve. "The prison is guarded."

"We know that," said Faro. "We see with our own eyes when we go there."

"So why haven't you freed them yourself?" said Steve.

"The cells are locked with magic," said Lucian. "Council magic. We do not know how to break that."

"But you," said Chiara. "You stop magic. You can open the cells."

"We take you now," said Argi, moving towards Steve. "Go free them."

"We could help you escape," said Lucian. "That is a fair deal, yes?"

"I can't go without my friends. I won't. Xav has made it clear that if I don't get him out of Venice, he'll hurt us."

"Not our care," said Faro.

"Well, it's my care," said Steve as Argi grabbed him by the arm. He struggled with the other boy, pulling himself free. "I won't put them in any more danger than—"

The door to the ballroom slammed open. Two of the guards stepped inside, batons outheld. When they saw Steve, they lowered their weapons.

"What are you doing in here?" said one.

"Nothing." Steve looked around. Lucian and his siblings had disappeared. "I just needed a break."

"You shouldn't be in here." The other guard grabbed Steve by the arm. "Come on."

As the guards dragged Steve from the room, he looked back into the empty space. There was no one to see, not even a glint.

Chapter Twenty-Seven

The early morning sky, or the space where the sky should have been above Venice, was painted in angry shades of scarlet and grey. The column of light in the Doge's Palace courtyard reflected those colours as if the device was itself annoyed. Steve shivered, his hands buried in his jacket pockets. Mary, Bodrn, and Hartley stood close behind him. Steve had counted the guards in the courtyard as more had filtered into the space. There were twenty-seven in all, silently waiting for Xav Mallorick's instructions.

The mind flayer was wrapped up in a thick padded coat, his thinning hair hidden by a trilby. He carried a small suitcase and an expression of eager trepidation. He was the only person in the space who wasn't still. Instead, he walked around and around the column of light, muttering to himself.

A guard appeared from the archway that led to the prison and hurried to Xav's side. Xav handed his suitcase to the guard, took a deep breath, and turned to Steve with a smile that was closer to a snarl. The mind flayer had dropped any pretence of pleasantry. He looked deadly, and determined, and totally focussed.

"Come here." He beckoned to Steve. "It's time to show everyone what you can do."

"But…" Steve hesitated until one of the guards grabbed him by the arm and thrust him forward. "I want your word," he said. "That you'll let us go."

"One step at a time," said Xav. "Take down the power source first."

"What'll happen to Venice if I do? Will everyone here be all right?"

"I have no idea," said Xav with a shrug. "And I don't care. They can all perish as long as I get to leave this damned place."

"That wasn't the deal," said Steve. "I don't want to hurt anyone."

"And maybe you won't," said Xav. "Now, get on with it."

"I need more time." Steve tried to retreat but the guard held him in place. "I've only just learnt how to use my powers. What if I do it wrong?"

"Then your friends will suffer."

Steve saw Xav nod to someone behind him. When he turned, each of his friends and his mum struggled in the grasp of the guards.

"Nothing ventured, nothing gained, Steve," said Xav. "I won't hold it against you if you get it wrong, first time. But you will take down the barrier. Let him go," Xav told the guard who held Steve's arm. "Let them all go."

Steve looked at his mum and friends as the guards released them. Mary took a step towards him, but Hartley took her hand and drew her back. Bodrn kept an eye on the guards.

"Okay." Steve nodded. "Just give me a moment."

"Only a moment, though." Xav retreated a couple of steps, waving for the guard who carried his suitcase to do the same.

Steve took a deep breath and closed his eyes. He could feel the vibration from the column of light. It gave him the same sensation in his chest as if he was humming. He curled his fingers into loose fists and felt for the tension in his stomach.

"Keep your eyes shut." The quiet voice was so sudden and close to his ear that he had to stop himself from jumping a little. "We will save your friends. The rest is up to you."

Even with his eyes closed, he found himself raising a hand to shield his face as a bright light seared through his eyelids, painting them a vivid pink. He heard shouts of alarm around him and scuffling feet. A hand grabbed his arm, shaking him and pinching.

"Where are they?"

"Ow!" Steve pulled free of Xav's grasp.

"I'll find them. I'm still in their minds." The guards rubbed their eyes and blinked blearily around the courtyard. Steve turned a full circle. Mary, Hartley, and Bodrn were nowhere to be seen.

"Where are you? Where are you?" Xav pressed a hand to his forehead, his eyes squeezed shut. "You'll suffer for this."

"What shall we do with this one, Mr Mallorick?" One of the guards grabbed Steve by the shoulder. A second guard pinned Steve in on the other side.

"Take him back to the hotel." Xav turned away with a dismissive flutter of his hand. "I need to concentrate."

As the second guard grabbed him too, Steve dug his hand into the magically-imbued pocket of his jacket and thought of the only item that could possibly help him. Immediately, he felt the cold plastic of the flare charm in his hand.

"Oi!" said the first guard as Steve elbowed him in the chest. "Get back here." He grabbed at Steve, but it was too late. Steve dodged the man as he pulled the flare charm from his pocket.

I'm not sure how this works, Steve thought as he backed away from the guards. *Maybe…*

He shook the flare charm. The liquid it contained sloshed and bubbled in response. Then he grabbed it with both hands and bent it until he heard a snap.

Is that it? he thought as the flare charm did nothing else. He gave it a final shake and threw it at the advancing men.

As the flare charm bounced off the forehead of one of the guards, Steve heard that all-too-familiar sound of a vacuum releasing, and then another, and another. Popping into existence, seven Hidden soldiers appeared in the courtyard. As one, they turned to face Steve.

"What have you done?" Xav stared open-mouthed at the Hidden. For a second, Steve took a little satisfaction that he'd ruined the man's plans. Then Xav Mallorick smiled. "What fun," he said. "My own army of Hidden to command. Thank you, Steve."

"You can't do that."

"Watch me," said Xav. "I've done it before. Why else do you think there are no Hidden in Venice?" He clapped his hands. "Just think of the possibilities."

As the instinct of the guards to protect Xav kicked in, they descended on the Hidden, fighting with truncheons and knives. The Hidden deftly dodged the attacks, standing back-to-back with each other.

"We can't have this," said Xav. "I don't want my Hidden damaged. They're too precious."

As he raised a hand and took a breath to speak, Steve did the only thing he could think of. He grabbed Xav's wrists and pulled the man around to face him.

"What are you doing?" Xav pulled away. He looked for help, but the guards were all involved in their attack on the Hidden.

"Hold still." It was Steve's voice, but it felt as if someone else was speaking through him. The vibration from the column of light and the tension that had started in his stomach had combined into a force that filled his body. His arms felt so heavy that they ached. His head ached too, with a ring of pressure that encased his skull. There was no sensation of the floor beneath his feet. His diaphragm swelled as he took a deep, deep breath.

"Stop it." Xav's normal arrogant tone had slipped into a frightened whine. "You can't hurt me. I'm in charge here. I am Xav Mallor—"

The mind flayer fell silent as Steve roared at him, but the noise that came from Steve's lips and lungs wasn't human. It was animalistic, brutal, and unforgiving.

Xav whimpered and recoiled, slumping a little at the knees. His face twitched. Tears ran from his eyes. His complexion paled, losing any tinge of health. His thinning, blonde hair dulled and then it turned pure white. Xav stumbled to his knees, trembling and gagging.

"That is enough." It took a moment for Steve to register the voice. "Stop. Serfs do not kill. Let him go."

"He deserves this." It was Steve's voice, but it seemed distant and detached from him. "For his crimes."

"I agree," said the voice by his ear. "But you have taken his magic. Leave him with his life. You are not a killer."

That last word—killer—dragged Steve's attention away from the fading mind flayer. With a sudden inwards gulp of air, he released the man's wrists. Xav Mallorick slumped to the floor, crying and wheezing.

"Steve." The eldest of the luminants stood at his shoulder. Lucian's hands were raised as if he didn't dare touch Steve. "Are you back, outsider?" The wide-eyed fear and worry in the teenager's eyes made him look younger than his years.

Steve nodded. His stomach muscles hurt and he had a stitch in his side, but he was himself again. "Where are the others?"

"Your mother is safe," said Lucian. "And your friends."

"She's not my…" Steve shook his head. "That's good. Where?"

"Come." Lucian beckoned to him. "To the prison. Before—"

His words were cut short as the guard who had carried Xav's suitcase swung a fist at the teenager. Lucian dodged, landing a blow in the guard's stomach. The man doubled up. Before he could recover, Lucian and Steve dashed away.

"Wait!" Steve stopped at the entrance to the prison. The fight continued in the courtyard. The guards were clumsy and ineffective compared to the Hidden. Already, half of Xav's people lay unconscious or injured on the ground.

"No time," said Lucian. "You must free our friends." He dragged Steve through the archway and as the courtyard disappeared from view, they began to run.

The imprisoned children and teenagers shouted and cheered in their cells. Some hammered on the windows. Others waved to Steve and Lucian as they ran past.

"Steve." He was engulfed in Mary's arms as he and Lucian finally reached the end of the long corridor. "I thought I'd lost you."

"I'm fine." He pushed her away as gently as he could.

Lucian's siblings stood with Hartley and Bodrn, but someone new watched from the tall archway beside the interview room doors. The golem looked exactly the same as those Steve had seen in the Council controlled area. It was tall, so tall that its head brushed the top of the archway. It was broad too, giving the impression of heavy muscle. It didn't smile but its face held an expression of watchful calm. Unlike the golems in the Confluence, however, this one wore a suit, shirt, and tie that matched the colour of its sandy hair. The youngest girl, Solana, held the golem's hand.

"What's the plan, my boy? No, don't tell me," said Hartley. "I don't want that man reading my mind."

"That is not a problem," said Lucian. "Steve saw to that."

"How?" said Mary.

"No time to talk." Steve didn't want to have that conversation now, if ever. "Where are the controls for the locks," he asked Lucian.

"This way," said the golem. He shuffled backwards through the archway, releasing Solana who followed at a skip.

"Can we trust him?" Steve whispered to Hartley. "Doesn't he work for Xav?"

"My purpose is to maintain the good running of the prison," the golem called back. "This is what I was created for."

"Golems have excellent hearing," said Hartley. "Sorry, I should have warned you. But yes, we can trust him. The Council made him and, being a golem, he can't be controlled by anyone other than his creator."

"I trust him," said Bodrn. "Golems may not be human, but they have a deep understanding of people."

"And they know right from wrong," added Mary. "I just hope he thinks we are in the right."

"We will stay here," said Lucian. "Keep watch for the guards or the Hidden."

"Thank you." Chiara took Steve's hand. "For what you will do. We will remember."

I haven't done it yet, Steve thought. *What if…?* He dismissed the thought and nodded to the girl. "Be careful," he said.

"You as well, serf," said Faro. He drew his sister away and before another word was spoken, the four older luminants disappeared.

Chapter Twenty-Eight

"This is the command console that manages the entire prison."

The golem gestured to a control panel on a raised platform in the centre of the large circular room. The panel was a mixture of technology that Steve was familiar with, like switches and dials, and other non-scientific items like crystals set into the metal surround and glowing symbols that hovered above the surface of the panel.

The walls of the room were lined with glowing screens that showed views of the corridor outside and many others, all lined with cells. Eight less impressive control panels sat beneath the screens. The ceiling above was domed and displayed a constantly changing series of symbols and words that Steve didn't recognise.

"How many cells are there in this place?" Steve turned around, looking at each of the screens in turn.

"There are four hundred and eighty-four cells in the prison," said the golem. "Currently housing one thousand nine hundred and two prisoners."

"Children," said Mary. "They're not prisoners. They've done nothing wrong."

"I make no judgement, ma'am," said the golem. "I am simply here to maintain the prison and its inhabitants."

"I can't open four hundred and eighty-four cells," said Steve. "It'd take too long. And the Hidden…"

"Are in the prison." Argi appeared in the archway. "Two are in the corridor. They walk slow, but…" He shrugged.

"We have to do this quick." Steve stepped up to the central

control panel. "If I remove the magic from the command console—"

"You will destroy the prison." The golem moved Steve away, placing itself between the boy and the console. "And everyone inside the prison."

"But there has to be a way." Steve suddenly felt the weight of the promise he had made to the luminants. *I'm not enough*, he thought. *Even with my powers, I'm not enough.*

"Can you open the cells?" Bodrn stared up at the golem.

"The clay remembers you, little sister," said the golem with a smile. "Even in this form. The answer to your question is yes."

"All at the same time?" said Steve.

"Yes," said the golem.

"Right. Fine," he said. "Do that, please."

"Unfortunately, I am prevented," said the golem.

"But you just said that you could do it." Steve could feel the tension rising in his stomach again. It was an angry sensation that buzzed under his skin.

"I can do what you ask," said the golem, "but the Council bound me to prevent that action." He held up his wrist. A thin, golden chain glinted against his dull skin.

"Let me see." Steve took hold of the golem's hand and placed a finger on the chain. He could feel the magic contained in the metal, pulsing against his fingertip. "Can it be broken?"

"Not with force," said the golem.

"But if I removed the magic, would that work?"

"Perhaps." The golem shrugged its heavy shoulders. "It has not been done before."

"If you're going to do this, Steve, then best be quick." Hartley nodded to one of the screens. In the corridor pictured, the one that led to the control room, two Hidden looked into each of the cells as they passed. Two more stood guard at the far end of the corridor. "If the Hidden catch us, they'll take us back to Darkacre. Or the Council will put me on trial. Or both."

"And we won't be able to find Dad." The words came from

Steve's gut, or his heart, so quickly that they surprised him. He looked at his mum and pictured the man he'd always known as his father standing beside her; the man he wanted to see again.

"It's now or never, Steve."

"Right." Steve closed his eyes. The tension was still there but it was weaker than before. It really was now or never. "I don't want to hurt you." He looked up at the golem. "I'm not sure how this works."

"You cannot hurt me," said the creature. "I exist or I do not. The only thing you can hurt is my purpose and I do not believe you would do that."

With a nod, Steve took the chain between the finger and thumb of one hand. He curled the other hand into a fist. It helped him focus on the remaining tension in his body. He found the anger—at Xav for his treatment of the children— and those feelings of protectiveness for his friends and Mary. He pinched the chain in his grasp, feeling the metal and the magic it contained fighting his touch. *Now or never*, he thought, and then he sent all of that tension, all of those emotions, into the chain around the golem's wrist.

The chain writhed in his grasp as if it were a living thing, and then with a hiss it shattered and disintegrated into nothing.

"Well done, Steve." Hartley took the golem's arm. "No harm there," he said, examining the wrist that had been bound by the chain. "Now, if you wouldn't mind. Could we please open the cell doors before the Hidden arrive?"

"As you wish," said the golem with a nod. "You might like to observe the screens," he added. "Evacuation protocol enabled. Opening all cells."

Steve and the others watched the screens that lined the rooms as the golem turned dials and pressed a number of the symbols that hovered above the control panel.

"It's working," said Mary as the cell doors opened. Each screen showed an outpouring of children and teenagers into the corridors beyond.

"Look!" Argi pointed to the screen that displayed the entrance corridor. Two Hidden struggled amongst a sea of children and teenagers. "That will stop them, right?"

"It will undoubtedly slow them down," said Hartley. "I don't suppose the prison has a back door, does it?"

"No," said the golem. "There is only one entrance to the prison."

"I was afraid that you'd say that." Hartley sighed, and then he clapped his hands and rubbed them together. "Right then, Steve, my boy. Do your stuff." He pulled back his sleeves and held out his bangled wrists.

"But I don't know if I can." Steve instinctively backed away from his friend.

"You freed the golem," said Hartley. "You can do the same for me."

"But that was just one small chain. This is different." He shook his head. "I don't have enough…" He wanted to say magic, but of course that wasn't right. "Enough power left."

"Perhaps," said Hartley. "But you won't know until you try."

"I might hurt you."

"You didn't hurt the golem."

"Golems don't feel pain," said the golem.

"Not helpful," said Hartley. "Steve, you have to try. It's our only chance of getting out of here unaccosted by the Hidden."

"Lucian and the other luminants can hide us. They did it before."

"That won't work." Faro appeared in the archway. "Hidden can feel our magic." He held out a hand to his youngest sister.

"Bad Hidden," she said as she took his hand. "Naughty."

"He's right." Lucian appeared at his brother's side, followed by Chiara.

"The Hidden will find us like that." Argi clicked his fingers.

"You can do this, Steve," said Hartley. "I believe in you."

"We all do," said Mary as Bodrn nodded her agreement.

"I don't know." Steve looked around at the others. They all

looked so sure of his abilities, as if it was the simplest thing to deal with the bangles. "Are you sure about this, Hartley?"

"As sure as I'll ever be, dear boy." Hartley raised his messy eyebrows. "You're our best bet at getting out of here."

"Right." Steve nodded and closed his eyes. The tension was still there, buzzing under his skin and clamping his stomach muscles, but it was weakening by the minute. He opened his eyes and reached for Hartley's wrists. For a second, his hands hovered over the bangles as he pulled on the emotions he felt: anger, the need to protect the people he cared about, and the smallest amount of belief in these new, terrifying powers.

When he touched the bangles, he expected the metal to react just as the golem's chain had reacted. Instead, the bangles sizzled as they turned white hot. He let go, shaking his fingers to cool them. Steve heard Hartley grunt in pain, then mutter, "Get on with it."

"Right." Steve lay his hands on the bangles again. He expected the heated metal to burn his fingers. Instead, it simply vibrated under his touch. Gradually, the bangles dimmed from white to a dull red.

Hartley's lips disappeared into his white beard as he clamped his mouth shut. His chest rose and fell rapidly. He blinked his watering eyes, staring up at the domed ceiling.

"Not long now, Hartley." Mary stood at the shopkeeper's shoulder. "Just a little bit more."

The vibration of the metal changed under Steve's touch. Now it felt like a wriggling creature trying to shake him off or escape. The dull red colour had changed to the original gold. A series of runes and symbols blinked into sight and disappeared on the surface of the bangles. With a sound of shattering glass, the bangles gave a final shake and slipped from Hartley's wrists.

Steve and Mary both grabbed one of Hartley's arms as his knees buckled. Bodrn took the weight of his torso as she broke his fall and gently lowered him to the floor.

"Hartley?" said Steve as the elderly shopkeeper took deep,

rasping breaths. "Are you all right?"

"All right?" Hartley examined the scorched skin on his wrists. "All right?" His shoulders shook and Steve assumed he was crying.

"Hartley?"

When Hartley looked up at Steve, that old familiar, face-splitting grin was back. "I am marvellous," laughed Hartley, wiping a tear from his eye. "Never better, my boy. Never better. *Ally-up!*" Leaning on them all, and with a great deal of noise, he climbed to his feet. "Now then, about that door."

"Will this do?" Lucian slapped a hand on the archway. "It is a door, right?"

"Absolutely." Hartley staggered forward. "Just the thing," he said as he touched a hand to the metal frame of the arch. "Of course, we have to make this journey count. I'm not sure I'll be able to do this again for a while. If only we knew where your father went after he left Venice. Any ideas, Mary?"

"Sorry, no." Mary shook her head.

"Steve?" said Hartley. "I don't suppose Xav Mallorick dropped any clues, did he?"

"He didn't know." Steve sighed. "All he read in Dad's mind…" He paused, unsure of whether he should still say 'Dad'. It felt right and wrong, all at the same time. "All he got was the middle of nowhere. Sorry. That's not very useful."

"To the contrary, my dear boy." Hartley pointed a finger in the air with a deep, reverberating chuckle. "He didn't say the middle of nowhere. He said the Midden of Nowhere."

"Is that better?" said Mary.

"Of course it is." Hartley placed a hand on each side of the archway and closed his eyes. "I know exactly where to take us."

Steve felt a hand slip into his. He looked sideways and then down as the youngest luminant, Solana, smiled up at him. "*Grazie*," she said. "Thank you."

"Come." Argi drew his sister away. "They are busy." He rolled his eyes at Steve.

On the other side of the archway, the other three luminant siblings, Lucian, Faro, and Chiara hugged each other and laughed. Chiara raised a hand to wave and then the view through the archway shifted to a scene of angry, dark clouds. Steve heard Hartley muttering to himself. The old shopkeeper's body shook as he leaned into the archway.

"He's in pain," said Mary. "We have to stop him."

"No," Hartley snapped. "It's working. I just—"

He threw back his head and roared. The scene in the archway changed in an instant. In place of the clouds, Steve could see blue skies and scrubby grass. He felt a hot breeze brush his hair.

"We're here," Hartley murmured. "Well done, me." His eyes closed and he fell forward through the archway.

The darkling was the first to follow, kneeling beside the shopkeeper on the parched ground. Mary was next, stepping through the archway as if it were the most normal thing in the world to do.

"Quick," said Argi, nodding to one of the screens. The Hidden had pushed or teleported their way along the entrance corridor and would be on the other side of the archway any minute.

"Will you be all right?" said Steve, looking at the golem and the two luminants. "When the Hidden get here?"

"I will protect them," said the golem. "All of them."

Without another word, Steve stepped through the archway and as his feet touched the ground on the other side, he heard a door slam shut behind him.

Chapter Twenty-Nine

The Midden of Nowhere sprawled out below the cliff-top vantage point that Steve found himself on. In a massive, crater-like basin below, what must have once been a small town lay in a wasteland of rubble and ruin. At the centre, buildings were reduced to little more than dusty footprints and piles of debris. Further out, partly collapsed and burned-out structures dotted the fractured streets. The single road leading into the town was ruptured by potholes and cracks.

Hartley lay face down on the cliff-top grass, arms outstretched. His eyes were closed and his nose whistled in a way that suggested he was having a doze. Mary and Bodrn crouched down on either side of him, watching with expressions of worry on their faces.

"You know, most visitors come in through the front door, not out."

Steve, his mum, and the darkling all turned around at the words. While Steve simply stared, Mary and Bodrn looked ready to fight.

Two men stood at the open door of a small, battered, circular log cabin. Both had tanned, leathery skin and were dressed in dusty, faded shirts and jeans. One was tall and thin, with braided long iron-grey hair. He wore wire-rimmed glasses. A tattoo of a star and crescent moon was visible above his open collar. The other man was a little shorter, broad, and muscular. He was completely bald, and his round face finished in a scruffy, white beard.

"What have you done to yourself this time, old friend?" The bald man knelt down beside Hartley, rolling the shopkeeper onto his back.

Hartley muttered something about not being old, puffed out a breath of air, and struggled to sit up.

"Stay down," said the man, forcing Hartley to lie back. "Let me look at you." He held out a hand to the other man. "Cin, I need your glasses."

"Again?" said the other, slipping them off his face. "You should buy your own, Az." He handed them over with a sigh.

"Sorry." Hartley huffed. "I'll be fine." His teeth chattered as he began to tremble. "In a min…" He closed his eyes and his head fell to one side.

"Hey!" Az slapped him across the face. "Wake up."

"Awake." Hartley's eyes flew open, and he blinked up at the man like a slightly offended owl.

"He's in shock," said Az. "Pain?" he asked.

"No, thank you," said Hartley.

"He's all right," said Cin.

"Best get him inside." Az hauled Hartley onto his feet and then lifted him over his shoulder as if he were no heavier than a sack of vegetables. "You too," he said to the others. "There's a storm on the way."

The inside of the cabin was more generous in size than the exterior suggested. The walls were constructed from rough, interlinking logs and smaller, woven twigs and branches. There were shelves carved into some of the logs, holding tiny wooden figures, two or three polished bone horns, and an assortment of pottery vases. The ceiling was, well, not really a ceiling at all. In its place, a cloud or fog or smoke—it was hard to tell exactly what it was—hovered above their heads. A stone firepit marked the centre of the space. Steve could feel the heat radiating from the flames but there was no smoke in the air. The room smelled of herbs and pine trees.

Two wooden rocking chairs, each draped with a blanket, sat on either side of a roughly-hewn table. There was a long, backless bench too, with a pile of blankets at one end.

"Sit. Sit." Cin gestured to the bench. "Have you travelled far?"

"I think so," said Steve. "Where are we?"

"Where do you think you are?" said Az as he kicked open the door at the back of the room. "Not long now, old friend." He bent a little to fit through the door, carrying Hartley with him.

"Not the Continent?" said Steve.

"*A* continent, for sure," said Cin. "This is the American Isles."

"Will Hartley be all right?" Bodrn hovered by the front door. "I have never seen him so injured."

"This is nothing," said Cin. "Hartley Keg is a battler and a survivor. My brother will make sure he is well in no time at all."

Steve beckoned to Bodrn as he and Mary sat on the bench. She watched Cin for a wary moment longer. The man gave her a pleasant smile as he lowered himself onto one of the rocking chairs. Her stance relaxed and she crossed the room, standing at Steve's side.

"Have you visited the American Isles before?" asked Cin, rocking his chair. It creaked a little as it moved, but the sound was soothing rather than annoying.

"No, I've only just visited the Continent," said Steve. "Our continent."

"We came to see the Midden," said Mary. "We think my husband might be there."

"I see." Cin suddenly had a pipe in one hand and shreds of some kind of herb in the other. "Not a typical place for a holiday." He stuffed his pipe and clicked his fingers. The pipe began to smoke.

"Hartley is settled." Az stood in the doorway, watching them. "He will sleep his pains away." He closed the door behind him.

"Can I see him?" Bodrn's hands had tensed into fists again.

"He needs no guard," said Az as he took the other chair. Unlike his brother, he didn't rock the chair. Instead, he leant forward, clasping his hands before him. "I am more worried about you. All of you."

"Why?" said Steve. He was finding it difficult to keep his eyes open. The sound of the rocking chair had settled into the rhythm of Steve's heartbeat, or maybe it was the other way round.

"Two of you have been enchanted up here." Az touched the side of his bald head. "And the other forced to change. I think you all need to rest."

"But my husband," said Mary.

"Quiet now," said Az, spreading his hands. "Questions are for tomorrow, as is the Midden."

"But I'm not tired at all." Mary covered her mouth as she broke into a long yawn. "Really, I'm not."

Her head dropped onto her chin, and she slumped back onto the wall. Bodrn buckled at the knees, slapping her hands on the mud floor as she fell.

Steve wanted to react, but his body and his eyelids had other ideas. He felt his torso slide to one side, coming to rest on his sleeping mother. His eyes closed and the world went away.

*

"This is preposterous. I came here in good faith and seeking help."

Steve opened his eyes. He pushed himself upright on the bench. He was alone in the log cabin.

"I'm sorry, my friend, but you weren't in any state to explain yourself or your companions."

"Barely conscious," said someone else. "And influenced by a mind flayer."

Steve recognised the voices. Hartley and the two men who lived in the cabin stood on the other side of the open doorway. He could hear his friend stomping up and down in front of the building.

"I would have done the same." That was Bodrn. "To keep my home safe."

"Thank you," said Az. "See?"

"No, I do not see," said Hartley. "It's just, well, frankly it's insulting."

"Stop waving your hands around. The bandages will come loose," said Cin.

"He's always like this," said Mary. "He likes to be in control."

Steve listened to the exchange as he crossed the room. He felt strangely cheerful and refreshed, as if he'd had the best night's sleep ever.

"Hi." He peered out through the door. "Is everything okay?"

"Fine," said Mary, at the exact same time as Hartley said, "Not at all!"

Bodrn stood apart from them all. Her posture was relaxed but her eyes were watchful.

"Good morning, Steve," said Cin. "How are you feeling?"

Steve wanted to say 'good' because that was the truth. But a grain of the energy that had surged through his body as he removed Xav Mallorick's magic still remained in the pit of his stomach. He had no idea whether that was a 'good' thing or not.

"Better," he said.

"Your mother has told us about your quest," said Az.

"Steve, he was here," she said with an honest, open smile. "Az and Cin can take us to him."

"We can take you to where we left him," said Az. "Whether he is still there…" He shrugged.

"Still," said Mary. "It's a good place to start."

"But not until Hartley's wounds are on the turn for the better," said Cin. "No arguments," he added as Hartley opened his mouth.

"My brother is right to be careful. Wounds and wild magic don't mix," said Az. "And the path through the Midden of Nowhere is threaded with wild magic. Remnants of the town's destruction. With a guide, it's almost safe if you're in good health. But the wild is attracted to injury and weakness."

"And how long will that take?" said Hartley. "We can't hang around here, you know. The boy wants to find his, his… He wants answers. Don't you, Steve?"

"Of course, I do," said Steve. "But I've got Mum back." He smiled at her. It felt comforting to call her that.

"You have." The tension around her eyes dropped away and she gave him an open, honest smile.

"And you need to heal, Hartley," said Steve. "I think we should wait, for a little bit. If you don't mind?" He looked at the brothers.

"Do we mind, Cin?" said Az with a grin.

"Only a little," said Cin. "No, not at all," he finished with a grin that matched his brother's. "It will be good to have younger people around."

"Even you, Hartley Keg," said Az.

As the others returned to the cabin, Steve took a moment to be on his own. The sky was swollen with dark, bloated clouds. There was a storm coming, just like Az had said. He could feel the electricity in the air and the cold wind that had carried the storm here. Before all of this had started—Hartley, Winters, magical devices, and mysterious doorways—he would have run indoors to shelter from that storm. But now, everything was different. He was different.

The Midden of Nowhere waited for him below and, with any luck, the man he'd always known as his father did too. But that adventure would wait for another day.

THE END (for now)

Acknowledgements

This is the third novel in Steve's adventure and I couldn't have completed it without all the wonderful people who help my creative mind keep on, well, creating.

Thank you to:

- my family, those marvellous people who inspire, love, and often keep me fed as I write
- the folks at Burning Chair who keep on believing in my authorly skills and releasing my books into the wild
- the writing community for their encouragement, support, and cheerleading
- Billy and Sarah who provided the inspiration for two characters in Haven's Deceit – your kindness and cups of tea will always be appreciated
- my readers, whose book reviews played a large part in shaping this novel
- Thank you to all you glorious souls.

About The Author

For many years Fi Phillips worked in an office environment until the arrival of her two children robbed her of her short-term memory and sent her hurtling down a new, bumpy, creative path. She finds that getting the words down on paper is the best way to keep the creative muse out of her shower.

Fi lives in the wilds of North Wales with her family, earning a living as a copywriter, playwright and fantasy novelist. Writing about magical possibilities is her passion.

You can follow her on Twitter - @FisWritingHaven

Or at **fiphillipswriter.com** – where you can also sign up for an exclusive short story from the universe of Haven Wakes – absolutely FREE!

About Burning Chair

Burning Chair is an independent publishing company based in the UK, but covering readers and authors around the globe. We are passionate about both writing and reading books and, at our core, we just want to get great books out to the world.

Our aim is to offer something exciting; something innovative; something that puts the author and their book first. From first class editing to cutting edge marketing and promotion, we provide the care and attention that makes sure every book fulfils its potential.

We are:

- Different
- Passionate
- Nimble and cutting edge
- Invested in our authors' success

If you're an author and would like to know more about our submissions requirements and receive our free guide to book publishing, visit:

www.burningchairpublishing.com

If you're a reader and are interested in hearing more about our books, being the first to hear about our new releases or great offers, or becoming a beta reader for us, again please visit:

www.burningchairpublishing.com

More From Burning Chair Publishing

The Casebook of Johnson & Boswell Series, by Andrew Neil Macleod
    The Fall of the House of Thomas Weir
    The Stone of Destiny

The Curse of Becton Manor, by Patricia Ayling

www.burningchairpublishing.com